The Bachelor's Fool

And

Life, Nothing but Drama

By

Kimberly McKenzie

Small Fish Big Sea Publications
August 2009

Kimberly McKenzie

Table of Contents

Small Fish Big Sea Publications
Paperback Fiction

PUBLISHER'S NOTES

First Printing

Printed in the United States of America

ISBN: 978-0-9801470-1-8

Cover Design by N'DigoDesign

ACKNOWLEDGMENTS

*This book is dedicated in memory of my father, Rufus Orr Sr.
and my Grandfather, Lilton Poindexter Sr.*

Chapter 1

<u>*Karen*</u>

Black folks either get together for a wedding or a funeral but not this time, Karen thought, as she stuffed some clothes into her suitcase at record speed, trying to hurry out of the house. She needed to get away; time to think whether or not she would tell her husband that she was pregnant. Their relationship had gone downhill over the last several months and the abuse had only gotten worse.

Karen popped the trunk open to her BMW, threw in her suitcase, then jumped into the car and backed out of the driveway. She looked up at what had been her home for the past two years. Looking from the outside in, it seemed she had the perfect life. She was a computer tech for a reputable firm and her husband was a construction worker, raking in lots of cash.

Karen fell head-over-heels in love with Jason the first time she saw him. He was working on the busy streets of downtown, Euclid Avenue, in Cleveland, Ohio. She'd been working on a major project, and it was the first time in weeks that she had taken a lunch break. It was a scorching hot summer day, ninety degrees to be exact, and when she walked out to pick up a sandwich from the deli across the street her eyes immediately centered on Jason's sweaty chest. He had the perfect physique and his six-foot three-inch chocolate frame was all muscle. She wanted to lick the sweat right off his chest but went inside the deli and bought him some ice-cold lemonade instead. That was over two years ago, and the way Karen's life was going now, she wished she had never taken that lunch break back then or fallen in love with Jason Townsley.

Chapter 2

<u>**Ray Ray**</u>

"Don't look at me that way," Ray Ray said, snapping his fingers up and down.

"Yes, I'm gay. If you ever need to be turned out then give me a call," he told Shelley's boyfriend.

"That will never happen," Ken told Ray Ray, turning his nose up in disgust. "Believe me, I wouldn't even be in here if Shelley hadn't insisted that you do her hair."

"Yes, well she knows who's the best damn beautician in the city of Cleveland," he said spraying some oil sheen in Shelley's hair.

"Ray Ray, I don't know why you are always bickering with Ken," Shelley said, cutting in.

"Oh girl, please. Ken knows he loves coming in here picking with me. If I didn't love you so much, I would be trying to hit on your man," Ray Ray responded, giving Ken a wink.

"Uugh—I think I'm going to be sick," Ken said, handing Ray Ray eighty dollars. "Shelley, I'll be out in the car waiting for you."

"If it was anyone else, my feelings would be hurt," Ray Ray called out to Ken before he left out.

Ray Ray just shook his head and finished adding the last minutes touches to Shelley's hair before handing her the mirror.

"Impressed as always," Shelley commented, while straightening out her short skirt.

"I'm flattered— now get out of here so I can close my shop up. You know Karen doesn't like to wait for anyone."

"Well thanks for opening up the shop just for me."

"Shelley, anything for you, darling. Now go give Ken a big juicy kiss for me and enjoy your one-year anniversary."

"Will do," Shelley told him as she walked out of the shop.

By the time Ray Ray was finished cleaning up, Karen was outside blowing her horn.

"Okay, Karen. I'll be right out," Ray Ray waved through the window. He grabbed his bags and glanced in the mirror to get a good look at his own hair. Damn, his fresh perm was looking on point and his feathered back curls were combed to perfection. "Just lovely," Ray Ray sighed as he locked up his salon and jumped into the car.

"Karen, I'm so glad you changed your mind and decided to come along with us."

"I need the break," Karen smiled.

"So what does Jason feel about you taking off?"

"He doesn't know."

"Oooh, Karen. Do tell," Ray Ray gasped, fanning his hand back and forth.

"Not now, Ray Ray. Maybe later," she told him, as they headed off to Hopkins International Airport.

Chapter 3

<u>*LuLu*</u>

"DeAndre, I told you to be here at 2:00," Lulu screamed through the telephone.

"Lucy calm down. I'm on my way," DeAndre told her.

"Well hurry up, I don't want to miss my flight. You know since September 11, folks have to check in at the airport early," she snapped. "And don't call me Lucy, you know it irritates me when people call me that—it sounds too white and I'm definitely a sister."

"Whatever, Lucy. Like I said, I'm on my way."

"*Whatever*," Lulu said, repeating his words. "DeAndre, just get your ass over here and quick. It's not often that I ask you to spend time with your son Andre. You should be glad to come get him and spend some quality time alone. Just like a man to want a woman to do everything."

"Did you tell the same thing to your other two kids' daddies?"

"DeAndre—"

"What?"

"I'll be waiting," Lulu said, before clicking off the phone. Right now she didn't have time for this baby daddy drama.

Why did DeAndre always have to give her problems? Rick and Tyrone never gave her any headaches. Whatever she wanted, she had. Rick had picked up their ten-year old daughter, Charmaine, over two hours ago, and Tyrone came and picked up their seven-year old son Tye Jr. the other day. DeAndre, on the other hand, was a different story. Why in the world did she ever give him the time of day? They met over five years ago when he boarded her bus on a cold December day. Lulu worked for the local transit system and was actually filling in for someone who had called off. It was just a few weeks before Christmas and Lulu didn't mind working a double shift for some extra cash. The bus was not crowded that day and before long, she and DeAndre were the only ones left on the bus. He came up near the front, introduced himself, and began talking his game.

Lulu remembered brushing him off. "I got two kids and no time for games." Her attempt to brush him off only made his desire stronger and eventually she broke down and agreed to go out with him. What a mistake, Lulu thought, looking at her watch. Just when she was about to peep out the window, the phone rang.

"Hello."

"Girl, you ain't left yet?" Ray Ray asked.

"I'm still waiting for that damn DeAndre," Lulu told him.

"Well you'd better hurry because Karen and I can't hold this plan for you. By the way have you heard from Delana?"

"Nope. I'm having a hard enough time worrying about myself; besides we're not close like we used to be so I doubt if she would call over here," Lulu responded.

"Now I've got to go, DeAndre just pulled in the driveway."

"All right then. And give that man a kiss for me. You know I don't like light-toned men, but that man is fine."

"Ray Ray, you're so crazy," Lulu said before clicking him off the phone. As fine as DeAndre was, he was nothing but trouble.

"DeAndre, about *time*," Lulu snapped pointing at her watch. "And since you're so late, I need a ride to the airport."

"For someone being so nasty, you're sure asking for a lot of favors."

"Come on, I'm really in a rush now." She had planned on catching the rapid but right now there just wasn't enough time.

"Where is Andre?"

"He's upstairs sleep. Now are you going to do me a favor and drop me off at the airport?"

"A favor! What favor do I get in return?"

"DeAndre, I don't have time for any games."

"Neither do I," DeAndre said, unbuckling his pants. "A quickie will do since you're so pressed for time."

Lulu just rolled her eyes, hiked up her sundress and rode him until he stopped yelling for more. She traced her tongue around the rim of his lips then parted them to brush her tongue up against his. She kissed him for a good five minutes before pulling her tongue back out.

"Oh, by the way—that kiss was at the request of Ray Ray," Lulu told him before heading upstairs to get their son.

DeAndre just turned up his lips and threw his hands up in the air. He was about to say something but decided against it. There was no point in arguing with Lulu because she always had to have the last word.

Chapter 4

<u>*Delana*</u>

Delana loved to make that almighty dollar. She should have been at the airport right now but instead she was finishing up a last minute job. Delana couldn't turn down a five thousand dollar job and was all too happy to coordinate the wedding design for one of her biggest client.

Everything had been set up and Delana walked through the big mansion where the reception would be held later this evening.

"Mrs. Crenshaw, is everything to your satisfaction?" Delana asked for the hundredth time.

"Things couldn't be more perfect," Mrs. Crenshaw replied. "Thanks again for working on such short notice. I never would have imagined that the reception hall we rented would catch on fire."

"Well unexpected things happen all the time. I'm just glad you entrusted me to design the décor for such a wonderful event."

"I wouldn't have it any other way," Mrs. Crenshaw said, handing her a check.

"Wonderful. Now my assistant Natasha will be here at four o' clock to help with the caterers and any other last minute things that you may need."

"Perfect. Now you hurry along so you won't miss your flight."

On that cue, Delana hurried out and jumped into her sporty red convertible Mercedes Benz and jetted down Van Aken Boulevard from Mrs. Crenshaw's illustrious estate in Shaker Heights. Thank goodness she had her bags already packed. Delana sped down the streets and jumped onto Interstate 271 and prayed she wouldn't get caught in rush hour traffic. It was a quarter to four and the boarding time for the plan was five o'clock sharp.

Delana sure hoped it wasn't Mrs. Crenshaw calling when she heard her cell phone. "Hello."

"So, I guess you wasn't going to call before you left."

"Corey, look, I don't have time to talk with you right now. I'm in the middle of the highway and almost late catching my plane."

"Damn, Delana, you sure have been cold lately."

"Well when you get your ass a job then maybe I will warm up to you again."

"Ouch! You sure know how to kick a brother when he is down. Do you think I wanted to be fired from my job?"

"Look, Corey, I know you didn't get fired on purpose. Companies downsize every day but it's been over six months. I'm going to be honest, there's no way in hell I'm going to support a man with my hard earned money."

"Did I ever ask you to support me?"

"No, but I'm not stupid, your unemployment will be running out soon."

"So let me get this straight, you mean to tell me that this relationship is all about me supporting you?" Corey asked.

Delana took a deep breath then slowly exhaled. Why was Corey trying to talk about all this now?

"Corey—"

"No, Delana, be honest with me," he said, listening to her long-winded sigh.

"Corey, you know when we met that this was not no love type relationship, so it really shouldn't bother you about the way I feel. I can't be there to hold your hand like a child while you decide on how to get your life back together. There's just too much other stuff going on in my life right now."

"Well maybe it would be easier if I wasn't in your life. Delana, I thought we were more than just a good fuck. If you can't stick with your man in hard times, then I truly question what type of woman you really are. You know a real woman would stick through the thick and thin, but instead you turn your back on me. You don't care about the hundreds of resumes I've sent out or even care about the interviews I've been on. It's all about the money for you. As long as you continue to be selfish like this, you'll never find a good man," Corey told her before clicking off the phone.

"No, he didn't just hang up on me?"

Delana threw her cell phone on the passenger seat. When the phone rang again, Delana took another deep breath. Corey wasn't that stupid, she thought to herself, trying to mentally prepare herself for more of his arguing. *Hello.*

"Delana, where on God's green earth are you?" Ray Ray asked.

"Ray Ray, I'm on my way," Delana told him annoyed.

"Girl, what's wrong with you?"

"Nothing," Delana snapped.

"Well, obliviously it's something. Maybe Turner can help you," Ray Ray said.

"Maybe so," Delana said before hanging up. She sure needed a therapist right about now. They were all going to Chicago to take part in their friend's graduation. Delana was so proud for Turner, a black doctor and a therapist. She was all too happy to see her folks moving up the ladder and maybe Turner would bend his ear for an old friend to help her with a life that seemed to be in shambles. Who in the hell did Corey think he was calling her selfish? Well maybe that part was true, but she had good reason to be selfish and she damn sure had no problems finding a man.

Chapter 5

<u>*Turner*</u>

Turner was nervous and excited about his graduation. If anyone would have told him years ago that a boy from the inner city of Cleveland could become a doctor and be a therapist, Turner would have never believed it. He had proved them all wrong; he was one of the few to make it out of the drug-infested neighborhoods in the inner city of Cleveland.

Turner wished his mother had lived to see this day. She had worked two, sometimes three jobs to support him as a child, plus she had gone to school. She always told him, "Turner, you have to get out of this ghetto. You have to make something of your life." Turner was glad his mother kept him from the mean streets that swallowed so many young men like himself. He was susceptible to falling prey to the streets, especially growing up without a father figure in his life. Luckily he survived, but many of his friends ended up in the streets, either selling drugs, using them, behind bars, or dead. In Turner's thirty-two years he had seen so much, and that's why he became a therapist. Turner wanted to give back; he wanted to help people who couldn't help themselves.

"Turner, you didn't hear me calling you," Natalie said, handing him the phone.

"No, I didn't," Turner replied, focusing his thoughts back to the present.

"Hello."

"Turner, it's Ray Ray. I'm just calling to let you know we're about to board the plane. We should arrive at Chicago's O' Hare Airport in about an hour and a half."

"I'll be there waiting."

"Yes, I know," Ray Ray, responded. "You've always been prompt; until then, ta ta!"

Turner snickered and hung up the phone. Ray hadn't changed one bit; he was still the same person he had met back in high school nearly twenty years ago. He remembered vividly the first time he saw him. Ray Ray was an outsider; being gay made him the prone to the daily bickering from many of his classmates, except for the girls. The girls bonded to him like glue, especially when he started doing their hair for little of no money. Even back then, Turner had an instinct to help others. He felt bad for the way Ray Ray was ridiculed, so he brought him into his circle of friends. To this day he still remained close to Ray Ray, Karen, Lulu, and Delana. They were his closet friends, his family, and he looked forward to their coming to Chicago to celebrate his graduation with him.

"Turner, I don't understand why your friends can't stay in a hotel," Natalie said, taking back the phone. She walked over to the table and set it on the base so it could charge up again.

"Look, I'm not debating this issue with you again. If you have a problem with it, then you go stay in a hotel at your own expense."

"Damn, Turner, you sure can be insensitive to my needs. I wish you'd show me as much love like you show your friends."

"You mean family," Turner corrected her.

"Whatever, Turner. It's no sense in arguing with you. I'll just pack up my things and leave."

"Then make sure you take all your stuff. If you can't be here when my family comes, then how can I trust you to do anything else?"

"Turner, you're just using this as an excuse to push me away. You can't fathom the idea of anyone loving you. You really need to analyze your own problems before you start working with anyone else."

"Natalie, I'm going to be the therapist here. Don't you start trying to play this game of reverse psychology with me."

"Turner, I'm just speaking the truth. If I can't come to you about problems I have then how can I trust you? This ultimatum crap is ridiculous, especially coming from you," Natalie said before she stormed out the room.

"Why now!" Turner yelled, throwing his hands up in the air. He plopped down on the couch and closed his eyes in thought.

"Turner, when you get yourself together, call me," Natalie told him as she lugged her suitcases to the door.

"So you're just going to up and leave like this?" Turner asked, focusing his eyes on her.

"Yes, Turner. This isn't just about today. I should have packed up and left a long time ago. We've been together for almost a year now and never once have you told me that you loved me. Every time I spoke those words to you, I meant it form the bottom of my heart. It tore me up inside when those words of affection were never reciprocated. I tried making excuses for you—*he's in school and working a full time job*, or *maybe losing his mother caused him to shut down his feelings for others*. Now I've come to realize that maybe you just don't give a damn and never loved or cared about me at all. I've run out of excuses and hope. Goodbye, Turner," Natalie said before walking out the door.

Turner just tilted his head back on the couch and let the tears slide down his cheeks. A part of him wanted to run after Natalie but it was easier to just let her go. Even though he loved her, it was too difficult to say those words to her right now.

****

Turner was at Chicago O' Hare Airport at five o' clock sharp. He was early but there was no use sitting around the house weeping over Natalie. No one forced her to leave; she did that of her own free will. If she truly loved him the way she said she did, then Natalie would have stayed— that was the bottom line.

Turner decided to blow off some time at the terminal's coffee shop. He ordered a chocolate mocha and sipped it slowly, enjoying the warmth it created inside his body. Right now he needed that after how cold Natalie had treated him.

"Excuse me, is this seat taken?"

Turner turned and stared at the beautiful woman, captured by her hazel green eyes. He scanned her fingers, no ring—good.

"No," he replied, motioning her to sit. "Can I buy you a cup of coffee?"

"No, that's not necessary."

"Well I guess I'll continue to celebrate alone for the moment," Turner said, raising his glass and then taking a few sips of his coffee. "By the way, my name is Turner," he smiled before indulging again in the rich taste of his chocolate drink.

"My name is Cynthia," she told him before ordering a cup of French Vanilla coffee. "And what are you having?" she turned and asked Turner.

"Chocolate mocha."

"One chocolate mocha for the gentleman," Cynthia told the attendant.

"Wait a minute, the guy is supposed to treat," Turner said.

"Well, it's good to see a few chivalrous men in today's society. Let this be my treat," Cynthia told him.

When the attendant brought their coffee, Cynthia raised her cup to his with a toast. "Congratulations, Turner."

"Thank you, but you don't even know what we're celebrating."

"Well it couldn't be to marriage because I don't see a ring on your finger."

Turner just snickered, enjoying Cynthia's company. Great minds think alike, he thought while he watched her drink.

"You know, it's not polite to stare."

"I'm sorry," Turner replied. "It's just that you're so damn beautiful. Your caramel skin looks so sweet— sweet enough to pour in my coffee and drink."

"I'm flattered," Cynthia replied. Usually men would worm their way out of her questions, but not Turner. She appreciated his honesty.

"So, what brings you to the airport?" Turner asked, steering the conservation into a different direction.

"I'm here to pick up my sister and possibly a good man too," Cynthia smiled.

"Love connection at the airport? I must say you definitely intrigue me," Turner said.

"Now, I have to go," Turner replied. He pulled out his wallet and handed Cynthia a business card.

"Turner, the therapist!"

"That would be me," he smiled. "Call me," Turner told her before he walked off. He had just a little over five minutes to make it to the gate his friends would be arriving at. Turner hadn't seen all of them together like this in years.

****

"Turner, Turner! Oh my goodness it's good to see you," Ray Ray hooted, dropping his bags. He ran right over to Turner and embraced him.

"Ray Ray, I'm glad to see you," Turner said with a brotherly embrace. He quickly broke free of Ray Ray's grasp to avoid any impression that he was gay. He welcomed the rest of the group.

"All right, enough with the meet and greet. I'm starved," Lulu said, directing everyone to move along.

"Lulu, stop acting so ghetto like you have never ate before," Karen snapped. She pulled Turner into her arms and gave him a kiss on the lips.

"Karen, I'm really glad you came. I was surprised when Ray Ray told me you were coming along."

"My plans changed— besides I wouldn't miss your graduation for the world," Karen told him.

"And Jason, you know he was more than welcome to come."

"Yeah, I know but he couldn't make it."

Turner just watched while the spark from Karen's eyes went dead. He could pick out a problem situation a mile away. Something was definitely wrong with Karen and her marriage to Jason, but now wasn't the time to ask, besides Delana had wormed her way up to him and wrapped her arms around him.

"Wow, I've never had so many women in my arms at one time."

"Turner, don't get a big head," Lulu responded with a slap to his butt. "I'm too much woman for you. Now let's get going," she motioned.

"All right. Let's get everyone's luggage so I can feed this woman," Turner said in a sarcastic tone.

On that note, everyone followed him and they were out of O'Hare International Airport in less than forty-five minutes.

"Delana, how many bags do you have?" Turner asked, trying to squeeze them in the back of his Lincoln Navigator.

"As many as the plane would allow," Lulu cut in.

"Whatever," Delana replied with a sharp cut of her eyes. "At least I brought some real clothes along," she said, running her hands along Lulu's thin sheer sundress.

"Girl—don't player hate because I got all the right curves in all the right places."

"Lulu, I'm not hating over that," Delana snapped. "You need to cover that up; why do you think you have so much baby daddy drama?"

"No you didn't just go there," Ray Ray said, cutting in.

"Ray Ray, stay your gay ass out of this conversation. You have your own love triangle problems," Lulu hissed like an angry cat. Although Delana was right, she didn't have to go there about her kids. That was an insult and she definitely wasn't hearing any of that.

By now Ray Ray, Delana, and Lulu were all bickering back and forth with one another. People in the parking lot were even starting to look on.

"*Ladies*," Turner yelled as everyone came to a complete silence. "We're here to have fun, not argue," he told them. "Now let's go," Turner said, instructing everyone to get into the truck. "Lulu, you ride up front with me."

Lulu shot Delana a smirk just like a little child as Turner helped her up into the front seat. Men always preferred her instead.

Delana and Karen sat near the window in the back, forcing Ray Ray in the middle, which suited him just fine since he enjoyed being the center of attention.

"Turner, after we get something to eat, can you drop me off over my best friend's house? It doesn't make sense to unload my things twice."

"Fine," he replied. He started the car and was surprised to enjoy a moment of silence. Maybe it was the coldness of the air conditioner that settled them down or maybe it was the smooth jams from the Body & Soul CD that was flowing from his speakers. Whatever the case, he was in no mood to hear any bickering. He thought Delana and Lulu had gotten their friendship back on track, but obliviously there was still some animosity there. Turner thought time would heal all wounds but he guessed Delana would never totally forgive Lulu for sleeping with her man, Tyrone. That was over seven years ago and to make matters worse, Lulu became pregnant and had his son, Tye Jr.

Turner would never forget that time. He remembered the day as if it had happened yesterday. He recalled Karen calling him frantically that Delana had gone insane. Delana sat quietly for nine months until Lulu had that baby and then all hell broke loose. Karen was screaming for Turner to meet her over Lulu's house before Delana arrived. Turner flew out of his office building on Euclid Avenue and sped his raggedy Metro mini car over to Lulu's, off of 93rd and Union. At the time, they needed his social worker's skills to defray an explosion that had been building up. He considered it an emergency and by the time he had made it, Karen had just arrived herself. The only problem was Delana's car was already there. When they reached the door, they could hear the fight had already started. They were going at it like cats and dogs. Delana's suburban etiquette went out the door as she matched Lulu's ghetto mentality. It was hard to tear the two apart and Turner was glad Ray Ray had arrived to help.

It took months for Turner to put that relationship back together but he did. He had a natural love of helping people, so he decided to enroll back in school to get his master's degree. He moved to Chicago over six years ago to attend the University of Illinois. Tomorrow he would be receiving his Ph.D. It definitely felt good to be out of school and even better to have achieved the highest educational status as a doctor. It's a good thing he could help his friends because they surely could use a doctor. Karen's marriage was on the brink of destruction, Ray Ray was in some kind of love triangle, and Delana and Lulu still harbored resentment over an incident that happened over seven years ago. Somehow throughout this weekend, Turner had to find time to deal with these issues, he thought as he pulled into a bar and grill restaurant.

Everyone was all too happy to jump out the truck and get their grub on. Turner was even hungry. Between his fall out with his girlfriend Natalie and the problems between his friends, he had worked up a big appetite.

Turner was surprised at how well their dinner went. Delana even sat next to Lulu. Sometimes Turner just couldn't figure women out. One minute they were going at it and the next minute they were talking like best friends.

After they finished their meal, Turner got back onto the highway and headed to the nice suburbs of Wheaton to drop Delana off. When they got there, she kept her friend Michael far away from Lulu while she made quick introductions. After Delana disappeared into Michael's big house, Turner backed out of the driveway snickering to himself— WOMEN.

Chapter 6

<u>*Delana*</u>

As soon as Michael shut the door, he grabbed Delana and thrust his tongue in her mouth. He hadn't been with her intimately for over a year and he definitely was going to take advantage of her now.

"Michael—"

"Delana, we can talk later," he said cutting in while stripping her clothes off. He immediately got an erection. He grabbed Delana's breast and suckled lavishly on her hardened nipples."

"Oooh, Michael, give it to me just the way I like it," Delana moaned.

"You know I will but first give me what I've been waiting for," he said, while he unzipped his pants.

"And what flavors do you like?" she asked, digging through her purse to find some condoms.

"Why don't you choose, you'll be the one doing all the tasting," he told her.

"Umm— this dark chocolate works best. You know I can suck on this tasty flavor all day."

"Well then I'd better stock up on a supply," he told her while she went to work.

Michael's six foot five frame weakened like Jell-O as he grabbed onto the door for support. Delana must have sensed his overwhelming desire because she went down on him even more. The rim of her mouth felt wonderful as it slid up and down his shaft like a piece of machinery. Michael tried to hold out on her good lovin' but he couldn't wait any longer. He grabbed her hair while he exploded in excitement. Michael stripped the rest of Delana's clothes off and returned the favor. He loved seeing her squirming erotically in his hands. They spent the next two hours making up for lost time.

"Umm— you sure know how to make a sistah work up a sweat."

"I wouldn't have it any other way," Michael told her. "If a man can't satisfy his woman in bed, then somebody else sure will."

Delana didn't respond while she laid her head on his chest and thought about Corey. She loved him but not nearly like she loved Michael. Besides she was not ready for a love relationship, especially now that Corey was jobless. He needed to get himself back together and until then she had no regrets about being with Michael.

"Delana, I know I've asked you before but why don't you reconsider moving up here with me?"

"Michael, we've had this discussion before. You now I'm not the settle-down-type— you know, the wife and kids at home."

"Who said you had to be a at home wife with kids?"

"Michael, those were the exact words that came out of your mouth before."

"Okay you're right— but tell me this, how many brothers do you come across that can allow their women to stay at home?"

Delana bit down on her lower lip in thought. "Not many," she responded.

"Exactly. Now I want you to seriously reconsider my proposal. To add some incentive, I want you to wear this," he told her.

Delana gasped at the two-karat diamond ring sitting inside the gold box.

"Michael—"

"Yes, Delana— I want you t be my wife."

"Michael, this is so sudden."

"No it's not," Michael told her. He took the ring out and slid it on her finger. "Just as I thought—a perfect fit," he said, kissing the tip of her fingers.

Delana didn't know what to say so she cried instead.

Michael pulled her closer in his arms and traced his finger across her face. "Delana, I love you so much. I was crushed when you refused to move down here with me the first time. You just were so hell-bent on being independent and all so I just let you go out of anger without a fight. Ever since we've been apart, my life has not been the same. Delana, marry me. We can have it all and I promise you can have your independence as well."

"Michael, we're both involved in relationships."

"Delana, it doesn't matter. That can easily be resolved for me. If you really loved this so called Corey than you wouldn't be in my bed. You need to trust your heart Delana. You've never been able to do that before."

"Michael, I'm not saying no to your proposal— it's just that I wasn't expecting this."

"Well give me your answer by the end of this weekend. If you turn me down again, Delana, I want my ring back and a promise that we'll be strictly friends."

"You mean no more booty calls?" Delana said, as if this was a deal breaker for the decision she would have to make.

"You damn straight," Michael laughed at her sarcastic comment. "That's what I love about you."

"And what's that?" Delana asked, slipping her tongue into his mouth.

"Your persona. You're so business like but you're also funny, loving, and don't mind getting your hands dirty if you have to."

"You got that right," Delana said, thinking about Lulu's deceitfulness. That's exactly what broke up their friendship in the first place. Since then, Delana was always on the look out when it came to Lulu and her boyfriends. She would never forget that day when Lulu slept with her ex, Tyrone. That was the worst day of her life. They had been close like sisters but that bond was broken forever. Thanks to Turner they had moved past the ordeal but that's as far as it would go. Every time Delana saw Lulu's child, Tye Jr., all the memories came flooding back. It was just too much, so Delana did what she does best—she moved on.

"Delana, I also have one more incentive for you."

"And what's that?"

"Some good lovin," Michael responded. He pulled Delana on top of him and they made wild passionate love all over again.

"Michael, you make it hard for a girl to say no. You love me, you can take care of me financially, and you definitely have it going on between the sheets."

"So I take it that you'll marry me?"

"I'd be a fool not to. YES— Michael Thorton, I'll marry you. I'd love to be your wife," Delana said, snuggling up next to him.

Chapter 7

<u>*Karen*</u>

Karen could barely make it to Turner's home before her cell phone began to ring. Her home number appeared on her caller I.D. She was not ready to talk with her husband Jason, but she couldn't ignore the call.

"Hello."

"Karen, where the hell are you at?" Jason screamed through the phone.

"Look, Jason you got my note. Why can't you just leave me alone?"

"Leave you alone! The last time I checked you were still my wife. Karen, where are you at so I can come and get you?"

By now Karen was crying. She sat down on the edge of Turner's bed in fear that her legs would give out. Her whole body began to shake. Just the sound of Jason's voice would do that to her when they argued.

"Karen, are you there?"

"Jason, I can't take any more of your abuse, especially now."

"Baby, I'm sorry," he said, lowering his tone. "Come back home so we can work through this together."

"Jason, you gave me a black eye. How many more punches will I have to take before you realize hitting a woman is wrong?"

"Baby, I apologized for that. I promise you it will never happen again."

"Jason, if you love me then you will give me this time alone. I need time to think, time to heal, and time to set priorities in my life."

"Baby, I'm afraid you're going to leave me. I promise I'll get help if you come home."

"Jason, I will be home but not today. Please respect my wishes to be alone right now. The last thing I want is to end up in divorce court."

"When will you be home?"

"In a few days. I'll call you every day to let you know I'm okay but please respect my privacy. We both need time. Jason, I really hope that you are serious about getting help because I won't give you a next time to hit me," Karen told him before hanging up the phone.

Karen folded her hands over her face and let the tears go. She was surprised to feel Turner's hands wrapped around her body.

"How long have you been standing there?"

"Long enough."

"Turner, I really didn't want you to hear that."

"Karen, I'm glad I did over hear your conversation. I knew from the moment I saw you that something was wrong, but this is the last thing I would have expected."

"Turner, promise me you won't tell the others."

"Karen, I would never step out of line with your private business. Besides, we've been through so much," he said, wiping the tears from her eyes.

"Turner, you've always been there for me," Karen said. The tears were still flowing from her eyes and Turner was steadily wiping them away.

"Karen, I'll always be here for you."

"Thank you," Karen told him, kissing him on the lips. It felt good to roam in familiar territory. Karen traced her tongue around the edge of his lips before parting and brushing her tongue across his.

Turner was surprised by Karen's actions but did not push her away. He pulled her body closer into his and relished in the moment as their tongues interlocked. It felt like old times. A moment of silence lingered between the two.

"Karen, I'm going to kill that bastard for laying his hands on you."

"Turner, no. The last thing I want is you sitting behind bars because of me. Turner, look at you— tomorrow you'll be graduating with a doctorate degree. You've come so far; promise me you'll never do anything stupid trying to protect me?"

"Karen, our friendship means more than any degree. I can't let you go home knowing this."

"Then help me," Karen told him. She took his hands into hers, "Turner, you're the therapist. Put your personal feelings aside and help Jason and me."

"Karen, that's asking a lot of me, besides it would be a conflict for me to provide therapy to my friends. I'm not sure how I'll react if I see Jason. Do you know how hard it would be to put my personal feelings aside? Karen, we lost our virginity together and now we are best friends."

"Turner, I'm pregnant. I know it's a lot to ask considering I didn't even want you to know about this, but Jason promised to get help. I think you would be the right person to help us. Turner, I wouldn't feel comfortable talking to anyone else."

"Okay," Turner said, caving in. "I'll give you some advice as your friend, but this is only for you and the baby. As far as I'm concerned Jason can go straight to hell."

"Turner—"

"Okay, Karen. I'm sorry," he told her as the phone began to ring.

"Hello."

"Turner, it's Ray Ray. We're lost," he said in an agitated voice.

"Ray Ray, where are you at?"

"I don't know Turner. Why don't you ask Ms. Lulu, the bus driver who had to stop to get some cigarettes," Ray Ray said before handing the phone over to Lulu.

Turner gave Lulu instructions on how to get downtown. When he was done he hung up the phone and cuddled Karen back in his arms.

****

"Lulu, press that pedal to the metal and stop driving like a bus driver. I can't be late for this hair show."

"Ray Ray relax; you'll get there on time," Lulu told him. "Besides, I'm not about to get a ticket on my record and on Turner's truck for speeding."

"Then you should have let me drive."

"Please, Ray Ray— you can barely handle driving your Ford Focus."

"No, you didn't just go there," Ray Ray proclaimed with a long-winded sigh. His eyes rolled to Lulu then to the highway and back to Lulu again.

"Look Ray Ray, I'm sorry. I've already gotten into an argument with Delana and don't want to get into one with you."

"Well, apology accepted. Now you want to tell me what's really going on with you and Delana?"

"Ray Ray, you already know what's wrong with me and Delana. She's never going to let me live down the fling that Tyrone and I had."

"Lulu, you know I'm your friend, but I can't say I blame Delana one bit for still being angry at you. It's bad enough that you and Tyrone slept together but an innocent child was born out of the affair. How do you think Delana feels whenever she sees Tye Jr.? It's a constant reminder of the affair you had and the bond of friendship you have broken."

"Ray Ray, I understand your point but it has been over seven years. If she can't find it in her heart to forgive me than why do she pretend that we're still friends?"

"Lulu, I don't think that Delana is pretending to be your friend. You know she don't stand for no bullshit and certainly don't have a problem with walking away. Hell, Delana and Tyrone didn't even have a relationship they were just sex partners. If it had been anyone else that had slept with him, then I'm sure Delana would have cared less one way or another about Tyrone. I think this whole thing is a trust issue, something you may want to talk with Turner about since he is the therapist."

"Maybe you're right. Delana and I can't continue down this destructive path if we want to continue being friends. It's not healthy for neither one of us and I hate that my son is caught in the middle."

"Yes, I can imagine how awful that must be," Ray Ray said, patting Lulu on the leg. "Just remember time can heal all wounds— you just have to nurture it properly."

"Ray Ray, for someone caught up in their own love triangle, you sure give some good advice."

"Girl, I don't even want to think about my problems. Turner's graduation couldn't have come at a more perfect time because I needed to get away."

"Me too," Lulu said. "This is the first time in years that I can just enjoy being by myself. No kids, no men, and definitely no headaches," she laughed as she exited off the highway.

"See Ray Ray, I told you we would make it on time."

"Yes, I see. Thank you," Ray Ray smiled as the car became silent for the remainder of the drive to the Chicago Hair Expo.

Chapter 8

<u>*Turner*</u>

Turner could hardly sleep so he decided to get out of bed instead. The time on the alarm clock read 4:45 a.m. He had another five hours to go before his graduation from the University of Illinois.

Turner decided to take a long hot shower and wondered if Natalie would be there. No matter what happened between the two of them, he was falling madly in love with her. How come he just couldn't tell her those words? Instead he pushed her away, something he was beginning to regret already. You would think his life would be under control since he was a therapist but it wasn't. Natalie had only been gone for one day and his life was already a mess. It forced him to face the past of losing his mother, his intimate relationship with Karen, and many other things in between that caused a wall to go up so he would not be hurt again. Turner knew what he had to do. He stepped out the shower, dried off, and then went to his bedside to pick up the phone.

"Hello."

"Natalie, I'm sorry to call you so early in the morning."

"Turner, is everything all right?" Natalie asked in a raspy tone.

"Yes, everything is fine. I just wanted to call and tell you how much I love you."

Silence— there was complete silence.

"Natalie, are you there?"

"Yes, Turner, I'm just surprised—"

"Surprised that I said those words," he said finishing her sentence.

"Yes."

"Well I'll admit that it took you walking out on me to realize the special bond we have. Natalie, I don't want to lose you," Turner told her thinking about all his friends' problems. Before he could help them he had to help himself.

"Turner, you know I love you too."

"I know. Natalie, I want you to come to breakfast and meet my friends— I mean family. They've been asking about you. I kind of lied and told them you were out of town on business and wouldn't be returning until this morning."

"You lied. Turner, I'm surprised," Natalie chuckled softly.

"I'm sorry— I promise I'll make it up to you."

"Oh, you can count on that. Now what time do you want me to be over there?"

"At seven o' clock sharp. You know we're going to need at least an hour and a half to feed a large group."

"Seven o' clock it is then," Natalie said, before hanging up the phone.

Turner felt positive about the steps he had just taken. It had been fifteen years since he last said those words 'I love you' to anyone.

****

Breakfast was a blast. Turner was especially pleased how well Natalie fit in with the group. Of course Delana was late and shocked everyone with her own good news.

"Oooh, Delana— do tell," Ray Ray told her while running his hand across that huge diamond rock.

"Ray Ray, what does it look like? I'm getting married silly."

"Delana, I'm no fool. I'm just surprised. I thought you and Michael were just friends. Just the other day you were madly in love with Corey."

"Mind your business," Delana told Ray Ray as she pulled up a seat next to him. "Today it's all about Turner," she smiled while Turner introduced her to Natalie.

"It's good to finally meet you," Delana said to Natalie. Since I'll be moving to Chicago, it will be good to have some friends here."

"Any friend of Turner's is a friend of mine. Here, let me give you my card."

Turner noticed the jealousy in Lulu eyes as they both exchanged cards. He definitely needed to help them bridge their relationship before it was lost forever. All these years it had been hanging by a thin rope and Turner needed to mend it together before it snapped. Furthermore, he needed to get in Delana's mind— the last thing he ever expected was for her to come down here and get engaged to Michael, the man she dumped to preserve her independence.

"Excuse me, everyone," Karen said, as all eyes centered on her.

"I just wanted to say a little something before we head off to Turner's graduation."

The table became completely silent. Karen prayed to God what she was about to do would not come back to haunt her. She took a deep breath before continuing.

"Turner, I can't say enough about how proud we all are of you."

Everyone nodded in agreement.

"And your parents would have been especially proud of you, too," Karen said, handing him a neatly wrapped box.

"Karen, where did this come from?" The only parent he had was his mother and she was dead.

"Just open it," Karen told him.

Turner was reluctant to open the box as he neatly tore at the seams of the wrapping paper. Inside was his mother's Bachelor's degree with a note inside.

"Karen, where did this come from?" Turner asked again.

"Your father gave it to me. I had no idea what was in the box. He just pleaded with me to give you this before you walked across that stage."

Turner slid his hand across the leather bond case that held his mother's degree. He slowly took out the note and began to read.

Turner,

I've asked Karen to deliver this because I know you would not have accepted anything from me. Anyhow, enclosed is your mother's Bachelors degree. The last time we were together she brought this degree to me and slapped me upside the head with it. She called me all kinds of 'no good for nothing,' names. I understood her anger, she basically wanted to say, she made it without me. Your mother boasted on and on about how successful you all would be. She loved you so much, Turner. She told me 'my son is going to surpass me and even one day get his doctorate degree.' Turner, even before your mother passed, she knew of your destiny. I want you to have her degree and stand it along side yours. Leila would have been so proud and so am I. You know your mother forgave me for all my wrongs and I hope that someday you will find it in your heart to forgive me too.

Robert.

Turner eyes watered but he didn't let any tears escape from his eyes. Why didn't Karen give this to him yesterday or when he was alone? He knew the answer to that— because he would have thrown the box away and besides she had on idea what was inside the box.

Turner slid his mother's degree back in the box and was glad the waitress brought out their food. Perfect timing— and for the next hour everyone got their grub on.

Lulu was glad the graduation ceremony was finally over. She stretched her sleeping legs and then made a mad dash to the ladies room before the crowd hit. When she was behind the comfort of the bathroom stall, she broke down in tears. Every one of her friends was doing well with their lives. Even though she was making good money as a bus driver, she couldn't help but feel a little envious. Delana and Ray Ray had their own business, Karen was happily married with a master's degree in Information Technology, and now Turner had just walked across the stage to get his doctorate degree. To make matters worse, Delana was engaged to be married. She always had the good men, the kind that a sister wanted to settle down with. Well from this point forward, Lulu decided she had to make a change with her life. There would be no more easy access for men when she got back to Cleveland. She also wanted to enroll into community college, and the one last thing, she promised herself was to be a better mother to her kids. No more running the streets or not being there to help with the kids' schoolwork or whatever. Lulu wanted her kids to do something with their lives, and if their own mother didn't help to make sure that happened, why would anyone else?

Lulu wiped the tears from her eyes, used the bathroom, and then made her way back to join the others.

"Is everything all right?" Ray Ray asked her, pulling her to the side.

"Yes Ray Ray, I'm fine."

"Well it looks like your eyes are a little teary," he told her.

"Really, I'm fine," Lulu told him before putting her sunglasses back on.

After taking a ton of pictures, everyone headed back over to Turner's to change into some relaxing clothes. Lulu was glad she had decided to come along to Chicago. This was a major factor in her decision to put her life back together. She wanted more, needed more, and would get more out of life. Once Lulu made her mind up to do something, she did it. From this point

forward Lulu was going to be a changed woman— and it felt
good.

Chapter 9

Ray Ray

"Jim, didn't I tell you not to call me anymore?" Ray Ray said with a long-winded sigh.

"Ray Ray, I'm in love with you. How can you be so cold and treat me like this?"

"I can do what the hell I want, Jim— besides you lied to me from the very beginning."

"Ray Ray, what would you have had me do— stamp a 'I have AIDS,' sign on my forehead?"

"No, but you definitely should have told me up front. That's the very reason why many people contract AIDS, because of all the dishonesty. My goodness, Jim, you let me tongue you and everything. If I hadn't persisted that you get tested before us having intercourse then you could have very well passed the disease on to me and my current lover."

"Ray Ray, I would have used protection."

"Oh no you didn't— like that's supposed to make me feel any better. Jim, condoms break and, furthermore, condoms are not a hundred percent guarantee that it will protect against the AIDS virus."

"Ray Ray, I'm sorry. I'm just scared to lose our friendship."

"Yes, Jim, it's just a friendship. You know I'm involved with someone else. I wish you would stop calling me like we're together or something."

"Ray Ray, we are together. I'm not going to let you give up on me," Jim told him.

"We're really good together, Ray Ray. If it wasn't for me having AIDS, you would have been dumped your lover and came to my bed."

"Jim—"

"Ray Ray, when was the last time you checked your lover Demetrius?"

"Hold up— how do you know Demetrius?"

"Let's just say he's not all that faithful as you think him to be. I hope you're protecting yourself with his ass because I know for a fact that he's been with several of my lovers," Jim said, before clicking him off the phone.

Ray Ray sank back on the toilet seat as his legs gave way. "Oh my goodness," he shrieked quietly to himself. Now he couldn't wait to get back to Cleveland so he could straighten out the mess that his life was in.

"Ray Ray, how long are you going to be in the bathroom?" Karen asked, knocking on the door.

"Just a minute, girl."

"Okay, I'll just stand here and wait," Karen told him. She did not want to lose her place in line. After the graduation and touring Chicago all day, Karen was in desperate need of a shower. In a few hours they would be heading out for a late dinner and dancing at some of Chicago's finest clubs. She also wanted to get into the bathroom for some privacy so she could call her husband Jason.

"NEXT," Ray Ray sighed with a half-looking smile on his face.

"Ray Ray, is everything all right?" Karen asked looking into his troubled eyes. She definitely recognized the signs of problems because she was going through some herself.

"Yes, Karen, I'm fine. Now hurry up and get dressed so I can throw a few curls in your sweated out hair."

"Oooh Ray Ray. Does my hair look that awful?"

"Yes, darling— but nothing Ray Ray can't fix."

With that Karen went in the bathroom and took a quick shower. She lotioned her body, threw a black silk sundress on, and then picked up the phone and dialed home. Karen was relieved when the answering machine came on. She was in no mood to talk with her husband. She left a message that she was okay and would be home tomorrow afternoon. Karen slipped her cell phone back into her purse and then cleaned the bathroom. After that she joined the others out back on Turner's enclosed porch, where Ray Ray set up shop doing hair.

"Wow— if I wasn't gay, Karen, I would try talking game to you," Ray Ray said giving her a wink. "Now, come sit in my chair," he said motioning Lulu to get up.

Everyone busted out in laughter but not even a shriek came from Turner's mouth. His eyes were all over her. She could feel the intensity of him as her nipples became rock hard and pierced through her thin dress. Thank goodness Ray Ray covered her up with his plastic slip protector— and thank goodness Natalie wasn't here to see the spark within their eyes. Any stranger would have picked up on their feelings, but the rest of the group had been friends for so long that they barely paid attention to a flame that had been extinguished so many years ago.

It took Ray Ray nearly an hour to put curls through her long silk hair. The length flowed down to the middle of her back, and when Ray Ray was done he handed her the mirror.

"Beautiful as usual," Karen told Ray Ray. "Now how much do I owe you?"

"Nothing. This one is on me."

Karen got up and Delana took a seat to get her short hair spruced up. Delana reminded Karen of Hallie Berry, from her hairstyle to her petite body frame.

Karen wondered where Turner had gone off to? She left her friends on the porch and went into the house to be alone for a few moments.

"Is everything okay?" Turner asked, circling his arms around her waist.

Karen did not turn around. "Yes," she told him looking out his bay window in the living room. His arms felt good around her. Turner turned her face to meet his.

"Karen, you're married and I'm involved with Natalie, and yet I can't shake these feelings I still have for you. Seeing you again just brought everything back."

"Turner, what are you trying to tell me?"

"I'm still in love with you. Is it possible to be in love with two people?"

"Turner, all the times we were together you never once told me you loved me."

"Karen, you had to know that deep down in your heart."

"Yes, and I'll always love you to. I never understood why you pushed me away in the first place."

"I was stupid— but the truth is when we were together I was dealing with a lot of pain over the loss of my mother. I never wanted to get close to anyone, I never wanted to experience that type of pain again. Between you and me, it took Natalie walking out on me to realize the problems I needed to deal with."

"I would have never imagined that you harbored these feelings for so long. Turner—your mother has been gone now for over fifteen years. She would have not wanted you to suffer like this; she loved you."

"I know. I told my mother I loved her on her death bed— that was the last time I used those words until the other day with Natalie and now you. I thought letting out my feelings would resolve my problems but it has only made me more confused, especially being here with you."

"Turner, I know you love me but that was in the past."

"Karen, I just picked up and left you all those years ago. At the time it was easier to do that than trying to explain my emotions."

"Yes, I was really hurt but I knew you were going through some things."

"Back then I felt all alone. My mother was the only one I had or could depend on.

"Turner, I wish you would have turned to me. Sometimes I wonder if we would have gotten married, had a family—"

"I'm so sorry for hurting you."

"Turner, don't apologize. All I ever wanted was for you to be happy. I know our lives went in different directions, but I'm content with us being friends. How many ex-couples do you know can say that?"

"None."

"My point exactly. Maybe it was meant for our lives to turn out this way. I couldn't imagine not having you in my life. Relationships come and go but friends are forever," Karen said, kissing him on the lips.

"Forever— then I'm glad we're friends."

****

Delana had too much fun bumping and grinding out there on the dance floor. It was five o' clock in the morning when Turner dropped her off over at her fiancé's house.

"Who the hell do you think you are walking into my house this late?"

Delana was surprised at his tone of voice. Michael got up from the couch and came over to her. "Michael, it's my last night here. I told you I would be out late."

"Yeah, but five o' clock, Delana. I guess you had no intentions of spending time with me."

"Michael, why are you tripping?"

"Tripping— you haven't seen any tripping."

"Wait, hold it one damn moment. You don't own me. I can do whatever the hell I want."

"Not in my house you won't."

"My house— oh, I see how this shit is going to be," Delana screamed, slipping the ring off her finger.

"The engagement is OFF," Delana said, throwing the ring in his face. She pulled out her cell phone and called Turner to turn around and come back to pick her up. It took Delana all of two minutes to pack up her belongings.

"A leopard never changes its spots," Micheal gasped in anger.

"It sure damn don't and I never told you I would change my spots. You either take all or have none of me," she yelled, smacking him across the face.

"Delana, what the hell is wrong with your drunk ass?"

"Michael how could you do this to me? You asked me to be your wife. You know how I am— you were the one talking all that shit about me being able to keep my independence. You never had no intentions of that?"

"Delana, this is not about your independence— it's about RESPECT. You don't come walking in somebody else's home at five o'clock in the morning."

"Somebody else's house! Michael, you sure keep putting the emphasis on the singular rather the plural, WE. And to think I was going to give my home and business up in Cleveland to move down here with you. Hell, I'm glad I did walk in here late to see your true colors. I'll be damn if I ever let any man control me."

"Delana, you'll never let a man have you."

"Hell no! He can be with me but he will never "have" me. Ownership went away with slavery."

"You're always twisting things around."

"No I'm not— and you're the stupid ass one. You better go get one of those poor ass sisters to control because this sister can get everything on her own," Delana shouted, waving her hand in his face.

"Well then take your ass outside and wait on your own," Michael said, opening his door. He pushed Delana out before she had the chance to walk out proudly on her own. Michael slammed the door in her face and all he could hear was her screaming, *son of a bitch this* and *son of a bitch that*. It was no use in arguing with that fool. As much as he loved Delana, he could never be with her on a permanent basis. She was too independent for her own damn good. He could have kicked himself for trying to do the right thing. Michael should have just hung on to Delana as a now and then booty call, because that sister was definitely a freak in between the sheets.

****

Turner was sad to see his friends go. After church service on Sunday, they headed directly to the airport so they could catch their flight back to Cleveland. He wished he was returning with them but his life was flourishing in the windy city of Chicago. Turner and Natalie said their goodbyes and headed back home.

Chapter 10

Ray Ray

Ray Ray had both hands full of luggage coming back from Chicago. One bag was full of hair products that he had received at a huge discount. That alone was reason enough to make a trip to the windy city but he was glad he went there to see his friend Turner graduate. It was both an honor and a blessing to have such good friends.

"Oh my goodness— Jim, how in the hell did you get into my house?" Ray Ray asked, dropping his bags.

"Ray Ray, I've been here all weekend waiting for you to return home."

"What! This isn't your home. I want you to leave," Ray Ray yelled in an agitated tone.

"No, we need to talk."

"Talk about what? The fact that you broke into my home?"

"Ray Ray, I have a key. This hardly constitutes as breaking in."

"Yes, if you stole it, and obviously you did, it's against the law."

"Look, Ray Ray, why are you trying to give me such a hard time? I went through a hard time trying to get this together," Jim said pointing towards the bedroom.

"Jim, I swear if you went through a single thing in my bedroom you're going to regret it," Ray Ray said, rushing into his bedroom to see what he was talking about.

"What in the world!"

"I take it you like everything?"

All the scented candles that were lit up stunned Ray Ray. Jim had champagne and rose petals thrown all over the bed. Ray Ray could do nothing but gasp as he put his hand over his mouth.

"Jim, I want you out of here," Ray Ray said coming back to his senses. He went around the room blowing out all the candles. Jim caught him off guard and threw him against the bed, binding his hands to the bedpost.

"You ungrateful bastard. I've done all this for you and this is the thanks I get?" Jim belted out, while he striped both of their clothes off. He became a wild animal thrusting his hard erection in and out vigorously from behind. Taking one hand, he gripped it tightly over Ray Ray's mouth to drown out his hollering. With the other hand, he straddled around Ray Ray to hold him from flopping around like a fish with no water. Jim pumped in and out confessing his dying love for Ray Ray. He hadn't been intimate in over a year and his thrust became harder and harder.

Jim never intended for the condom to break. He rushed and got a towel and tried to wipe his fluids quickly out of Ray Ray. All Jim could hear was, "You mother fucker bastard have given me AIDS." Scared, Jim retrieved his clothes and ran fast out of Ray Ray's place.

Ray Ray couldn't break free from the handcuffs to pick up the phone but he was able to stretch his neck to the base of the phone. He depressed the help button using his nose.

"911."

"I've been raped, please help me," Ray Ray screamed out frantically.

"Please calm down and tell me where you are and who did this."

"Don't tell me to calm down," Ray Ray shot back. "The guy who raped me have AIDS. Please get someone over here quickly to unlock my hands."

Ray Ray stayed on the phone with the dispatcher until the police and paramedics arrived. They already had latex gloves on when they came into his bedroom.

"Oh God, please don't let me have AIDS," Ray Ray prayed while the police helped free his bruised hands from the handcuffs.

Ray Ray was immediately taken to the emergency room where he was poked and prodded by the hospital staff. They ran a series of test, one that would determine if he had been infected with the HIV virus.

"Mr. Fields, do you have someone who can take you home?"

Ray Ray just looked at the nurse with a blank stare. He couldn't get the words out and hot tears formed in the corner of his eyes.

"Take all the time you need," the nurse, told him, handing him a box of Kleenex. She set the phone on his bed and then walked out of the room to take care of the other patients who occupied her time.

After ten minutes elapsed, Ray Ray picked up the phone.
"Hello."
"Turner, this is Ray Ray. I've been raped."
"What did you say?"
"Turner, I'm in the hospital. Remember that love triangle that Lulu mentioned I was caught up in?"
"Yeah."
"Well when I got home he had broken into my apartment and then raped me. Turner, he has AIDS. Oh my goodness—I'm going to die," Ray Ray cried through the phone.
"Ray Ray, I'm on the next flight to Cleveland."
"Thank you Turner. I really need your help."
"No problem. That's what family is for."

Chapter 11

<u>*LuLu*</u>

"DeAndre, you're the last person to pick our son up and the first person to bring him back."

"Lulu, stop tripping. I have things to do," DeAndre told her.

"Things to do!" Lulu mimicked back. "DeAndre you ain't shit. I haven't even been back two hours. You could have at least given me time to settle in."

"Whatever. So how was your trip to Chicago?" he said, trying to change the subject.

Lulu just looked at him and rolled her eyes. "I thought you had something to do."

"Yeah, I do but not before I get in between your legs," DeAndre said, kissing her on the lips.

"Hell no," Lulu said, slapping DeAndre in the face.

"Woman, have you lost your mind."

"Yep. I lost my mind the day I let you crawl up in between my legs. Going to Chicago finally knocked some sense back into my head. Being away from everyone gave me time to think of the things that are really important in my life."

"Meaning?"

"Meaning no more booty calls for your ass."

"Lulu, you know you can't resist this," DeAndre said, grabbing his crotch and then giving it a squeeze.

Lulu just stood there and laughed. For the first time in her life she realized that she didn't need a man to fulfill her life, at least the wrong kind of man anyway. As fine as DeAndre was, he was no good, not as a man nor as a father.

"DeAndre, I'm not even going to partake in your foolish games but I will tell you this, there are going to be some changes."

"Changes."

"Yes, you heard me right," Lulu said, cutting him off.

"Starting next month I want a hundred dollars a week for child support by money order or cashiers check."

"What?"

"DeAndre, I didn't stutter. Either you start taking care of your child or I will go downtown and let the courts do it."

"Lulu, what the hell is wrong with you? I do take care of my son."

"DeAndre, I hardly call buying a few outfits here and there and spending a few hours whenever you can fit it into your schedule as taking care of a child. I am busting my ass working double time to take care of my children."

"Well no one told you to lay up and have three kids."

"You're right about that but I'm damn glad all my kids are not from you because your sorry ass can't take care of one. At least the money I get from Tyrone and Rick helps me out a lot, even with taking care of your baby too. And don't forget that it takes two to make a baby. Why do women get stuck with all the responsibilities?"

"Lulu, I don't have time for this," DeAndre told her, heading out the door.

"Well you better make time," Lulu yelled after him. "You should be happy that I'm trying to work something out with you. Most women just haul their baby daddies down to court. DeAndre with your new job's salary I could easily get over two hundred dollars a week, but all I'm asking you to pay is a hundred dollars for your child. You can at least do that."

DeAndre just looked at Lulu with hate in his eyes. As mad as he was, he wasn't stupid. He nodded his head in agreement with her terms and then walked off muffling angry words to himself.

"Yeah, that's right," Lulu said underneath her breath. Do that fool think he can ride around in a new truck and not pay for his child? Well not any longer, Lulu thought to herself. She was tired of carrying the entire load and time was changing starting today. It was definitely going to be for the better.

Chapter 12

<u>*Karen*</u>

Jason was sitting on the couch watching television when Karen came in.

"So, you're finally back," Jason said without even turning his head to greet her.

"Jason, can we talk?"

"That's a good idea, and you can start by telling me where the hell you were all weekend."

"Look, Jason, I don't have the time or the energy to argue with you."

"Well you wasn't over your mother's or sister's house because I checked. Karen, where did you go?" Jason asked, flicking the television off.

"I was in Chicago visiting Turner."

"You were where?" Jason stated, leaping out of his seat.

"Jason, Turner has agreed to help us work through some of our problems."

"No, I didn't just hear you say that," Jason said, pushing her up against the wall. "What the hell were you thinking telling him our business and then getting him involved without my permission?"

"Stop, Jason! You're hurting me," Karen screamed, trying to wiggle herself free.

"Hurting you! I ought to slap the shit out of you," Jason said, tightening his grip. "You are unbelievable going off to another man's house and telling him our business."

"Jason, I didn't go off to another man's house. Turner is like family and besides, Lulu, Delana, and Ray Ray also came along."

"And that's supposed to make it better?"

"Jason, we went down for Turner's graduation. I didn't tell anyone our business. Turner just happened to overhear our conversation when I called you."

"Well he wouldn't have if you would have stayed your ass at home."

"Jason, I would have stayed home if you hadn't beat me. Now get your hands off me," Karen said, pushing him to the side. She wasn't about to get cornered into a situation that she couldn't get out of. She had her baby to think about.

"Karen, why do you make me do these things to you? You always drive me to do crazy things. Why?" Jason hollered, grabbing Karen from behind.

Karen tried to escape from his grasp but he was too strong as she went plummeting to the floor. All she could think of was protecting her stomach. Karen placed her hand in front to take the initial blow from the fall. Before she had a chance to move, Jason's large frame was already on top of her. Karen was pinned down to the floor. She was trapped and had nowhere to go. Hot tears started to stream from her eyes.

"Jason, please stop— don't hurt me."

"You should have thought of that before you went telling our business. When will you learn? Do you think I enjoy hitting you?"

Karen could feel the hit coming and the only thing she could do was yell out, "I'm pregnant. Jason, please don't hurt our baby," Karen pleaded.

It took a moment for the news to filter through his mind but just as quickly as Jason flew in a rage, his anger dissipated within seconds. Instead of hitting her, he circled his arms around her body with a gentle embrace.

"We're going to have a baby?"

"Yes," Karen stated, scrambling off the floor. She grabbed her luggage and headed for their bedroom. She didn't unpack any of her belongings she had taken to Chicago. Instead, she started emptying her drawers and stuffing them into the already full suitcases.

"Karen, what are you doing?"

"Jason, I'm leaving you. It's one thing for you to hit me but I can't risk you hurting the baby, and that's exactly what you're doing. This is just too stressful."

"I would never do anything to hurt you or the baby. Please don't leave. I'm sorry I lost control."

"You're giving me no choice. I promised myself I would never be your punching bag again. Do you think I just want to pick up and leave?"

"Karen, please."

"Jason, stop!" Karen said, cutting off his sentence. "I don't want to hear anymore. You didn't even let me get through the door before starting up with me."

"It's just that you've been gone all weekend. How do you expect me to act when you were staying with another man?"

"Another man. Turner and I are just friends and Delana, Lulu, and Ray Ray was there too. Why can't you just understand that I needed to be away from you for a few days?"

"A man is a man, whether a friend or not. Did you enjoy being away from me?"

"Yes. Jason, I'm tired of all this arguing and fighting. It seems like no matter how hard I try, I can't please you."

For the first time in their marriage Karen felt sorry for Jason. He just sat on the edge of the bed and cried. Silence washed over the room. He rocked back and forth as if his life was over.

For some reason Karen felt a need to comfort him. She wrapped her arms around his thick muscled frame and whispered softly in his ear how much she loved him. Those words made the tears spill from his eyes even more.

"Karen, I don't want to lose you or the baby," Jason whispered in a faint tone.

"I don't want to lose you either but we need help."

"I know," Jason told her while reaching for the phone. He scrolled through the pre-stored numbers before hitting the send button.

"Hello."

"Is this Turner?"

"Yes."

"This is Jason, Karen's husband."

There was an awkward moment of silence. Jason bit down on his pride and admitted for the first time that he needed help.

"Karen told me that you were willing to help us through some of our problems."

"Yes, that won't be a problem for you, will it?" Turner asked.

"No it won't be a problem. When do you think you'll be able to come up? If it's not feasible, we can arrange to come down there."

"Actually, I have an emergency and will be in Cleveland later tonight. Is tomorrow morning a good time to drop by or do you want to make it later in the evening after work?"

"No, tomorrow morning is fine," Jason, told him. He confirmed their appointment and then clicked off the phone.

"Karen, Turner said he'll be in Cleveland later tonight on some type of emergency. He's going to stop by tomorrow and began our therapy sessions."

"Thank you," Karen said, kissing him on the lips. "Now come help me unpack my things," she told him with a sense of relief. Jason had finally made the first step and admitted their marriage was in serious jeopardy. Maybe there was some hope for them after all, Karen thought, rubbing her belly.

Chapter 13

<u>Turner</u>

Turner had planned spending two weeks vacation after his graduation just relaxing, but his friends needed him so now he was on his way to Cleveland, Ohio.

The flight went by fairly quickly and before he knew it the plane was landing at Hopkins International Airport. It was eight o'clock when Turner picked up his luggage. He rented a car and was on his way to see Ray Ray within the hour. The May weather in Cleveland was breezy but Turner enjoyed the cool air caressing his face. He made a right turn onto I-480 East and headed towards Ray Ray's house off of 123rd and Kinsman. These roads were all too familiar, bringing back old memories of when he had worked as a social worker for the City of Cleveland for five years. He ran his car ragged going from home to home with an overwhelming caseload. There were so many problem families, he was able to help some of them. Turner sure hoped he could do the same for Ray Ray and Karen.

Turner couldn't fathom the idea of a man being raped by another man but nothing surprised him after being in the social services field. He encountered problems ranging from incest to the extreme of things he could not even mention. These were all issues that he had to help people deal with, and he was sure he would be able to help Ray Ray through this ordeal.

Turner was so deep in thought that the thirty-minute drive to Ray Ray's house passed by in no time. He pulled into the narrow driveway looking at the rainbow colored flag that hung at half-post. This was a bad day for Ray Ray, Turner thought, walking up the front steps to the porch. Turner knocked on the front door a few times before Ray Ray opened up the bar gates in tears.

"Turner, thank you so much for coming," Ray Ray said, motioning him to come in.

"Not a problem," Turner replied, taking a seat.

"Can I get you anything to eat or drink?"

"I'm fine, Ray Ray. Right now I'm more concerned about you. Have a seat and tell me exactly what happened," Turner said, pulling out his note tablet. "And take your time, Ray Ray. Remember that I'm your friend and I'm here to help you."

Ray Ray could hardly get the words out but managed to tell Turner the tragic events that took place today.

"Did the police take a report from you?" Turner asked, in a sympathetic tone.

"Yes. In fact they just called me a few moments ago and informed me that they had apprehended Jim."

"Good, now tell me what happened at the hospital?"

"They basically ran a bunch of tests to collect evidence and also drew some blood so they could check to see whether or not I was infected with the HIV virus."

"Ray Ray, I'm so sorry. Did they tell you how long it would be before you get the results back?"

"It'll be about a week or two before they can tell me anything. Turner, I'm so scared," Ray Ray said, folding his hands over his face.

This was going to be a long night, Turner thought stretching his hands. Right now he had to play two roles as friend and therapist. He knew eventually he would have to refer his friends over to a trusted colleague because he was too close to the case. As a therapist it would be a conflict of interest to treat his friends, but right now he was there to listen, console, and direct them on the right course of recovery and finding the help they needed. Turner was determined to break the myth for African Americans that it was bad to seek counseling to help deal with the problems they were facing.

Chapter 14

Delana

Delana was furious with her fly by night engagement with Michael. That kind of drama was for the Hollywood celebrities. Delana never imagined she would be in the same ranks with this kind of entertainment. Damn! Right now Delana needed some attention so she picked up the phone and dialed Corey's number.

"Hello."

"Corey, it's me, Delana."

"Yeah, Delana— I know your voice. What do you want?"

"Why do you have to sound so harsh?"

"How do you expect me to talk after the way you spoke to me a few days ago? You treated me like a damn dog."

"Corey that's not true. I may have been a little rude but I never treated you like some kind of dog. Look, that's why I'm calling, it didn't feel right how we left things. Can you come over?"

"You want me drive way from the West side to your fancy condo in Gates Mills to get dogged out again? I don't think so," Corey told her, before she had the chance to respond.

"If you don't want to come over here than at least let me stop by there. Is that all right, Corey?"

"Delana, it's ten o' clock on a Sunday night and I have to be at my new job early tomorrow morning."

"Corey, you found a job?"

"Yep. Right after you belittled me on Friday, I received a call that I got the job at Graphics-Consultant firm."

"Wow, I'm really proud for you," Delana said, kicking herself. Why in the world did she curse him for not having a job the other day? It wasn't like he was lazy and didn't want to work. He had just fallen victim to the harsh economy where companies were downsizing just to survive. Instead of being supportive, she scratched her claws into his back just when his unemployment was about to run out. Damn, she thought again. Now Corey had a job at Graphic Consultants, a huge Fortune 500 company that made top revenue. With Corey's skills, he had to get a good benefits package, Delana thought, biting down on her lower lip.

"So, can I come over?" Delana asked, breaking the long silence.

"Fine, Delana, whatever you want. Besides I don't think you would take no for an answer anyway."

"That's right. I really want to talk, Corey. I'll be over in about an hour," Delana told him before hanging up.

She rushed through the shower and put on a cute little Victoria's Secret sheer panty and bra set. Corey was no match to Michael's wild ass in bed but he was nothing to laugh at either; he was just a gentleman and sometimes Delana liked it rough. Right now she could picture Corey's dark bronze six-foot muscular frame on top of hers, caressing and touching her just the right way. She loved how delicate Corey was with her. He treated her just like a porcelain doll, careful not to do anything to break her body, mind, or spirit. Delana was crazy not to realize the special relationship she had with Corey. She had to somehow find a way to make it up to him.

Delana packed her overnight bag and then headed out of her condo and raced on the other side of town to Corey's house.

****

"You could look happy to see me," Delana told Corey who had reluctantly let her into his house. Corey rented the second floor of a three family house off of West 125th Street. This place looked so bare and drab before Delana met him. All she could remember were white walls, but with her creative hands, she had turned Corey's place into a work of art. She had gotten rid of all his hand-me down furniture and refurbished his whole place. In the living room there was now a tan leather sofa, a love seat, and a recliner she purchased especially for

59

him. A flat screen television was mounted on the wall with a surround sound system hooked up to it. On the decorated black cocktail tables there was a selection of sport magazines along with *Ebony*, *Essence*, and *Black Enterprise*. Delana did let him keep his old rustic lamps, which gave the room an overall man appeal. Black artwork adorned the rest of the once blank walls, and to this day Corey still moaned and complained about how much debt he was in, especially after losing his job.

"Delana, whatever you have to say better be important," Corey told her. Even though he was mad, he was glad to see her, though he would never admit it. After the way Delana had spoken to him the other day, he wondered if he should be re-examining his mind for giving her the time of day.

"Corey, do you think I would even be over here if it wasn't important?" Delana asked. "Maybe this wasn't a good idea," she said out loud before he could speak. Although she didn't want to be alone right now, Delana begged no man for anything. She dumped Michael earlier today and had no problems adding Corey's name to the list if need be.

"Delana, wait," Corey said, grabbing her around the waist. The sweet scent of her perfume and the cleavage showing from her fitted halter-top gave him an instant erection.

"Corey, I know you're upset with me but I just wanted to come over and apologize for the way I treated you the other day," she stated, batting her beautiful brown eyes. For some reason she got all-emotional and began to cry. Delana quickly wiped the tears from her face; she never wanted anyone to think she was the submissive type.

"Delana, why do you always have to be so headstrong? Just let it all out," Corey told her.

For the first time in over seven years, Delana cried like a baby. She let it all go— the hurt and the pain of Lulu sleeping with and having a baby by her ex-boyfriend, all the bullshit she took from her jobs before she packed up and left and started her own business, and the fiasco of letting Michael catch her off guard with his marriage proposal that went sour.

"Corey, I act the way I do because I never want to be hurt again," Delana sobbed. For the next few hours Delana told Corey everything, including her relationship with Michael. If he wanted to still be with her, it was all or nothing.

After what seemed like forever, Delana gathered her belongings and got ready to go. Corey had been relatively quiet; why she thought he would ever understand, she would never know.

"Where are you going?"

"Home. Corey, this was a mistake," Delana told him. Talking to Corey lifted a heavy weight off her shoulders, but she should have never opened herself up totally to a man, just to be rejected all over again.

"Delana, look, you just laid a lot on me. I'm sorry if I'm not reacting the way you want me to but this isn't just about you. I can tell you, however, that despite what happened I'm still in love with you."

"Corey, I'm sorry I hurt you. Is there a chance we can get back together?"

"Let's just take it one step at a time. It's hard enough that you didn't support me when I needed you but you ran into the arms of another man."

"That was a big mistake," Delana said, trying to salvage what little hope she had of hooking back up with Corey.

"I was so upset when you told me that maybe it was better for you to leave me alone and that I would never find a man who could love me."

"Look, we both said some hurtful things but I just didn't jump into bed with another woman because of an argument we had."

Delana couldn't control the tears that poured from her eyes. "You're right, Corey. If it was reversed, I don't know if I would be so forgiving either."

"That's where we differ," Corey told her, sitting down. He motioned for her to sit next to him and then pulled her into his arms.

"If you really love someone than you can work through any problems. It has to be a two-way relationship, Delana. Everything can't revolve around you and whatever you think you deserve. You have to give yourself to me— it's not about owning you, Delana, it's about you trusting in me whatever the situation may be."

"Corey, that's asking a lot of me. I not sure if I can trust anyone completely."

Delana just snuggled in Corey's arm while the room became quiet. It seemed like he wanted to say something but pondered for a few moments on how to articulate the right words.

"Whatever you want to say— just tell me," Delana told him. "I'd rather be hurt with the truth than lied to and hurt later on down the line."

"Okay, fine," Corey said, letting out a long sigh. He knew what he was about to say would send Delana flying right out the room, but if they had any hopes of getting back together then certain things were going to have to be changed.

"Delana, I— um, I think you should get some counseling to help you deal with some of your issues."

"You're right, Corey, and I know of just the person who can help me," Delana said, picking up the phone. She punched in the numbers and then waited while the phone rang.

"Hello."

"Hi, Natalie, this is Delana. Sorry to bother you but can I speak with Turner for a few moments?"

"He's in Cleveland right now," Natalie responded. "There is an emergency that he had to take care of."

"Oh. Is everything all right?"

"Yes, Turner is fine. He's helping a patient," Natalie told her. "Why don't you give him a call on his cell phone. I'm sure he'll enjoy hearing from a friend."

"Great," Delana told her before hanging up. Maybe there would be some hope for her and Corey after all. It was too late to call Turner right now but she was definitely going to call him first thing tomorrow morning so she could get the help that she desperately needed.

Chapter 15

Turner

Turner was mentally and physically exhausted. He wished he hadn't let Ray Ray talk him out of staying at a hotel. Right now he would have loved to be in a fancy hotel, taking a leisurely swim in the pool or soaking in the whirlpool to release some of the tension from his body. Instead, Turner folded out the sofa bed and stretched under the multi-colored bed sheets. Turner flicked on the television and watched the late night news until he drifted off into some much needed sleep.

****

It took Turner a few moments to realize where he was at when his eyes focused on his ringing cell phone.

"Hello."

"Turner, it's me, Delana. I spoke with Natalie who said you were in Cleveland on an emergency. Is everything all right?"

"Yeah. I'm just helping a patient of mine work through some things."

"Well I hope you'll have some time to visit me," Delana said. "Turner, I could really use your advice about some things right now."

"From the sound of your voice I should be asking you whether everything is all right."

"No, it's not," Delana told him. "I know you're probably exhausted from the graduation and then coming up here to Cleveland, but if you have the time I would really like to talk with you."

"Delana, any time you need me I'll be there. I know you wouldn't ask for help unless it was something really important. What time do you want me to stop by?"

"Well I have a meeting this morning that I can't reschedule. How about you stop by my place for lunch? I'll pick up some Chinese food if that's okay."

"Sounds good to me," Turner said, before hanging up.

He sat up in the bed surprised from all the problems his closest friends were having. First he dealt with the issue of Ray Ray being raped and now he had to go over to Karen's house to deal with spousal abuse issues. He was shocked when her husband Jason had phoned him personally. He really sounded sincere about getting help. Karen must have either threatened to leave him or told him about the baby. In either case, Turner had to make sure they received the proper help even long after he left to go back to Chicago. He had to make sure that Jason would never lay another hand on his wife. Karen was too special to him, even though he had reservations about stepping into his friend's personal affairs. He had to find a way to put his personal feelings aside because Karen was too important to him.

Turner didn't want to think about anything for the next few hours. He buried his head underneath the soft pillow and went back to sleep.

Chapter 16

<u>Lulu</u>

"Turn the television off and get in here," Lulu screamed at her three children.

"From now on there are going to be some changes around here," she quipped, giving some reading books to them.

"But Mamma, it's summer time. Can't we just relax and play?" her youngest son Andre asked.

"Play!" Lulu said, mimicking her son's words back.

"Your studies come first. From this day forward there will be one hour of reading every day," Lulu announced, looking her children in the eyes.

They just continued to sit there quietly, wondering what in the world was wrong with her. The point of the matter was that Lulu was appalled to hear that so many black children lagged behind or couldn't read at all compared to other children of different ethnic groups. The truth is parents had to get more involved and there was no way in hell that her children would fall in the statistical category of those having problems or not being able to read at all.

"Not only do you have to read, but you will write a paragraph regarding what you've read. Do I make myself clear?"

"Yes, Mamma," Charmaine, Rick, and Andre repeated in unison.

"Good, now get to reading while I prepare lunch."

"Mamma, will we have to read when you get off vacation and go back to work?" Andre asked.

"Yes Andre," Lulu sighed. "Every day means every day and you've just wasted a minute," Lulu said, tapping at her watch. When their books covered all three noses, Lulu left out the room.

Lulu shuffled over to the refrigerator and took out some eggs and added them to some water to boil. She threw some

French fries in the oven to go along with the tuna salad that she would be making for lunch.

When the phone rang, she looked at the caller ID before answering. Lulu was in no mood to be hassled by any bill collectors today. Seeing Turner's name displayed on the screen, she picked up the line on the third ring.

"Hello."

"Lulu, this is Turner."

"Yep, I know. Your name came up on my caller ID"

"Technology sure has come a long way over the years. Anyway, I was wondering if Delana and I could stop by."

"Stop by," Lulu said, with a puzzled look on her face.

"Yes, I forgot to tell you that I'm in Cleveland."

"Cleveland. Turner we just left you in Chicago the other day. You miss us that much?"

"I certainly do!" Turner chuckled.

"I bet. Now what's this meeting about and what time are you talking about coming over?"

"You'll find out when we get there. Is it okay to come over now?"

"Nope," Lulu said proudly. "Give me an hour or so. My kids have to finish reading and get their lunch. By the time you all get here I can send the little ones upstairs to work on their writing assignment."

"Homework in the summer?"

"Yes— just because they're not in school doesn't mean they should stop studying, and that goes for me too. Tomorrow I have an appointment to find out about enrolling into community college."

"Wow, Lulu, you seem to have made some positive changes in your life. Our talk will be along those same lines," Turner said, before hanging up.

Lulu put the phone back on the hook and wondered what this was all about. Well, there was no use speculating, so

Lulu went back to chopping some onions to put in her tuna salad. By the time she was finished preparing lunch the kids were wrapping up their reading assignments. They all sat down to the kitchen table and Lulu prayed before everyone dug into their food. Lulu just looked on as a good feeling swept over her body. She really was blessed to have healthy kids who would grow up to be somebody; she promised herself she would make that happen.

After lunch Lulu sent the kids upstairs then washed the few dishes they had soiled. The doorbell rang and she took a deep breath and exhaled before answering. Whatever this was about with Delana, Lulu knew her affair with Tyrone was bound to come up.

"Turner, Delana, come right in," Lulu said.

"Lulu, it's always good to see you," Turner stated, kissing her on the cheek.

"Same here," Lulu replied, blushing. Why couldn't she find a man like Turner? He was caring, educated, and made good money. Besides all that, Lulu knew he would make a great father one day.

"So do you all want something to drink before we get into whatever you came to talk about?"

"Yeah, do you have any of that famous lemonade you make?" Turner asked.

"Sure do. I'll fix you a nice tall glass of it. What about you, Delana?"

"Sure, I'll have the same," she replied in a nervous tone.

Delana took a deep breath and exhaled. She gathered her composure while Lulu was in the other room getting their drinks. She definitely needed something to cool her down after the explosion that was about to take place.

"So, what is it that you wanted to see me about?" Lulu asked, handing them both a glass of lemonade.

"Before we began, are the kids upstairs?"

"Turner, sometimes I swear we think alike," Lulu replied. "They're all upstairs working on their homework assignment."

"Homework assignment!" Delana cut in. "I thought the kids just got out of school. Are they in a summer program?"

"Yep— they're in my summer program," Lulu said, filling them in on her changes. "From this point forward my life is heading in a positive direction and if anyone don't like it they can stay behind," she added.

For a moment there was total silence. Delana wiggled in her chair while Turner looked to be deep in thought.

"Well, we've known each other forever so I'll just get straight to the point," Turner said. He glanced over at Delana and then towards Lulu. He prayed Lulu had really changed like she said because he didn't want to be in the middle of a cat fight like the one nearly seven years ago.

"When you all came to Chicago, I noticed right off that there was still some animosity between the two of you. We all know what this is about and I think it's best to talk and completely deal with this issue before it spins out of control and beyond repair."

"I agree," Lulu said, looking Delana in the face. "I know sleeping with Tyrone was wrong and I've apologized a million times for my mistake. Somehow, I never think Delana will forget and forgive," Lulu said, cutting her eyes back to Turner.

"How do you ever expect me to forget and forgive?" Delana asked, before Turner had a chance to speak.

"Lulu, I considered you my best friend, my sister. I never thought I'd see the day of you stabbing me in the back by sleeping with my man— and to make matters worse you conceived a child out of the affair," Delana cried.

"WAIT," Turner said, interrupting. "Let me just make a few things clear," he motioned, trying to defray the emotions that were beginning to spin out of control.

When Turner had their full attention, he moved on.

"First, while it is important to get everything out in the open, there will be no fighting between you two. Secondly, there are kids in the house, so unless they have somewhere else to go, we're going to have to keep our voices down."

On that cue Lulu raised her hand while she grabbed the phone. She quickly dialed her next-door neighbors to see if Melana could watch the kids. She was glad she caught her before she left. Lulu stood up and scurried to the stairwell.

"Chairmaine, Rick, Tye— come down here now."

Lulu stood there while the loud stampede of their feet clattered down the steps. When they reached the bottom, Tye said, "But mommy I thought we had to finish our assignment before coming out our room."

"I know what I said, but Melana wants you all to go with her to get some ice cream."

"Ice cream!" Tye Jr. repeated, with his eyes getting wide.

"Yes, and after that you all are going to the park. Now come in here Charmaine and get this money," Lulu told her. While Lulu reached into her purse, the kids ran over to Turner and Delana. Lulu almost fainted when Tye Jr. ran into Delana's arms and gave her a hug. She didn't know how Delana would react, but she kept her cool. Lulu gave Chairmane twenty dollars and then walked them to the door.

"Thank you, Melana," Lulu yelled, while the kids crossed the street and scrambled into Melana's truck. Melana backed out the driveway and Lulu watched her kids wave goodbye with a huge grin on their faces until they disappeared out of sight.

"Okay, we have the house to ourselves," Lulu said, sitting back down.

Turner breathed a sigh of relief. The last thing he wanted was for her kids to overhear any of their conversation. With that taken care of he proceeded on.

"Now, before we move on there is going to have to be some order," Turner said, looking at the two.

"First, I want Delana to talk and get everything off her chest with no interruptions. When she's done then you can speak," he told Lulu. "After both of you get done then we can talk interactively about the issue at hand. Can the both of you agree to that?"

Both Lulu and Delana agreed to his instructions. There was a moment of silence and then Turner motioned Delana to proceed.

Delana took a long sip of the ice-cold lemonade to clear her throat. It had been over seven years and she wanted to make sure Lulu heard everything she had to say.

"Lulu, not only was I devastated about you being pregnant with my man's child but it was also the way I found out, which upset me even more," Delana said, thinking back to that horrible day.

Delana and Tyrone had been going through some problems but they finally called a truce— or so she thought— and made up. Delana could remember Tyrone's hands all over her body as they made passionate love. Right after the sex, Tyrone fell his ass to sleep, so Delana got out of bed to tidy up the room and picked their clothes up off the floor. Delana wasn't intentionally snooping through his belongings but all women at some point and time went through their man's wallet. Delana was shocked as hell to find a baby ultrasound picture and even more surprised to see Lucy Pierson's name imprinted on the side. It took a moment for Delana to digest the information and regain her composure. She abruptly woke Tyrone up and all hell broke loose.

Tyrone was caught and there was nothing he could do to wiggle his way out of this damn lie. Delana remembered tearing his house up. She snatched the covers off and then jumped on top of him, clawing like a wild animal trying to kill her prey. Her petite body was no match for Tyrone's large frame and he quickly turned over, pinning her arms and legs down with his weight. Since she couldn't move she screamed and cursed all kind of vulgar names at him. Tyrone just let her get it out and when she was done Delana broke down in tears. That moment was the first time Delana ever saw a man cry and it made her feel good to have some kind of power over him. Tyrone really loved her but he knew their relationship was as good as gone. Delana told him to let her go and then she got up from the bed, gathered her belongings and left. The truly sad part about this whole matter was Lulu was four months pregnant. Four months of lies and deception from her best friend who she considered to be her sister.

Delana's mind came back to the present and Turner handed her some tissue. There was a moment of silence while everyone absorbed the emotional state that Delana was in.

Even Lulu was sitting there crying tears of regret.

"Lulu, I'm going to let you speak now," Turner said, motioning her to begin.

Lulu took a deep breath then exhaled. "First of all I want to say what I did was wrong. I can't take back the events that happened but I've tried everything to makeup for what happened. Since this is the first time you're really listening, I want to explain exactly what happened over seven years ago," Lulu stated, thinking back to her side of the story.

She remembered it was twenty degrees below zero when Tyrone came ringing her doorbell on a cold winter day in December. Her child, Charmaine, was gone with her father for the weekend and Lulu had enjoyed the downtime, snuggling up to the fireplace with a near empty bottle of wine.

"Tyrone, is everything all right with you and Delana?" Lulu asked.

"No," Tyrone answered, coming in.

Lulu took his coat off and then listened to Tyrone drown her with his problems with Delana. Since she was Delana's best friend he thought she could help him figure her out. With a half empty bottle of cognac, neither one of them should have been left alone with one another.

"Why can't Delana be more like you," Lulu remembered Tyrone saying. He ran the tip of his finger across her cheeks. Lulu should have seen the signs then and made Tyrone leave but when he kissed her it was all over. The first kiss was just their lips touching but when Tyrone saw that she was responsive, he parted her lips and interlocked his tongue with hers. His hands started roaming all over her cream-colored skin and before long they were both naked, caressing one another in front of the fireplace. Lulu's eyes glistened while Tyrone's perfect physique intertwined with hers. She knew what she was doing was wrong but she was jealous of Delana getting the good men all the time. It made her feel even more special that he wanted her. Tyrone touched and explored all over her body. He started from her lips then licked down to her chest, belly button, and then in between her thighs. He swallowed up her juices as she went into a state of excitement. When she erupted in ecstasy she got on her knees and pleasured him. It didn't take long before Tyrone was moaning in pleasure, a much better state than when he first came in. All the excitement helped to relax her nerves as he thrust his shaft in and out of her mouth. When his legs began to fold, he released and then pulled her on top of him where they had sex for the rest of the night.

Those memories were one that she would never forget but she didn't go into all those details with Delana and Turner. She did, however, tell them when the wine and cognac had worn off the next morning, they both realized that they had made a huge mistake, one which they would regret for the rest of their lives. Lulu loved her son with all her heart, but the way he was conceived was wrong and would always haunt her for the damage their one night of passion caused.

After Lulu finished talking, another moment of silence washed over the room. Before Delana had a chance to respond, Turner cut in.

"Well, now that everything is out in the open I want to begin the interaction part of this therapy. I want the discussion to remain civilized, so we'll start by having Delana ask a question, Lulu you can respond, and then I will offer some comments and solutions."

Everyone agreed to the stipulations before Delana began.

"Lulu, you told us the events that happened but I want to know why you really slept with Tyrone and why didn't you tell me you were pregnant?"

Lulu took a deep breath again and then sipped down some cold lemonade to sooth the knot that had formed in her throat.

"Delana, I don't know why I did what I did, it just happened."

"But there had to be a reason," Delana responded, cutting her off. Before she could say anything else, Turner cut in.

"Delana, remember the rules now," he reminded her. "You need to let Lulu finish her statement before interacting."

With that being said, Lulu took the floor again.

"The truth is you've always had the best of everything, Delana. You went to college, found jobs that paid you good money, and had the top choice in men. I love you to death but deep down I resented you. I was jealous. When Tyrone came over that night I had no intentions of sleeping with him. When he started complimenting me and saying he wished you were more like me, I must have became hypnotized that he wanted me more than he wanted to be with you."

Lulu eyes flooded with tears. She took some tissue from Turner and dabbed at the corner of her eyes. It was no use, the tears kept coming, so she just decided to continue on.

"I didn't tell you I was pregnant because I was seriously contemplating getting an abortion."

By this time Lulu's tears became uncontrollable. She started gasping for air when she thought about her son, Tye Jr. and the fact that he would have not been here because of a decision she almost made.

"Lulu, calm down," Turner said, interceding. He gently massaged the back of her neck to sooth her nerves. In any other case he would never touch a patient but Lulu was a friend. He lifted her glass and made her take a few sips of lemonade.

"I'm okay," Lulu told Turner. As difficult as this was she was glad to finally be able to get everything out in the open. Whether Delana decided to forgive her or not, she knew she had tried everything in her power to make things right.

"Delana, I didn't tell Tyrone I was pregnant until I was three months along. He was so angry with me because he was still in love with you. By the time the shock subsided I was four months, and he told me it would be unethical to get rid of the baby at that point. We were both thinking of the best way to tell you but I never had the chance since you found out yourself."

"Delana, is there any other questions you want to ask Lulu?" Turner asked.

"No."

"Lulu, is there anything you want to ask Delana?"

"No, but there is something I would like to say," Lulu responded.

"Okay, than the floor is yours," Turner told her.

Lulu took a deep breath like she had so many times since they had begun talking, and she tried to figure the best way to say what she had to say. Either way Delana's feelings may be hurt, but since they were all being honest about everything, she would just get straight to the point.

"Delana, I've apologized a million times for the mistakes I made. I still love you like a sister, but you need to truly decide if you can forgive me or not. If you can then we need to move on in a positive way. If you want to continue counseling, then I'll be more than willing to go as well. More importantly, I will not continue to bring my son in the middle of this nightmare. Delana you're going to have to accept the both of us or none at all."

"Wait a minute, Lulu," Delana snapped. "I've never done anything to hurt Tye Jr. or any of your kids."

"Not physically but I can feel the resentment. Delana you're so cold with my children. You didn't used to be that way."

"Why do you think I'm here today?" Delana responded.

"Every since you broke my trust by sleeping with Tyrone, I haven't been the same person. It's also affecting the current relationship I'm in now with Corey."

On that cue, Turner jumped in. "Delana, I'm glad you recognized that you need some help. That's the first step in getting better. There's a lot of things that we need to work through and we can discuss the issue with Corey later in a private session. As far as your relationship with Lulu, it's up to you. Lulu expressed earlier that she wants to continue being friends with you and now you'll have to do the same. You don't have to give us an answer today or tomorrow but you should consider everything we've talked about today and decide whether or not you can move forward," Turner told her. Just when he was about to wrap the session up, his cell phone rang.

"Excuse me one moment," Turner told them while he took out his phone.

"Hello."

"Turner, it's Ray Ray."

"Is everything all right?" Turner asked, noticing a difference in his voice.

"Yes, everything will be fine real soon. I just wanted to thank you for everything. Turner, I love you like a brother and tell my sisters Delana, Karen, and Lulu, that I love them too."

"Wait a minute," Turner said, getting up. He went into the kitchen for a little privacy.

"Ray Ray, what's going on?   You're not talking like yourself."

"Turner, I can't live with the HIV virus. I just can't," Ray Ray said, swallowing the rest of the pills from his prescription bottle.

"Forgive me, Lord," Ray Ray said, before clicking Turner off the phone.

"Nooo!" Turner screamed. He clicked over and dialed 911.

"Oh my goodness, why are you sending an ambulance over to Ray Ray's house," Lulu asked.

She was standing in the doorway with Delana who was also waiting for his response.

"I can't talk about it but Ray Ray's in big trouble," he replied, hurrying towards the front door.

Lulu and Delana rushed right behind him and scrambled into his rental car. Turner didn't argue with them to leave so they just remained silent as they sped over to Ray Ray's house.

Chapter 17

<u>*Turner*</u>

By the time Turner reached Ray Ray's house off of 123rd in Kinsman, the paramedics were lifting him into the ambulance.

"Where are you taking him?" Turner asked, rolling down the window.

Turner made a quick U-turn in the middle of the street, just missing the curb. He sped to the hospital.

When they arrived at the emergency room, Ray Ray was rushed back where a group of nurses and physicians began to treat him.

Turner stepped away from Delana and Lulu to speak privately with the attending nurse. He gave her details about Ray Ray's possible HIV infection, the reason for his suicide attempt. The nurse jotted down the information and then rushed off again to the room where they had Ray Ray.

When Turner returned to the waiting area, Karen was sitting there with Delana and Lulu. They were so busy chit chatting about what could be wrong with Ray Ray that they didn't notice his arrival until he literally sat in between them.

"Turner, what in the world is going on?" Karen asked, standing up.

"Ladies, I'm not at liberty to say," he told them.

"Not at liberty to say!" Lulu repeated, now standing.

"Turner that's bullshit. Look, Ray Ray is just as good of a friend to us as he is to you. Now tell us what's really going on," Lulu snapped.

"Look— I know all of you want to know what's going on with Ray Ray, but I can't discuss any confidential matters with you since what we spoke about was through counseling."

"Turner, we understand," Karen said, taking Lulu firmly by the arm.

Karen certainly understood the importance of confidentiality. She would not want Turner discussing her marital problems with Delana or Lulu if they had asked, so she appreciated his stance right now, even though they were all worried and curious about why Ray Ray was in the hospital.

Whatever Karen said to Lulu, Turner was relieved when they sat back down and didn't press him for information. At least Delana wasn't pressing the issue and right now two cool heads were better than none. Lulu was bound to follow suit and conform to avoid being the *shit starter*, especially after their session today.

"Turner, have you contacted Ray Ray's parents?" Karen asked.

"No. I'm trying to wait to see his prognosis before calling. I'd hate to worry his mother who has enough health problems of her own. Besides, she's in a nursing home and I wouldn't want to tell her this over the phone. As for his father, you know they haven't talked since Ray Ray was in high school and admitted that he was gay," Turner responded.

"That's so silly," Lulu replied. "That's his child no matter what," she said in disgust.

"I agree," Turner replied. "However, you can't force a parent to take care of his child. That's why we have so many children in the system now."

"Yeah, but Ray Ray's situation is different. He had both his parents in his life until he revealed his lifestyle. It's been over twenty years, you'd think he would accept his son in all that time," Lulu complained.

"Well, sometimes it's not that easy to forgive people," Delana jumped in. "Remember there is two sides to every story," she added rolling her eyes.

Delana hated how Lulu just spoke without thinking about things. If she had, maybe she wouldn't have become pregnant by Tyrone.

Lulu was about to reply but then became silent when the doctor came out.

"Dr. Turner Worthington."

"That would be me," Turner said, getting up.

They stepped off to the side to speak privately.

"I'm Dr. Smith," he said, extending his hand.

Turner shook his hand, "So how is Ray Ray doing?"

"Well thanks to your quick response and getting him the proper care, it looks like he's going to pull through. How are you related to Ray Ray?"

"I'm a therapist and long time friend," Turner replied. "Ray Ray just informed me of the crisis he has been going through. The medical information is already documented in the hospital system when he was here the other day."

"Yes, I've read through his records. Does he have any family here?"

"He has an elderly mother who lives in a nursing home and he doesn't have contact with his father."

"Do you know if he has designated anyone to have power of attorney over his health?"

"Come to think of it his parents do," Turner told Dr. Smith.

"Ray Ray had surgery a few years ago and he had some documents drawn up. His mother insisted his father be put on the documents in case something happened to her, even though his father doesn't know it. Ray Ray is a stickler for having everything in order."

"Good, then maybe you wouldn't mind contacting his father. We can't release him unless he can be with someone who can monitor him around the clock so there won't be another suicide attempt."

"He hasn't had contact with his father for some time."

"Well his mother cannot look after him in a nursing home, so our only other recourse is to send him to a mental hospital for further observation," Dr. Smith replied.

"No, let's hold off on that option," Turner suggested.

Even though it was normal practice for suicidal patients to be observed by a mental health provider, he knew Ray Ray did not belong in a place like that. He had so much pride that no counselor would be able to get any information out of him. That was the main reason Turner was helping him in the first place. He never would see his friends as his patients so he just listened and give advice as a friend instead. He had to break this barrier that counseling was a bad thing. Sometimes talking with someone was just the thing you needed to set your priorities and refocus again. Turner pulled out his cell phone to make a couple of phone calls. If push came to shove, he would just have to stay in Cleveland until Ray Ray could recuperate from the problems going on in his life right now.

Chapter 18

<u>*Karen*</u>

Whatever problems Ray Ray was facing were private and there was nothing Karen could do about it. Right now she had her own issues to deal with as she headed out of the hospital and went home. Unfortunately, she had to drop Delana and Lulu's bickering behinds off since they had ridden with Turner, who had stayed at the hospital.

Karen dropped Lulu off first and then took Delana home to her condo in Gates Mills since it was closer to her own residence in Cleveland Heights. Karen must have been deep in thought because the person behind her began to beep impatiently letting her know the light had changed green. When he had enough room, he cut over in the next lane, flipped Karen the middle finger, and then sped off.

Gee wiz, talk about road rage, Karen thought to herself while she continued driving up Richmond Road. Her mind quickly drifted back to Jason and she wondered if he would really be able to change his violent ways. He had apologized for his behavior so many times before but somehow always found an excuse to use her as his punching bag. Now that he knew she was pregnant he would not dare lay a hand on her, but what about after the baby was born? With so many domestic violence cases ending up in murder, she had to be sure she would be around to raise her child.

Karen made a left off of Richmond Road to Monticello and was home in no time. When she walked through the door, Jason was waiting for her.

"So how is Ray Ray?"

"He was sleep the whole time we were there but he is going to make it. We decided to leave since his father was on the way. Turner stayed, and I'm sure they need the privacy considering his father hasn't seen Ray Ray in over twenty years."

"Karen, I can't imagine being away from you and our son," he said, embracing her in his arms.

"I know," Karen replied, pulling away and taking a seat on the couch.

Her mind drifted back to thoughts she had before. A chill ran up her spine. Tears suddenly began to roll down her eyes.

"Karen, what's wrong?" Jason asked, sitting beside her.

"I don't know— its just— Ray Ray is in the hospital and then I saw on the news yesterday that this beautiful young woman was killed by her husband."

"Come here," Jason said, pulling her on his lap.

"Ray Ray is going to pull through this and it's a shame what happened to that young woman. Karen, you don't believe I could be capable of doing such a thing?"

When silence washed over the room, Jason's heart fell to the bottom of his stomach.

"Look at me," Jason said, tilting her head towards his. He was now looking into those beautiful brown eyes that first attracted him to her and confirmed what she feared most.

"Jason, I would never want to believe that you would resort to that but looking at the man who killed his wife yesterday on the news was shocking. He totally did not strike me as a violent man but whatever happened between them, he just snapped. I can't help thinking that it could have been me. Jason, I'm not accusing you but that incident really scared me."

How could Jason be mad at his wife for feeling that way? Up until now he never imagined hitting a woman was a problem. He grew up in a violent environment and thought nothing of it until Karen threatened to leave him. She was not his property and he did not and should not think he could control her. Now that he knew he had a baby on the way, he had to do everything in his power to get his marriage back on track.

"Karen, I don't want you to be afraid of me," he said, kissing her lips. "I know that's hard to ask of you but I will prove to you how much I want to change."

Karen wrapped her arms around his neck. "I know you're trying. You made the first step by admitting you had a problem and getting help. Jason, I really want our marriage to work," she told him, kissing his forehead. She then kissed his lips and let her tongue trace gently over the edge before he opened his mouth and brushed his tongue against hers.

"I love the way you kiss me," he whispered, running his hands through her silky long hair.

The bulge between his legs became rock hard as he positioned her on top and lifted her sundress up.

"See what your kisses do to me?" he told her, while loosening her bra.

"It's good to know my simplest gestures entice you. Some women have to dress, splash on perfume, and do all kind of crazy things just to get their man going."

"Not you, baby. Now don't get me wrong, I enjoy when you give me those extra bonuses but your beauty alone is all I need to get me going," he said, engulfing her hardened nipples in his mouth. He went from breast to breast, teasing and suckling on each of them.

Karen let out a soft moan in pleasure. "Jason, make love to me."

"Is it okay to have sex? I don't want to do anything to harm our baby."

"It's perfectly fine. I checked with the doctor."

"Good, but we're going to have to slow it down. None of our off the wall stunts," he said, easing her dress off.

"Gee wiz, then I guess your going to have to make up for time after this baby comes."

"You know it, but for now I'll have to treat you like a porcelain doll," he said, laying her on the couch.

For the next hour, Karen enjoyed Jason's magical hands as they caressed over her auburn skin. He kneaded, pressed, and rubbed massage oil relieving the tension she had built up from earlier. When she was ready, he eased inside and made love to her.

Chapter 19

Ray Ray

Turner paced back and forth in the in the hospital room while Ray Ray slept peacefully. All hell was going to break loose when he opened his eyes to see his father standing in front of him. Turner hoped Ray Ray would wake up now and Turner could warn him but it was too late. Mr. Fields walked into the room and came over to his son's bed.

"So, how is he?"

"He's going to be just fine Mr. Fields. I'm not sure if you remember me, my name is Turner, Ray Ray's friend from high school."

"Yes, I remember," he said, with a firm handshake. "And call me Reggie," he told Turner.

"Will do," Turner smiled.

"So how is life treating you?"

"Very good. I'm living in Chicago now?"

"You sure are being very vague. Are you married, do you have any kids, what are you doing with yourself?" Reggie asked, taking a seat.

"Well I just graduated with my doctorate degree and I have my own counseling practice. I'm not married and have no kids but am involved with a beautiful woman named Natalie," Turner told him.

Turner just looked at Mr. Fields— Reggie, wondering why in the hell he cared about what was going on his life. He should be more concerned with his own son who was thankfully lying here in the hospital bed rather than a coffin at some funeral home.

"Turner, I always knew you would turn into a fine young man. I always wished the same for Ray Ray," he said, taking his son's hands and wrapping them in his own.

"Reggie, Ray Ray is doing very well for himself."

"Evidently not or he wouldn't be in here. Did he try to kill himself over some gay lover of his? I warned him that living this kind of lifestyle openly would only lead to self-destruction."

"Reggie, I don't want to seem argumentative but you have no idea of the things Ray Ray has been through recently. Only he can go into these details with you but, being gay is the lifestyle he chose to live. I personally don't look down on him as less of a person, and today it's more widely accepted within our society. I really hope you can get past this and have some type of relationship with your son."

"Dr. Worthington, I don't need you telling me what I should do," he snapped, standing up. He turned to walk out of the room but froze in place when he heard the sound of his son's voice.

"Dad, is that you?" Ray Ray asked, wiping his eyes. Even though his dad wasn't facing him, his father's stature stayed glued in his mind over the years. Twenty years had passed by and his father still stood six foot, three inches tall with broad shoulders. His russet skin was still smooth as ever with the exception of some aging wrinkles. Tears began to pour from Ray Ray's eyes as his father walked towards him.

"Ray Ray, I called your father to come here," Turner said, stepping in. "I'm going to step out in the hallway and give you two some time alone."

"Turner, you don't have to do that," Ray Ray told him with a worried look on his face.

"Ray Ray, I think Turner has the right idea. Don't worry, I'm not going to bite," Reggie told his son.

After Turner and the nurses left out, Reggie took a seat again.

"Ray Ray, it's been twenty years since we last spoke."

"Why did you come then?" Ray Ray asked, in a scratchy voice. When he began to cough, his father held a water bottle up to his lips.

"I'm here because your friend Turner called and said you needed me."

"Well, he wasn't speaking for me because I don't recall such a thing," Ray Ray said, looking out the window.

"Ray Ray, look at me." When he had his attention he spoke again.

"Do you want me to leave?"

"Dad, what do you want me to say? I mean— you denounced me as your son because I'm gay. It's been twenty years. I've learned that I can't depend on anybody but myself."

"Well, I can certainly understand your anger but I'm here now and we need to deal with it. So, tell me what's been going on with your life."

"Fine," Ray Ray responded, filling him in on his life's events. His father's mouth hung open in shock when he told him about the rape and the possibility of him having HIV.

"Good Lord! Thank heavens Turner had the sense to contact me instead of your mother. She would die worrying about you and Lord knows she has enough health problems of her own."

"Glad you still care so much about mamma. I wish you had the least bit of concern for me," Ray Ray said, gazing back out the window.

Right now he wished he could scream at his father for all the pain he had caused him. They lived the perfect life until Ray Ray came out of the closet with his gay lifestyle. He remembered vividly the day he told his parents. His mother just sat there calm as usual but his father jumped on him like he was his worst enemy. He could still feel the sting as his father pounded and punched on his chest. That day Ray Ray could have taken a bullet, because the words that spewed out of his father's mouth were much more lethal. 'You fagget, sissy, punk! Why the hell do you want everyone to know you like fucking men?' His father was on a rampage and his poor mother got knocked around in the process. Ray Ray wanted to call out and tell him, "Dad I learned this from you," but those words would have only gotten him and his mother killed the way his father was acting. At the time, Ray Ray just sucked it up and took all the pain that his father was giving. After his father stopped hitting him, Reggie packed up his bags and left his wife and only son. That day was the last time Ray Ray had spoken to his father; it had been over twenty years ago.

"Ray Ray, no matter what you think, you're still my son and I'll always love you."

"If you loved me then how come you walked out on us?"

"I just had to. Ray Ray, I never intended on walking out but I did. Your mother was so angry at me. We'd been having problems for years and the night you revealed your sexuality gave me the excuse to leave."

"So I was the scapegoat? There is no excuse for leaving the way you did. Momma was devastated, and didn't you ever want to talk to me or see how I was doing?"

"Ray Ray, I was dealing with my own problems. I didn't have the strength or the energy to deal with yours."

"I don't have any problems with my sexuality, if that's what you're referring to. Besides, I never did understand why you of all people would cast judgment on me. Like father like son, isn't that right dad?"

"What the hell are you talking about?" he asked standing up.

"Dad, don't play games with me. I know you're bisexual. I saw it with my own eyes—you were kissing and making love with that light-skinned friend of yours. What was his name? Oh, I remember, it was Newton."

Ray Ray must have sucked the life out of his father with those words. Reggie nearly crumbled over as he fell back into the chair. He was at a loss of words and his dark skin got at least two shades lighter. Tears started to bead from the corner of his eyes and his body began to tremble uncontrollably. The cat was out of the bag and Ray Ray had never seen his father break down like this before. A part of him wanted to put his arms around his father and comfort him, but he decided not to.

"Dad, I never thought any less of you as a man. In fact, seeing you and Newton together helped me deal and understand my own issues that I was going through at the time. Do you know how cruel people can be knowing you are gay? The gossip, looks of disdain, and pure hate are a lot to put on a person, especially as a child. Instead of disowning me, it would have been nice if you were there to support me. I wasn't asking you to accept my open lifestyle— just me. Dad, all I ever wanted was for you to be there for me."

"Ray Ray, I'm still trying to take in everything you just told me," Reggie stated. He pushed the button on the recliner then laid back in thought.

"Why didn't you come to me about Newton?"

Ray Ray just looked at his father and shook his head.

"Dad, that isn't something you just bring up in a discussion. I realized after you left that it wasn't my fault that you skipped out on our family. These problems you were having with my mother revolved around your own sexuality. Unlike me, you would rather die than let others know you're bisexual. The truth of the matter is, Dad, you'd rather be straight than gay."

"Yes Ray Ray, you're right. However, I never wanted this lifestyle for you. I didn't have a choice— I was molested by my father's best friend as a child. I never had a choice back then, and by the time I grew up, my self-perception was all screwed up."

"Dad, I'm sorry," Ray Ray told him, trying to get up. His father motioned him to lie down and then sat on the bed next to him. For the first time in what seemed a lifetime, Ray Ray and his father clung to one another and let out the tears of all the hurt, pain, and anger that they both had suffered throughout the years.

Chapter 20

<u>*Turner*</u>

By the time Turner left the hospital, nighttime had already approached. After a full day of being there for his friends he was tired. He drove straight to the hotel he was staying at in Beachwood. Right now, Turner needed a good night's rest. After the sleeping on Ray Ray's pull out sofa the previous night, he was in much need of comfort. Besides, he didn't want to stay in anyone's home in their absence. He also didn't want any surprises from Ray Ray's friends who were caught up in a love triangle.

Turner checked into his hotel room, flicked on the television, and then crawled into bed with nothing but his under clothes on.

"Damn, who is this calling?" Turner said, picking up his cell phone. He didn't recognize the number that appeared on his caller ID.

"Hello."

"Is this Turner?"

"Yes, who's calling?" Turner asked, in an agitated tone.

"This is Cynthia. We met at the airport a few days back. Is this a bad time to be calling?"

"No," Turner replied, softening his tone. "It's just that I've had emergency after emergency today."

"Long day, huh— is there anything I can do to help?"

"Only if you can come to Cleveland, because that's were I am right now."

"You're joking, right?" Cynthia asked.

"Nope."

"Turner I can't believe this, but I'm in Cleveland right now."

"You are?" Turner replied, sitting up.

"Yes, my sister lives here in Shaker Heights. She came to visit me in Chicago a few days ago but her son was in an accident so I came back to Cleveland with her. Where are you staying?"

Turner gave her the information and rushed through the shower and put on some relaxing clothes. Thank goodness he hadn't left his bags in his trunk, he thought, spraying on a little cologne. By the time he gave himself a once over in the mirror, Cynthia was knocking at his door.

"Turner, I still can't believe this coincidence," Cynthia said, coming in and hugging him.

"Neither can I."

For the next few hours Turner enjoyed Cynthia's company. They talked about everything from their childhood to their dreams for the future. It didn't hurt that he was able to glaze from time to time in her beautiful hazel eyes. Her caramel colored skin was so smooth and Turner couldn't believe his need to have her in his arms. He pulled her close and covered her lips with his own. Cynthia was so sweet; he parted and interlocked his tongue with hers. Turner could have kissed her all night long, but the thought of Natalie popped in his mind and he pulled from their embrace.

"Turner, don't stop— that really felt good."

"Cynthia, as much as I want to, there's something you should know."

"Don't tell me you're married," Cynthia said, looking at his fingers. There was no ring but he could have easily taken it off.

"No, I'm not married but I am involved."

"Are you engaged to her?"

"No."

"Then you're fair game in my book. Turner, it's so hard to meet a decent man these days. I've really found someone worthwhile. I feel so comfortable with you, like we've known each other our whole lives. If you're truly committed to this person and want me to leave, then I will," Cynthia said, brushing her lips against his again.

"No, I don't want you to leave," Turner told her.

He eased his tongue back in with hers and before he knew it they were both naked in bed. Cynthia was so beautiful. Every inch of her body was in perfect form. His hands melted into her caramel skin. He followed with gentle kisses and when he came to her large, firm breasts, he suckled on each one like the morning honeydew. Turner took his time exploring the newness of her body and when she couldn't take it anymore, he strapped on some protection and glided his hard erection inside of her.

Cynthia was so tight that Turner wondered if this was her first time. She wrapped her arms around him tightly as he gently eased in and out of her. When she became relaxed, Turner increased the intensity of his thrusting. Their bodies became one as the room heated with their love making. Cynthia's moans were so intoxicating; her hazel eyes put a spell on him and they continued making love for the next hour until Turner couldn't take it anymore. He exploded shortly after her release and they both collapsed on the bed in exhaustion.

"Cynthia are you a—"

"Virgin?" she said, finishing his sentence.

"Yes, Turner, I was a virgin before tonight happened."

"Why did you give yourself to me?"

"Because it felt right," she said, kissing him on the cheek.

It was only a matter of minutes before she fell asleep in his arms.

Turner just stared at her. She was so beautiful, but what in the hell did he just get himself into? He remained deep in thought until his own tiredness turned into sleep.

Chapter 21

<u>*Lulu*</u>

Lulu took a sip of some vodka and plopped down on the couch in front of the television. It was midnight and she could not go to sleep with all the events that had taken place today. Ray Ray was in the hospital for something she was clueless about, and she felt that she and Delana had finally opened up a wound that had been haunting them for the past seven years. Out of nowhere tears started strolling down her face as she relived everything going on in her life. There was too much pain swirling through her mind and the vodka seemed to do wonders in relieving or masking her problems.

"Who the hell is ringing my doorbell this time of night," Lulu slurred, going to the door. She peeked out the peephole.

"DeAndre, what are you doing over here this time of night?" Lulu asked.

"Please, don't start up on me," DeAndre told her. "I really need a friend right now."

"What's going on?" she asked, seeing tears form in the corner of his eyes.

"It's my father— he's in the hospital. It doesn't look good, Lulu, he had a stroke."

"Oh, DeAndre, I'm sorry," she said, wrapping her arms around him. All the bullshit she'd been going through today instantly faded from her mind.

"Lulu, I don't know what I would do if something happened to my father. He's always been there for me."

"I know, DeAndre. Your father is a good man. Let's pray for him," she said.

Lulu just opened up her heart and started to pray. Afterwards she put on a pot of coffee to sober herself from all the liquor she had drunk.

"Lulu, I don't want to be alone tonight."

"Neither do I. Come on, lets go upstairs," Lulu said, grabbing him by the hand.

****

Lulu was at the hospital bright and early the next day. She visited DeAndre's father, who slept the whole time she was there. She couldn't take sitting there watching his life slip away, so she told DeAndre she would be back and went to see Ray Ray.

"So how long are you going to be in here?" Lulu asked, giving Ray Ray a kiss on the forehead.

"Not long. They are going to release me today. I'm going to spend the next few weeks with my father."

"What! So your father really came to see you last night."

"Yes, and we talked and straightened a lot of things out. Lulu, after twenty years, I've finally got my father back."

"Well it's better late than never. I'm happy for you. Family is everything," Lulu said, filling him in on what happened with DeAndre's father.

"Oh, I'm so sorry to here that. What room is he in?" Ray Ray asked.

"I forget but he's on the ICU floor. I'd better be getting back. I'm glad you're feeling better and going home with your father. Make sure you call me and give me the telephone number and address where I can reach you."

"You know I will."

"Good. And, Ray Ray, I don't want to see you in this hospital again. Whatever is going on, know that you have friends that love you."

"I know, Lulu. We'll talk soon and I'll fill you in on everything. Until then— ta ta!"

"Ray Ray, you're going to be just fine," Lulu winked, before leaving.

Chapter 22

Karen

Karen was glad she had taken a week off from work to get her house in order. For the past few days she stayed in the house working on her marriage with Jason. Turner was great, stopping in and out between visiting and working with Lulu, Delana, and Ray Ray. Thank goodness he was a therapist, because Karen wasn't sure if she would have been able to talk with a total stranger, as Turner suggested they do when he returned back to Chicago.

"Karen, lunch is ready," Jason called out from the kitchen.

"You better stop spoiling me like this," Karen said, taking a seat to the table.

"Well, a woman needs to be spoiled every now and then. Besides, you better taste the food first before you say I'm spoiling you."

With that, Karen prayed over the food then twirled her fork in the spaghetti pie. She put a bite of the food into her mouth then looked at Jason.

"So, how is it?"

"Jason, it's wonderful. You know how much I love this dish."

"Well it was the easiest thing I could make. I followed your exact cooking directions: boil the spaghetti noodles and cook the ground beef. When that's done, drain both, add the noodles to the casserole and combine a package of Philadelphia cream cheese and some milk to loosen the noodles; spread the meat on top, then pour the spaghetti sauce on top and bake. A few minutes before it's done I just sprinkled the mozzarella cheese on top— and like magic, you have spaghetti pie."

"Perfect—and it tastes good," Karen said, filling her stomach. She had a salad and a glass of milk to go along with it.

After they ate, Karen helped clean the kitchen and then they went out on the deck to enjoy some fresh air. Summer would be approaching in just a few weeks and Karen looked forward to spending some time outdoors, especially after the harsh winter they had.

"So, what are you thinking about?" Jason asked, massaging the back of her shoulders.

"About our baby and the change in our lives once he or she arrives."

"I think about that a lot, too. Karen, nothing is more important to me than my family. I'm really trying to change my behavior and I hope you'll never leave me."

"Jason, we got married for better or for worse. Through these difficult times we have to work together. I love you and never wanted our marriage to end, but at the time you were leaving me with no options until you agreed to seek therapy."

"Well, I'm just glad you opened my eyes. I'm not too egotistical to not own up to my problems. Karen, I can't promise you everything will be smooth sailing, but I promise I'll never put my hands on you again. Do you believe me?"

"Yes, Jason. The past few days have been so great but we have a long road ahead of us. I think we'll be just fine. Let's focus on the positive things like our baby. Do you think it's a boy or a girl?"

"Hmmm— let me take a look," Jason said, coming in front to look at her.

"Jason, stop acting silly," Karen laughed. "I'm not showing yet. I still have a few months before my stomach starts protruding out."

"It doesn't matter, I've always had sound judgment," he replied, rubbing her stomach. "I think this baby will be a girl."

"A girl. I thought you wanted a boy."

"I just want a healthy baby," Jason said, kissing her on the forehead. "As much as I would like our first child to be a boy, my gut feeling is that this is a girl growing inside of you."

"Well, we'll just have to wait and see," Karen told him.

For the next few hours they enjoyed the fresh air. Karen actually fell asleep in her husband's arms before he carried her into the house to put her to bed for an afternoon nap.

Chapter 23

Delana

With everything going on, Delana forgot about her appointment. She could not miss this meeting with a potential client. This could boost her revenue into the tens of thousands and the thought of all the money was making her feel good as her cell phone rang.

"Hello."

"Delana, this is Turner."

"Yes, I know. What can I do for you?"

"Well I was wondering if you want to have one more session with Lulu before I leave for Chicago tomorrow morning."

"What time were you thinking? Right now I'm on my way to an important business meeting."

"Well it can be later on because Lulu is still on vacation. You know DeAndre's father is in the hospital and not doing well."

"Oh, I'm sorry to hear that," Delana responded. "What about meeting at 5:30? After that I want us all to go out to dinner and relax before you leave Cleveland."

"That sounds great. I'll call Lulu and we'll meet over to your place."

"Fine, until then," Delana said, hanging up. Too bad Ray Ray would not be able to come, but he needed to focus on getting better, she thought as she headed down Euclid Avenue to her meeting downtown.

****

"Delana, welcome to Designer's Inc.," Mr. Henderson said in greeting.

"Yes, same here," Delana said, with a firm handshake.

After all the introductions they sat in the high-tech conference room with the best cushiony leather chairs she had ever sat in.

"Coffee?" the receptionist asked.

"Sure, can I have one cream with two sugars," Delana replied, glad at the excellent service.

After everyone had finished their bagels and coffee, the meeting officially began.

"Well, Delana, I'm sure you're wondering why we've set up this meeting," Mr. Henderson said.

"Yes, I must say my curiosity has gotten the best of me."

"Well then we'll get straight to the point. Your reputation has been superb in this line of business, and we would like to bring you on board as Vice President of Sales."

Delana's eyes bucked while she read through the neatly bound report. The job title alone was great, especially being black, and the six-figure salary was a great incentive for jumping on board.

"Well, Mr. Henderson, this is certainly a great proposal," Delana said, going into detail and asking as many questions as possible. She wanted to know the full extent of the position being offered to her and not just what was being presented on paper.

After an hour of negotiations, Delana shook his hand and told him she would need some time to think over their proposal. Mr. Henderson walked her to the elevator with small talk to encourage her to come on board.

Luckily Delana was on the elevator by herself and let out a sigh of relief. A hundred and fifty thousand dollars a year! That was great money but was it worth giving up the freedom of running her own business? Yes, sometimes being the boss had its own headaches, but working under somebody else was one too. At least with her business she could take on the clients she wanted and do whatever she pleased. She wasn't bound to any corporate policies or politics. Was she ready to get back into this game? Delana had some serious thinking to do, she thought, heading to the garage to get her car. She let the convertible roof to her shining red Mercedes down and then headed back to her apartment. Today she would take the rest of the afternoon off before meeting up with Turner and Lulu. She wasn't in the mood to deal with that issue, because she wanted to stay on her high of somebody offering her all that money to work for their organization. Damn, jobs like that in Cleveland were hard to come by, especially for black folks.

****

"Coming," Delana called out, going to answer the door.

"Turner, punctual as usual. Hello, Lulu," she said, inviting them to come in.

"I'm sorry to hear about DeAndre's father. Let me know if I can do anything," Delana said.

"Thank you. We're just praying that he'll pull through. I don't even want to think about what will happen if he doesn't."

"Well I'll keep him in my prayers. Do you all want anything to eat or drink?"

"I'll wait until we go out to eat," Turner said, "but if you have some iced tea that will be fine."

"What about you, Lulu?"

"That will be cool with me, too."

Delana disappeared into the kitchen and returned with their drinks and some chips to munch on.

"Well, we all know what this is about so let's get right to the point. The last time we met we were discussing the affair Lulu had with Tyrone," Turner said, facing Delana.

"Before we rushed off to the hospital to see about Ray Ray, we ended the session with you, Delana. Have you had time to think whether you want this friendship with Lulu to continue on?"

"Turner, between everything that has been going on, I actually have found time to do a lot of soul searching," she replied.

She looked directly in Lulu eyes and said, "Yes, I would like to continue being friends with Lulu. We have so much history together that I don't want to give it up without at least honestly trying to make this work. For the past seven years I have been angry, vindictive, and jealous that you had Tyrone's baby. The fact is, we probably would have broken up anyway, but it just hurt so bad that you ended it for me rather than me being able to make that decision."

"Delana, where do you see this friendship going from here on out?" Turner asked.

"Well I know a miracle is not going to happen over night. I still have a lot of issues with trust. Thanks to our few sessions together and alone, I have been able to confront some of these issues head on. Only time will heal all wounds and I'm asking that Lulu be patient."

"Is that acceptable with you, Lulu?" Turner asked.

"Yes, that's fine with me."

"Good. Now here's what I suggest. I think both of you need to spend some quality time alone. Just the two of you need to hang out and start bonding and building your friendship back on track. Talk with each other; be honest about all of your feelings. The other main issue is Tye Jr.," Turner said, looking at the two.

"Delana, I think it would be wise to spend some time with Tye Jr. You need to learn more about him and not look at him as a mistake that happened between Tyrone and Lulu. The fact is, he is here and he is not the blame for anything his parents did. He's an innocent party and the sooner you come to grip with that the better your relationship will be with Lulu."

"Do you think we need to continue counseling?" Lulu asked.

"Yes, I'd prefer you get real therapy sessions with one of my colleagues here in Cleveland, but I know Delana will not agree to that. Remember I can't counsel my friends but I'm glad I've been here to lend an ear and give you some sound advice."

"No, Turner, let's keep this all in the family. I really appreciate you just being here for us," Delana told him.

"I agree," Lulu chimed in.

"You're both very welcome. Now since we're finished for today, let's go get our grub on," Turner suggested. He was sure looking forward to an ice cold martini.

Chapter 24

Ray Ray

After all these years it felt funny being back in his father's home. His dad lived in a two-bedroom apartment down in the flats. Ray Ray walked around from room to room, familiarizing himself with the place that his father called home.

"So, how long have you lived here?"

"For the past couple of years. When Cleveland started renovating the flats, I knew this was where I wanted to be."

"I never would have imagined. There is so much I don't know about you."

"Well, we will have plenty of time over the next few weeks, but for now I want you to get settled in so we can talk about this situation you're in."

On that cue Ray Ray grabbed his things and settled into the guest bedroom. He unpacked his suitcase and then stretched out on the queen-sized bed that was decorated in rustic earth tone colors. Ray Ray wondered what his life would had been like if his father had been there. Sure, he was damn near grown when he left, but a son never stopped needing his father.

"Ray Ray, are you all right in there?"

"Yes, Dad, I'm all right," Ray Ray responded, getting up.

Ray Ray joined his father in the living room. He had a table full of beer and chips to snack on.

"So, Ray Ray, let's not beat around the bush. What exactly is going on with you, Demetrius, and Jim?"

"Dad, Demetrius and I have been together for the past two years. Jim and I were just friends before he attacked and raped me."

"Do you know he is out of jail?"

"No," Ray Ray gasped.

"Well he is. He claimed he didn't rape you. Jim said your sexual encounter was consensual, so they had to let him go."

"But how could they do that?"

"Ray Ray, it's your word against his."

"That's bullshit," Ray Ray said, standing up. "Why in the hell would I sleep with someone who has AIDS?" Ray Ray hollered.

"He said that he wore protection and that you got mad and screamed rape when the condom broke."

"So that's how it's going to be. They're just going to let Jim walk the streets after what he did to me."

"Basically, yes. I even called and spoke to my attorney and he said how difficult it would be to prosecute such a case, especially considering the circumstances."

"Circumstances— you mean because I'm gay man?"

"Yes. You can pursue legal action if you want, but I'm just telling you up front all of the ramifications."

"Dad, I was the one violated."

"I know, Ray Ray," Reggie said, taking a sip from an ice-cold beer.

Silence washed over the room for a few moments while Ray Ray wondered deep in thought. If Jim wasn't going to jail, he damn sure wasn't about to let him get away with what he did.

"So, where is this Demetrius guy?" Reggie asked, interrupting his son's thoughts.

"He's out of town on an important business meeting. I couldn't tell him what had happened, otherwise he would have been on the first plane home to see about me."

"Sounds like a serious relationship."

"It is, Dad. Demetrius asked me to move in with him before he left. I told him I would give him an answer when he returned."

"So, what's your answer?"

"Well, before Jim raped me, the answer would have been yes. Now that all this has happened, how could I possibly move in with someone?"

"Ray Ray, I don't think Demetrius will think any less of you because of what happened."

"Dad, how could you think that? It is a possibility that I'm infected with the HIV virus."

"If this relationship between you and Demetrius is really serious, the way you say it is, then he will stand by you no matter what the outcome of those test are."

"Dad, you really believe that?"

"Yes, I do. Now why don't you go in the bedroom and call your mother. I'm sure she'll start to worry if you don't call soon."

With that Ray Ray went back to the guest room he would be staying in for the next few weeks. He stretched back out on the bed and wondered if Demetrius would really be supportive like his father said. He couldn't fathom the thought of Demetrius walking out on him, but he knew that could be a possibility. If it was the other way around, Ray Ray didn't know whether or not he could continue to stay involved with someone who may be infected with the AIDS virus. He would never stop loving Demetrius, but having that disease would change their whole lifestyle, not to mention the high cost of healthcare and dealing with death. Ray Ray wasn't sure if he could let Demetrius go through this, and quite honestly it scared him because he wasn't ready to die. Tired, his eyes began to sting from the tears that clouded his eyes. He slipped down on his knees and did something he hadn't done in years, prayed.

Dear Lord,

I know I'm not living a righteous life by your words and I have tussled with my gayness so many times throughout my life. It was not a decision I made for myself. It's just the way I am. Now I find out it runs in the family— there are no excuses but I pray that I'm not being punished because of my lifestyle. I really am a good person and pray that this disease hasn't infected me. I've been so careful, taken every precaution, and don't understand how this could be happening to me. Thank you for listening, Lord.

Ray Ray pulled himself back up on the bed and fell asleep.

Chapter 25

Turner

Turner was glad to be back in the windy city of Chicago, but he was not ready to go home and deal with Natalie. The last time they had spoken to each other had turned into a heated argument. Turner felt like she was pressuring him into marriage, so what did he do? He ran into the arms of another woman.

Cynthia was a beautiful woman with a great ear to listen to whatever he felt like talking about. Even though they had just met he felt like he had known her forever. She understood his needs; however, he felt guilty for taking her virginity. Why in the world had she given herself to him? If he had known she was a virgin he would have never slept with her. Did she want anything in return from him? Right now he didn't need any more drama in his life. He had to see Cynthia again to see if she had any ulterior motives hiding behind those alluring hazel eyes of hers.

"Turner, I'm glad you're home," Natalie told him, with a juicy kiss.

It was hard for him to concentrate with the sheer negligee she had on. Right now he was not in the mood to be with her.

"Natalie, we need to talk."

"Honey, I know you are angry with me. Let me make it up to you," she said, wrapping her arms around him.

Turner pushed her away. "Natalie, I want you to pack your bags and leave."

"What! Is this some kind of joke?"

"No."

"Turner, what in the hell is going on with you?" Natalie screamed, losing her composure.

"You're smothering me."

"Smothering you? Fuck you, Turner. I'm tired of this shit. The first time I left was because you put your damn friends before me. What is it this time? Have you found another bitch to warm your bed?"

"Natalie, please don't go there."

"Fuck you, Turner," Natalie said again, slapping him across the face.

Tears welled up in the corner of her eyes. "You said you loved me. After all this time, you finally said those words to me and now you want me to pack and move out."

"Natalie—"

"No— don't say shit to me. You're fucking crazy," Natalie shouted, cutting his sentence off.

"You call yourself a therapist trying to help *everybody* when you can't even help your damn self!"

"I see I can't talk to you right now," Turner told her, flicking on the television set.

"You're damn right," she hollered, snatching the remote control out of his hand.

She threw the control so hard at the television screen that it cracked.

"Are you out of your mind?"

"No, but you are," Natalie erupted with a devilish smile. She stormed out of the room, packed her bags, and then walked out of his life forever.

Chapter 26

<u>*Karen*</u>

Karen should have known that her marriage was going too smoothly. Tears flooded the corner of her eyes as she ran upstairs to their bedroom. She packed every last damn item of Jason's then hurled the suitcase down the stairs. Karen stumped down the steps angrily, pacing the floor until Jason arrived home.

When the keys clicked in the door, Karen took a deep breath. She knew all hell was about to break loose, but that bastard was leaving this house tonight.

"Why is my suitcase sitting on the floor?" Jason asked.

Karen smacked Jason so hard across the face that he staggered back.

"Don't play games with me JASON. Not now," she said, throwing the envelope in his face.

"Just get your shit and get out," Karen hollered, running back up the stairs.

Jason stood there speechless while his wife went on a rampage. Whatever was in this envelope had sent her into a crazed state as he flipped the envelope over. It was from Monique. Damn.

The letter read:

You're not the only one pregnant with Jason's baby. Yes, as you can see your husband and I have had sexual relations. Jason loved getting between my legs. Said I gave him everything a man ever needed. The way he caressed then ate the sweet juices from me was all a woman ever needed. I'm in love with your husband and he said those same words to me. Now that I am pregnant, he just wants to all of a sudden dismiss me. Well that will never happen and as long as you continue to be in Jason's life, then you'd better get used to having an extended family.

Monique

Jason's body collapsed against the front door. Over the past few weeks his marriage had been perfect and within minutes everything had fallen to pieces again. First abuse and now adultery; Jason wasn't too sure if he would have a marriage after this.

Karen felt Jason's hand caress the top of her back. She loved the way that felt— she loved him, but the thought of him being with another women sent chills down her spine.

"Jason, just leave," Karen said, without moving.

"Please, Karen, turn around so we can talk."

It nearly killed him to see her red strained eyes reflected in his. She had been crying and to make matters worse her body was trembling.

"Tell me one thing, is that letter true?" Karen asked.

"The affair, yes, the baby, no."

Karen's body felt like exploding into a million pieces. Her heart was shattered, her marriage was crumpling apart right before her eyes.

Right now she had to pull herself together. The only important thing right now was her baby. She had to calm down. Karen closed her eyes and wished this whole ordeal would just go away.

"Baby, you're scaring me," Jason told her. He expected her to be argumentative, anything other than lying there still.

He wrapped his arms around her and kissed the tears falling from her eyes. His touch only made her sob more.

"Why did you cheat on me?" Karen asked, opening her eyes.

"Honestly— I was running away from our problems."

"How long has this affair been going on?"

"Six months."

"When was the last time you two were together intimately?"

"It's been over two months. I guess this letter of Monique's is her way of getting back at me."

"Why do you say that?"

"Because I ended the affair. Karen, you and the baby are the most important thing in my life."

"Let me ask you this— "

Karen took a deep breath before proceeding on.

"If I hadn't told you about the baby, would you have continued cheating behind my back?"

"I can't honestly answer that question. All I know is when you left for Chicago to get away from me, that was the first time I realized that I could lose you. You forced me to do a lot of thinking about our marriage and all the problems we were having. News of the baby made matters more clear. Karen, I want to raise my child with both of us together. I want us to be happy. If only I could take it back— the bottom line is I'm sorry."

"I'm sure you are," Karen said, looking into her husband's eyes. Every word he spoke was the truth; she could see it in his eyes. Why didn't he just lie to her today? It would have made it easier to just push him away.

"Jason, I need time to think. If you don't want to leave then I'll pack my bags."

"No. I'll leave," Jason responded. Tears clouded his own eyes. There was nothing he could do or say. He dug himself into this mess and he only hoped his wife would find it in her heart to forgive him.

"So, where will you go?" Karen asked.

"A hotel. I hope you don't want me gone for too long. If you find it in your heart that you cannot forgive me, then I'll have to make other arrangements."

"Jason, why did you do this to us?" Karen cried. "I love you so much, but how do I decide where we go from here?"

"Baby, only you can answer that," Jason answered regretfully. "Just know that I love you and whatever it takes to get our marriage back on track, I'm willing to do. Please don't let our marriage go," he pleaded before walking out the room.

Jason hurried down the steps, grabbed his suitcase and left the house. Right now he felt so low and he was to blame. Their problems should not have sent him running into the arms of another woman.

Chapter 27

Turner

Turner missed Natalie, but Cynthia fulfilled all his needs. She didn't ask or require anything from him, which was a trait Natalie did not have. Natalie was always pressing him saying, "Why can't you tell me you love me?" When he finally talked himself into believing that, he spoke those three little words to her. Then she was going off on this _marriage_ tangent. Natalie didn't come out and directly say it but ever since she became involved in her best friend's wedding plans, she came back home making subtle hints. "Oh, Maria picked out the most beautiful wedding dress today. I can't wait until the day I can try on my own." Every day she was talking about that damn wedding. Turner became so irritated that he finally told her he didn't want to hear anymore about it.

"What do you mean you don't want to hear anymore about it?" Natalie asked him.

"Just what I said. This is something you talk with your girlfriends about. I could care less about what type of dress, flowers, or food Maria is picking out."

"Oh, Turner, how can you be so cruel? I hope you don't act like this for our wedding?"

"Our wedding! Who said anything about us getting married?"

"Turner, how can you be so cold? If you don't have any intentions of marrying me, then tell me now. My biological clock is ticking. I'm not getting any younger."

"Neither am I but I will not be forced into marriage."

"Forced!"

Turner couldn't believe how quickly that argument spiraled out of control. He was glad to go to Cleveland so he could have some space. Helping his friends work through their problems and his encounter with Cynthia helped take his mind off of Natalie. It also gave him time to think and he wasn't ready to be in the serious relationship that Natalie wanted. He had hoped that they could work things out but since he asked her to move out, he hadn't heard a word form her in weeks. Turner damn sure wasn't about to cry about her, especially when he had a young beautiful lady like Cynthia to keep his bed warm. In fact, he had a date with her tonight. He slipped into the shower to get dressed.

****

Turner enjoyed taking Cynthia out to one of the finest eateries in Chicago. On her college budget and part-time job, she could hardly afford such luxuries. He understood that, it hadn't been too long since he was in her position. Cynthia was twenty-six years old and in her second year of graduate school at the University of Chicago. Her course studies were in social science administration, where she was heavily involved in community activities. Since they both worked with people in their line of business, they were able to easily communicate and understand one another.

"Turner, will you stay the night with me?" Cynthia asked, drinking down the rest of her wine.

"Sure."

"Great. I normally go to church service around 11:00 a.m. You're free to go if you'd like."

"I'll pass," Turner responded.

"The way you said that sounds like you harbor some resentment."

"Yes— the last time I was in church was the day I buried my mother. I promised myself I would never go back."

Silence.

"Turner, may I ask what your mother died from?"

"Cancer. She died from breast cancer. By the time she found out about the cancer, it was too late. It had already spread to other organs in her body. She died a few months later."

"Turner, I'm sorry to hear that, but if you look at things from another perspective, maybe God freed your mother from all the pain and suffering that's associated with that illness. She didn't have to go through the chemotherapy, or deal with all her hair falling out. She didn't have to pump her body full of medication just to keep her body functions going. Most of all she didn't have to see you suffer by watching her die a painful death. Turner, you were everything to your mother. God never hurts anyone, even though you think he has. Even after all these years, Turner, God still loves you. He loves all his children."

Silence.

What Cynthia said struck a chord. Tears started to escape from the corner of his eyes. Out of all the years since his mother's death, Cynthia was the only person he had ever opened up to.

"I know this sounds crazy coming from a therapist, but how do I move on?"

"Turner, even therapists have problems and need someone to talk to," Cynthia said, taking him by the hand.

"The way you move on is to forgive. You have to forgive God for taking your mother away. You have to forgive your mother for not being here with you. You have to forgive everyone that you have hurt from the bottled up anger inside you. Most of all, Turner, you have to forgive yourself," Cynthia said, taking him in her arms. She was glad they were in a private section of the restaurant as she comforted him while he shed all the years of tears pent up inside of him. When he was done letting them out, she packed up their food and went back to her place.

Chapter 28

<u>*Ray Ray*</u>

"No, Demetrius, don't kiss me," Ray Ray said, pushing him away.

"What's wrong? Did anything change between the two of us while I was away?"

"Yes— a whole lot has changed," Ray Ray told him.

"Please don't tell me it's somebody else. Ray Ray, I thought what we had was special. For goodness sake, I asked you to move in with me."

"Demetrius, before a week ago, I would have loved to move in with you but after what happened to me, I can't," Ray Ray cried.

"What happened? Tell me what happened," Demetrius said, concerned.

"I was raped."

"What! Ray Ray, tell me what in the world is going on," he said, motioning Ray Ray to sit down.

Demetrius was stunned at the information coming out of Ray Ray's mouth. When Ray Ray was done saying everything that happened, Demetrius kissed him and pulled him into his arms.

"Ray Ray, you did nothing wrong and I'll be here for you whatever the outcome of the HIV test. When will you get the results?"

"Tomorrow."

"Do you want me to come along to the doctor's office with you?"

"Yes, Demetrius, that would be wonderful. I'm just surprised at how you're taking all this."

"Ray Ray, I am upset that you never told me about this so called friend of yours. However, I know you're telling the truth. If it was just a friendship then I have nothing to be angry about. Whatever the case, you didn't deserve to be raped. And by the way, I still want you to move in with me."

"Let's just hold off on any decisions until tomorrow."

****

Ray Ray was terrified as he sat in the doctor's office waiting for the results of his HIV test. He wished Demetrius was in the room with him but they decided it would be best for him to wait in the waiting room.

"The doctor will be right in," the receptionist smiled, before leaving him alone in the office.

"Thank you," he responded nervously. It took all of Ray Ray's energy to sit in the chair. He was a nervous wreck. This was the worst situation he had ever been in. Ray Ray had been so careful with his sex life and couldn't believe he was sitting here waiting for the results of an HIV test. His body began to tremble at the sheer thought of that virus running rampant through his body. He had seen the deadly effects this disease had on others and he vowed he never wanted to be in that situation. "Why Jim?" Ray Ray said to himself in anger.

"Mr. Fields, I have the results of your HIV test," Dr. Benson said, taking a seat. He ruffled through his chart for his notes.

"The results of your HIV test came back negative."

"Negative," Ray Ray repeated, with a smile appearing on his face.

"Yes."

"Thank you, God!" Ray Ray said, closing his eyes in gratitude.

"Well, I certainly understand your enthusiasm. This is good news to be thankful about today, but you'll need to come back in six months to be retested."

"The results should be the same, right?"

119

"Let's pray they are. In the meantime, please practice safe sex and I will have the nurse bring you a packet of information you'll need to read before your next visit."

"Thank you, Doctor," Ray Ray said, shaking Dr. Benson hand.

Ray Ray ran straight into the arms of Demetrius.

"Well, I take it from the smile on your face that everything is going to be all right."

"Yes, Demetrius, my test came back negative for the HIV virus."

"Good, now let's get out of this hospital and celebrate."

"Sounds good to me. Lets eat down in the Flats and after that I want to take you to meet my father," Ray Ray said, grinning from ear to ear.

Chapter 29

<u>*Delana*</u>

Delana couldn't turn down all that money and decided to accept the position at Designer's, Inc. When she arrived at her office she was pleased to admire the nameplate that neatly adorned on the door: Delana Smith, Vice President of Sales. Smiling, Delana sashayed into her office and twirled around in the comfortable leather chair. She was about to pick up the phone and call Corey when she heard a knock on the door.

"Come in."

"Ms. Smith, would you like a cup of coffee?" Olivia asked.

"Only if you'll join me. And call me Delana."

"Okay," Olivia smiled. "I'll be right back with your coffee.

Delana nodded as she watched Olivia disappear from the office. Like herself, Olivia was one of only a few African Americans that worked in this company and Delana was the highest paid. Whatever the case, she wasn't about to act like an uppity bitch to her people like so many others do when they make it to the top. Besides, Olivia had been working here for some time and would be very valuable as a friend and colleague.

"I hope you don't mind but I grabbed us a few bagels to go along with our coffee," Olvia said, sitting down.

"Not a problem because I'm starved. I didn't have time to eat before I came here. So tell me about yourself?" Delana asked, while spreading some cream cheese on her bagel.

"Well I've been working here for five years now. I started out as the secretary and was promoted to Executive Administrator about a year ago. My responsibilities are basically the same, though I get paid more."

"More money is always good," Delana smiled. "And I'm glad to see that they promoted a sister because you know we are always last on the totem pole."

"I hear you. I was pleased when they hired you. There's never been a black person in that position before, but I'm not surprised because things have been good ever since Mr. Henderson took over this company. His father, on the other hand, I can't say the same for."

"Get out of here," Delana said, sucking in every last detail.

"When Mr. Henderson married a black woman, his father had a heart attack and died. I'm sure he would have changed his will if he had time, but Mr. Henderson was the only surviving son and inherited everything."

"You're kidding. Mr. Henderson is married to a sister?"

"Yep. I was surprised myself. Hell, everyone was surprised, and the people who treated us like crap before changed their attitudes real quick."

"Well I'll be damn— ooops sorry about the language. I'm just shocked."

"Not a problem. I'm just glad you are a *real* sister, otherwise I wouldn't be telling you this."

"Olivia, what you say in my office won't leave this room and I'm thankful for any information. You never know what direction people are coming from, especially when they're undercover— if you know what I mean. Can you tell me who those people are?"

Delana listened intently while Olivia gave her the inside scoop. When she left, Delana wrote down every name on her black list. Over the next few days she would make it a point to meet with them personally. Delana would rather them spit daggers in her face rather than behind her back. She went through that drama with her best friend Lulu, and she would be damned if she dealt with this mess at work.

****

"Delana, why are you trying to entice me wearing that sexy ass lingerie?" Corey asked, while he watched her sashay over to the dresser drawer.

"Well, if you weren't trying to hold out on the sex, then there would be no problems," she said, fumbling through the drawers.

She walked back over to the bed and handed Corey some massage oil.

"I want you to massage me down," Delana told him. She unsnapped her bra and let it fall to the floor.

Delana crawled on top of Corey and dangled her breasts in front of his face.

"You really are trying to break me," Corey said, starring at her cinnamon-toned complexion.

"Baby, I just want a message. It has been a long day," Delana sighed, wiggling a few times on his hard erection.

She slid her panties off and positioned herself on the bed, stomach down.

The oil felt good as Corey let it drip over her back. His hands felt even better as he kneaded them over her skin.

"You really are tense," Corey said, continuing to massage her shoulders.

"Between starting a new job and you holding off on the sex, what do you expect?" Delana crooned.

"I'm not holding off on the sex."

"Corey, it has been weeks. What do you call it then?" Delana asked. She let a moan escape her mouth while his magical bronze hands glided down her butt.

"Delana, I just want to be sure about us," Corey replied. He kissed the roundness of her butt and then worked his hands down to her legs.

Delana sat silent for a few moments thinking about Corey's last statement.

"Corey, I'm sure about us," Delana said, flipping on her backside. "I love you," she told him.

"How much do you love me?" Corey asked, looking into her flaming dark brown eyes.

"Enough for me to spend the rest of my life with you. Corey, will you marry me?"

"Marry you? Isn't the man supposed to ask the woman?"

"Oh, I keep forgetting how traditional you are. Well, just know that my love for you is that strong. Corey, I can't imagine my life without you. It almost took losing you to understand the special relationship we have."

"A good lesson learned then. Delana, don't ever cheat on me again. I'm a fool in love but I will not tolerate your infidelity again."

"I know. Please let's move past this. Corey, make love to me," Delana pleaded, in a faint whisper.

"You don't have to beg me to do that," Corey said, tracing his tongue over her lips.

"So, I take it the time is right?"

"Yes Delana, the time is definitely right. I see your sincerity, and your commitment to this relationship," Corey told her.

"Therapy has forced me to face a lot of issues."

"I know, baby, and I love you even more for that," he said, wiping the tears from her eyes.

Corey let his tongue intertwine with hers as he sank into the abyss of her sweetness. He kissed her so long. He never wanted it to end but he had other parts of her body to pleasure as he slid his tongue down to her breasts. He licked each hardened nipple playfully before engulfing his mouth over it and suckling while she whined for more. Corey had Delana right where he wanted her to be. She needed a man in every sense and he was glad he was the one pleasuring her as they continued to make passionate love over and over again.

Chapter 30

<u>*Lulu*</u>

Lulu never imagined that she would be comforting DeAndre at his father's funeral. He could barely walk back to the limo as they proceeded in a slow line out of the cemetery.

"Lulu, he's really gone," DeAndre cried, laying his head on her shoulder.

"I'm sorry," Lulu replied, rubbing his back in comfort.

Lulu didn't know what to say to his mother, Andrea, who was lost in her own thoughts. The remainder of the ride to his mother's house was relatively quiet. DeAndre had two sisters who just stared out the limousine window as they drove through the familiar neighborhood of Cleveland. It was mid-August and a cloudy day. Lulu was grateful that there was no rain.

"You know Alexander's birthday was just a few weeks away," Andrea said, breaking the long silence.

"I had planned on throwing him a big surprise birthday party but instead were giving him a home going instead," she wept, as tears continued rolling from her eyes.

"I know, Mom," DeAndre replied. "I still can't believe he's gone."

Lulu didn't open her mouth as she sat there listening to his family grieve. When they arrived to the house she kept herself busy helping arrange and serve food. After DeAndre's family and friends left, she helped clean the house. When she was done, she kissed DeAndre on the forehead and went home. Right now he needed to be with his family. They all would need each other as they tried to move on without the presence of their father. Alexander was a good man. Lulu hoped DeAndre would straighten himself out and become more like his father was. She hated to say it but sometimes it took a tragedy like this to open someone's eyes and Lulu prayed that it would eventually help DeAndre.

Chapter 31

Turner

It was 9:00 p.m. and Turner had just seen his last client for the day. He wrote some case notes for about an hour and then made sure his office was in order before closing shop. He took his time strolling to the parking garage and the clock on his truck read 10:15 before he pulled out of the lot. He prayed no emergencies came up because he was looking forward to spending his Labor Day weekend with Cynthia.

****

"Turner, where are you taking me?" Cynthia asked, excitedly.

"You'll see. Just sit back, relax, and enjoy the ride."

"Okay, but you owe me one for this."

"Trust me, it'll be worth the wait," Turner said, heading onto the freeway.

Six hours later they arrived in Cleveland, Ohio. Turner checked into their hotel suite then ran some hot water in the Jacuzzi. He stripped Cynthia's clothes off and then his own before they stepped into the hot bubbly water.

"Turner, why didn't you tell me we were coming to Cleveland," Cynthia said, massaging his back.

"There's no place like home. Besides I have a weekend full of surprises for you," Turner replied, pulling her on top of his lap.

"Weekend full of surprises! Turner Worthington, what do you have up those sleeves of yours?"

"You'll just have to wait and see. Now let's stop all this talking," Turner said, sliding his tongue into her mouth.

His long kisses made Cynthia's heart flutter. She let Turner take full control as he worked his tongue down to her breast. He suckled on each of her hardened nipples before lifting her bottom halfway out of the water and suckling between her legs. The more Cynthia shuddered, the more

Turner circled his tongue around the spot that sent her to a state beyond control. When they were done dallying in their lovemaking, they snuggled in the warmth of the bed.

"Cynthia, I love you," Turner said, pulling her in his arms.

"I love you, too," Cynthia said, turning on her side to face him.

Turner kissed her on the lips and let silence wash over them.

"I know those words haven't come easy for you in the past. Turner, this truly is a surprise. Thank you for opening up to me."

"No, thank you. Now close your eyes, I have more surprises up my sleeve."

"More surprises!" Cynthia smiled.

"Yes."

With that Cynthia closed her eyes. What in the world did he have in store for her?

"Turner, what in the world is that?" Cynthia asked, feeling something cold on top of her stomach.

"Can you guess what it is?"

"Is it food? I know how much you like to lick all over my body."

"Nope. I'll give you a hint. I'll kiss the part of your body that this goes on."

When Turner picked up her hand, Cynthia was about to lose control.

She thought Turner was going to kiss her index finger but he ran his lips over her wrist instead.

"Okay, it's either a bracelet or a watch," Cynthia said. "Can I touch it?"

"Yeah, I guess," Turner said, sarcastically.

"You guess! I see. You want to play psychology, don't you?" Cynthia laughed.

"Okay, I can roll with that," she said, putting her arms behind her head. "Now, let's see," Cynthia said, wiggling her stomach slightly.

"Hmmm— It's a bracelet."

"Is that your final answer?" Turner asked.

"Yes, it's definitely a bracelet."

"Well since that's your final answer you can open your eyes."

"Oh, Turner, a diamond tennis bracelet."

"Yes, do you like it?"

"Of course," Cynthia told him.

She gave him a kiss on the lips and then wrapped the shining diamonds around her wrist. Turner secured the hook on the bracelet and then pulled Cynthia back in his arms.

"Turner, I still can't believe you bought this extravagant bracelet for me."

"That's only the beginning," Turner said, yawning.

They both laid there talking for the rest of the night until they drifted off to sleep.

****

"Cynthia, remember not to wear any perfume," Turner reminded her.

"Are we going to the park?"

"It's a surprise. My lips are sealed," Turner replied, running his finger across his lips. He pretended to zip them shut.

"You and your surprises. I guess I'll be a good girl," Cynthia told him.

She slipped her beige Capri pants with a snug black shirt to show off her figure. Cynthia slipped into her sandals, looked herself over in the mirror and was ready to go.

"Beautiful as always," Turner said, giving her a pinch on the butt.

129

"Thank you. You don't look bad yourself," Cynthia responded, pinching him the same.

"Yeah, we do look good together," Turner said, opening the door.

They headed out the hotel to begin their adventures for the day. Turner headed down Van Aken and made a quick stop by the store. He had to restock his supply of condoms for the rest of the weekend.

"We're so close to my sister's house; can we stop by?"

"Later on, right now I want you all to myself," Turner said, running his hand along her thigh.

"Okay," Cynthia sighed. "I'm not sure how long I can take all of these surprises. Turner, don't you go spoiling me," she smiled.

"Every woman deserves to be spoiled at some point in their life. Enjoy it because I don't do it often."

"You don't!" Cynthia said acting surprised.

"Ha ha. I didn't know you were so comical."

"Sometimes I can be. I want to have many more laughs with you," Cynthia said seriously.

"Me too."

Turner came to a stand still at the red light and took this opportunity to plant kisses on Cynthia's juicy lips. He got so caught up in the moment that the honk of the horn from the car behind brought him back to reality. He turned onto Fairhill to make his way to Euclid Avenue. The red convertible mustang behind him rushed to the side of him on the three-lane street, flipped him the middle finger, and then sped off.

"Don't worry, she's just mad because she doesn't have a man," Cynthia said.

Turner usually didn't go for that disrespect but he wasn't about to spoil his mood and get into any road rage with that lunatic. He took Cynthia's words to heart, which brought an instant smile to his face. That's what he loved most about her.

She knew him. Cynthia could read his mind even before it happened. She understood him even though they had only been together for a short time. He really caught a good one. Some women he had dated for a while never understood him. Turner was definitely going to hold on to her.

"The Botanical Gardens," Cynthia said unbuckling her seat belt.

"Yep. My mother used to bring me here all the time when she was living. She loved looking at all the beautiful flowers. She said they were relaxing. This was a special place where we would come hang out and let all of life's worries escape us."

"Oh Turner, I can't wait to see the gardens," Cynthia replied, getting out the truck.

Cynthia was flattered that Turner was taking her to a place his mother thought was special. Even though she would never get to know her in person, she felt a special closeness to her through Turner's eyes.

After an hour of walking through the beautiful gardens, she and Turner rested at the rose garden display.

"Turner, these roses are absolutely breathtaking."

"Just like you," Turner said, running his finger across her lips.

"Close your eyes. I have another surprise for you."

Cynthia complied without argument. When she opened her eyes, she began to cry.

"Cynthia, will you marry me?" Turner asked, while he was stooped down on one knee.

"Yes, yes, Turner I'll marry you! I can't believe this," Cynthia cried, while Turner slid the two karat diamond on her finger."

"Cynthia, I love you so much," Turner said, standing. He embraced her in his arms and then slid his tongue in her mouth.

Cynthia melted, as their bodies remained intertwined. Was this some kind of dream? Right now she was riding on cloud nine and never wanted this moment to end.

"Turner, I'm so surprised by all of this."

"Well they say when you find the right woman you want to marry, you'll definitely know. Cynthia, a month ago I would have never thought I would be saying these words to anyone. It was the furthest thing from my mind until you stole my heart."

The tears kept rolling from Cynthia's eyes. Turner pulled out some Kleenex and wiped them dry. Cynthia was definitely the woman he wanted to marry and spend the rest of his life with, he thought, as they continued strolling through the beautiful gardens.

Chapter 32

<u>*Ray Ray*</u>

Between working in the hair salon and moving in with Demetrius, Ray Ray was busy. That was good because that gave him less time to think about Jim and the awful rape that had occurred a few months ago. Just when Ray Ray was about to start putting a perm in his client hair, his cell phone rang.

"Hello, this is Ray Ray speaking."

"Ray Ray, it's Turner."

"Turner! Good to hear your voice. What have you been up to?"

"I'm here in town. Can you meet me for dinner? The rest of the crew will be there as well."

"Sounds great to me. What's the occasion?" Ray Ray asked, taking down directions.

"It's a surprise. Can you make it by 7:00?"

"Only for you, Turner. I'm going to have to close shop early. Thank goodness my last appointment is in my chair now."

"Good, until then—"

"Ta ta," Ray Ray said, finishing Turner's sentence before hanging up.

"Ray Ray, so you never finished telling me about you and Demetrius," Shelley said.

"Girl, things have been so hectic," Ray Ray replied, parting Shelley's hair into sections and applying the perm to the new growth of her hair.

"Details, details."

"Okay," Ray Ray replied, with a long-winded sigh.

"If you must know, Demetrius and I have taken our relationship to the next level. He asked me to move in with him and I said yes."

"Were you surprised that he asked you to move in with him?"

"Yes, girl! Demetrius knows that I have my own place and love my independence. He really loves me, girl— aren't I special," Ray Ray said, fanning his hand back and forth.

"You are a trip," Shelley laughed. "But seriously, he must really love you. Thank goodness you picked a brother with some money. You both can bring something to the table."

"Our relationship is not about money," Ray Ray told Shelley.

"I know, but it doesn't hurt to have it. You never want to put yourself in the position of depending on somebody else. That only opens you up to be hurt."

"Sounds like you're talking from experience."

"Yep, before I met Ken I was in a horrible relationship."

"Details, details," Ray Ray asked this time.

"Not today. Let's keep things on a positive note."

"All right then, let's talk about Ken because that man is so hot!" Ray Ray fanned.

"Oooh, should I be jealous?" Shelley asked.

"Since we're friends, no. Besides, I'm in love with Demetrius."

"You'll have to introduce me to Demetrius since I hear so much about him."

"In due time. Now lets get this relaxer rinsed out of your hair. I have to close shop after you leave because my old pal Turner is here in town and wants to meet with the crew for dinner."

"Sounds like fun," Shelley said.

"Yeah. From the sound of Turner's voice he is up to something, because when I asked him what the occasion was he said it was a surprise," Ray Ray replied.

"Well, you'll have to let me know the 411 the next time I come in to get my hair done."

"Will do," Ray Ray told her.

For the next hour, Ray Ray spruced Shelley's hair to perfection. When she left he began to quickly clean up so he could close shop. Luckily he had a change of clothes there so he would not have to go home. It was already going on 6:30 p.m., when he looked at his clock.

"What in the hell— " Ray Ray gasped. He stopped cold in his tracks.

"Hello, Ray Ray."

"Jim, how in the hell did you get in here?" Ray Ray asked. Memories of the rape flooded back to his memory. That was the same question he asked Jim when he appeared in his house several months ago.

"I have a key," Jim smiled, showing all of his pearly white teeth.

Sweat began to bead off the top of Ray Ray's head. He ran to his drawer and pulled out a gun.

"Don't make me use this," Ray Ray said, pointing the gun straight towards Jim's head.

"I just want to talk."

"Talk! I have nothing to say to you," Ray Ray hollered. "Now get out. The next time I call the police it will be to pick up your dead body."

"Now you're talking insane. Why would you kill me when I'm dying anyway?"

"Jim, don't move any closer," Ray Ray warned.

"Do you really want to spend the rest of your life behind bars? Ray Ray, please— I just want to talk."

"Get out, Jim."

Ray Ray took a few steps back with the gun still pointing at Jim's head. With one hand, he nervously picked up the phone and dialed 911.

"Help," Ray Ray shrieked as Jim lunged at him.

The gun went off as Jim grabbed the phone from his hand. He clicked the police off and then leaped on top of Ray Ray in one swift motion.

"Why do you force me to do these things?" Jim screamed in a heat of rage.

Ray Ray could not answer as he watched blood gush from Jim's body.

"Oh my God! Demetrius."

Demetrius dropped the gun to the floor and ran over to Ray Ray.

"Don't touch anything," Ray Ray hollered.

He pushed Jim's body off his and got up. Blood covered his body. Jim's HIV blood was scattered all over the place.

"Are you okay?"

"Demetrius you have to get out of here," Ray Ray told him.

"No, I'm not leaving."

"Demetrius, please! You have to leave now. The police are on their way."

Reluctantly, Demetrius left. Ray Ray ran to the back and threw the clothes he had just changed into in the washing machine. He rinsed the tainted blood off his body and then ran back to Jim.

"Jim, you're still alive," Ray Ray jumped frantically.

"Give me the gun," Jim gasped in a faint voice.

"Are you crazy?"

"Ray Ray, don't you hear the police sirens. Give me the gun. Let me make everything right before I die."

Ray Ray stood there frozen in place.

"Ray Ray, please. If you don't give me the gun then your friend will pay for my death. The police will figure it out. Now give me the gun, damn it!"

"Jim, how can I trust you?"

"Because I love you."

For some crazy reason Ray Ray believed Jim words were sincere. He walked over and handed him the gun.

"Jim, don't," Ray Ray pleaded as he held the gun to his head.

"Quiet, Ray Ray. Let me do this," he said in a raspy tone.

The loud sirens of the police cars stopped right outside Ray Ray's shop.

"Stop right there," Jim warned the police officers.

Ray Ray watched in disbelief while the officers drew their weapons.

"I didn't mean for things to come to this," Jim cried.

"I raped Ray Ray a few months ago. No one including the police believed him so I came back to rape him again. I have AIDS. Damn it, I just wanted somebody to love me."

Ray Ray couldn't believe the words coming from Jim's mouth. He was confessing and for some odd reason he felt sorry for him.

"Ray Ray shot me in self-defense but I'm still alive. Don't make him pay for my sins," he said before pulling the trigger.

Ray Ray legs nearly gave out. Blood splattered all across the mirror.

After what seemed like an eternity, everyone left and he was finally able to close shop. When he arrived home Demetrius was waiting with open arms. He wanted to run to him but instead he headed straight for the shower. After scrubbing his skin raw, he curled up in bed and told Demetrius that everything would be okay.

Chapter 33

Karen

Karen couldn't believe Turner was getting married. He was just involved and living with Natalie; now he was introducing a new woman by the name of Cynthia to be his wife. Was Turner making a huge mistake? A thousand questions began to race through her mind as she pulled up in her driveway. She didn't look forward to being alone in her empty house. Karen felt guilty for kicking Jason out of their house but it was the only way she could make up her mind on whether to keep her marriage or let it go altogether. Karen thoughts were interrupted by a knock on the door.

"Turner, what are you doing here?"

"I wanted to speak with you alone."

"Is everything all right?" she asked him.

"I should be asking you that same question. Your mind seemed to be elsewhere at dinner today."

"I'm dealing with a lot," Karen said, retrieving the letter from the drawer.

Turner stood there in silence. His blood began to boil. First, her husband Jason was being abusive and now he was caught having an affair.

"Karen, I'm sorry."

"It's not your fault," Karen said, breaking down in tears.

Turner embraced her in his arms. He became her post as she vented all the anger and frustration going on in her life.

"Turner, I don't know what to do."

"Karen, first you need to calm down. You don't need all this stress with a baby growing inside you."

"I can't help it. My life is falling apart right before my eyes. Turner, I can't take losing you too."

"Why would you think that?"

"Because, you're getting married. Turner, how could you just go off and get engaged like this? You never even told me anything about this woman you're seeing."

"Karen, that's partially why I'm here. I need to explain everything to you but maybe now is not the best time."

"Yes, it is a good time. You are an important person in my life so out with it," she told him.

Turner sat down on the couch. Where should he begin? He clutched the bottom of his chin in thought before beginning.

"Karen, before now I've only been in love once and that was with you."

Karen tears started to flow even more. If Turner had just been honest about his feelings all those years ago, then maybe they could have worked things out. He was the perfect man— kind, respectful, and most of all, loving. Yes, Turner was loving; he had a heart of gold even though he kept it locked for all those years.

"You must really love Cynthia to make this kind of commitment."

"I do," Turner replied.

"How did you come to this decision? I thought you were in love with Natalie?"

"No. Natalie forced me to believe I was in love with her. She wasn't the right person for me. I was comfortable in my relationship with her but she wanted more and it was something I could not give her. It seemed like we were always arguing about everything. As difficult as it was, I'm glad to have ended the relationship with her."

"So, tell me about Cynthia."

"Oh my goodness, where do I began?" Turner said, with a smile.

"Well from the grin on your face you can start with how you met."

"Cynthia and I met at the airport when I was waiting for you all to arrive for my graduation."

Karen listened as Turner spoke about Cynthia. He was so compassionate and caring. Cynthia was a lucky woman. Deep down Karen was envious, she wished it were her. She should have waited for Turner. She let him slip away and settled with his friendship instead. Karen had moved on with her life. She got married and now had a baby on the way. She could tell Turner how she truly felt, but what gave her the right? She had no right. Turner was a free man. He had finally found someone that could truly make him happy. Karen couldn't fathom stealing his joy.

"Turner, I'm so proud for you," Karen said, kissing him on the forehead.

"I know."

"One more kiss for old time sake?" Karen asked.

For a moment Turner hesitated. He should have listened to his first mind. Turner let his hands comb through Karen's silky long hair. Her kiss sent him into an abyss while his tongue locked passionately with hers. Turner was out of control as his hands traced lightly over her auburn skin. He unsnapped her bra and slid off her lace panties. Turner glided his tongue across her hardened nipples and then to her belly button. Her stomach was faintly protruding with a baby growing inside of her that was not his. He should have stopped then but he had to have her one last time.

"You'll always be my first love," Turner whispered in her ear.

"I know, now make love to me."

Turner slid his hard shaft into her as memories of their past raced to his mind. They were so happy together. Karen fulfilled all his needs in every way. She was a good woman, someone who deserved the best. Turner loved her; Karen was more than just his friend. She was his soul mate, the one person who understood him completely. Turner loved every inch of her body. He had to make her realize that she was special. No hands should ever touch her abusively, only gently through lovemaking. He could kill Jason for making her life so miserable. How could she tolerate being in such a wretched relationship? Karen deserved better, and he wanted a better life for her.

"Karen, are you all right?" Turner asked, as she snuggled against his chest.

"Yes, when I'm with you everything is always fine," she said, twirling the hair on his chest.

After Turner left, Karen straightened her living room up. She was interrupted by the sound of the doorbell.

"Turner, did you forget something?" she said, opening the door.

Karen was surprised to see her husband Jason standing at the door.

"Jason, what are you doing here?"

"I came to check on you. What was Turner doing over here?"

"Come on in. Why didn't you just use your key? This is your house too," Karen told him nervously.

"I didn't want to startle you," he replied, following her into the kitchen.

Jason watched her pour a tall glass of milk. She gulped all the contents down in a few swallows.

"Turner came to town to introduce us to his new fiancée."

"Fiancée?"

"Yes, Turner's getting married," Karen, told him.

A smile appeared on Jason's face as he sat to the table. Thank goodness he didn't come by a half hour earlier, Karen thought to herself. If he had, Jason would have caught her and Turner's bodies intertwined naked in the living room. In some way deep down she wished he had walked in on them, so he could see that somebody else could love and want her. She wanted him to pay for all the pain he had caused her. Karen could tell him what happened but what would be the sense. He was already jealous of her friendship with Turner and if he knew the depth of their relationship, he would forbid her from seeing him altogether.

"When did all this happen?" Jason asked, curiously.

"Well evidently Turner brought his girlfriend Cynthia to Cleveland and proposed to her today at the Botanical Gardens. He told all of this over dinner today."

"So what was he doing here then?"

Karen didn't like his line of questions. He had some damn nerve, she thought, wiping the milk stain off her lips.

"He wanted to speak with us about getting counseling with one of his colleagues. I was reluctant at first but he feels that this is best since we are friends."

"It makes sense."

"Yes, I guess. He says ethically he shouldn't be talking about our problems since we are friends. He just wanted us to be comfortable with speaking to someone about our problems since I felt so strongly against talking to a total stranger. Now I see how important it is for us to have counseling, how can I refuse? Besides, Turner lives so far away."

"Does he know I moved out."

"No," Karen lied.

She did not feel like explaining herself to him right now. Karen just wanted to go to bed.

"Oh, so have you had time to think about our marriage?"

"Yes, but I have not come to any decision. Jason, I honestly don't know where to go from here."

"Baby, you can start by giving me a second chance."

"You could have another baby on the way."

"It's not mine," Jason told her.

"How am I supposed to know for sure? Jason, I need to speak with her."

"No."

"Why not? If you don't have anything to hide than let me talk with Monique."

Jason got up from the table and paced back and forth for a few moments.

"Karen, I don't like this especially in your condition but here is the number if you absolutely feel the need to speak to her."

Jason kissed her on the forehead and then left. Karen picked up the phone and then hung it up. She contemplated for a few moments longer and then picked up the phone to call Monique.

Chapter 34

<u>*Lulu*</u>

Lulu was nervous and excited about being back in school. It had been over ten years since she had last opened a textbook to do any work. Lulu wasn't sure what field of study she wanted to go into but she started out with the basic classes of math, reading, and science.

"Is this seat taken?"

"No," Lulu replied, as a tall gentleman sat next to her.

"Hello, my name is Keith," he smiled, shaking her hand.

"My name is Lucy but everyone calls me Lulu."

"Well it's nice to meet you, Lulu."

"Same here."

Lulu tried her best to concentrate on the class lecturer but her eyes kept drifting over to Keith. He was a handsome gentleman, a coffee-colored skin tone, medium build, and a nice personality to go along. She knew he was different right from the beginning than any man she had ever dated.

By the time Lulu packed up her school materials, Keith was waiting for her in the hallway.

"Would you like to grab some lunch?"

"Sure. Where do you want to go?" Lulu asked.

"We can go anywhere you like. There is a strip of restaurants right up the street."

"Okay," Lulu replied.

She enjoyed Keith's company as he walked her to her car. She followed him to the restaurant and had an equally good time.

"So tell me about yourself?"

"Keith, I'm going to be upfront and honest with you. I have three kids by three different daddies. I make a good living driving a bus full time for the transit authority and I decided to go to school to make something more of myself. I'm trying to turn my life around," Lulu told him.

"Wow."

Silence. Lulu watched Keith as he sipped down a glass of iced tea.

"A handful, huh," Lulu said, biting down into her chicken sandwich.

"Yes, but you must be a strong woman to be that up front and honest about everything."

"Yep. I don't have time to waste. My main priority is being a good mother to my kids."

"So you're not looking for a good man?"

Lulu laughed. "Keith, I'm in my early thirties and haven't found a good man yet. I've all but given up. Besides, who wants a woman with three kids?"

"Somebody does," Keith answered. "God has a person for everyone out here."

"Really, well I wish he would send him my way."

"Maybe he has already."

"Keith, are you talking about yourself?"

"You want to give it a try?"

"Oh my goodness, you're serious, aren't you?" Lulu asked.

"Yes, it's not like we're getting married. We can start off as friends and go from there."

Lulu pondered his remarks for a few moments. "Keith, to be honest I don't know anything about you."

"Well I can change that."

For the next hour Lulu listened to a brief overview of Keith's life. He married at the age of twenty-five and got a divorce over two years ago. His marriage ended because he was unable to give his wife any children. Keith was thirty-five, had his own computer consulting firm, and he was taking a refresher course in English to improve on his writing skills.

"Keith, quite frankly you can do much better than me."

"Lulu, don't ever sell yourself short. If you don't believe in yourself then who will?"

"You got a point there."

"I know," Keith responded. "You're a beautiful woman. The first time I laid eyes on you, I knew I wanted to get to know you better."

Lulu was at a loss for words. No one had ever made her feel special like this before. All men wanted to do was get in between her legs. For the life of her, she didn't understand why she gave herself so freely, because now she was paying the price being a single mom to three kids. Maybe this friendship with Keith was the beginning of something new. Lulu decided to at least give it a try anyway.

****

Nearly two months had past and Lulu had fallen in love with Keith. He treated her and the kids so good. Was this all a dream?   Lulu had to pinch herself to make sure this was a reality.

"Mommy, where is Daddy?" Andre asked impatiently.

"He'll be here soon," Lulu smiled, patting him on the back.

"Now run along upstairs and get your things."

"Okay, Mommy."

Lulu watched as Andre skipped up the stairs. That damn DeAndre was never going to change. He was always the last one to pick up his kid and the first to drop him back off to her. Little Andre was looking forward to going trick or treating for Halloween. DeAndre better not screw this up, Lulu thought to herself. Besides, she had a special evening planned with Keith.

"ABOUT TIME," Lula yelled at DeAndre.

"What's your problem?"

"DeAndre, you were supposed to be here at 4:00. It's now going on 5:30."

"Look, why are you always on my case?"

146

"Why don't you grow up? If you're going to be late you can at least call."

"Damn, you're always bickering. Just be glad I'm here."

"Glad you're here! DeAndre you act like it is a chore to spend time with your son. You are messed up. You need to get yourself together and be half the man your father was."

Lulu didn't have time to brace herself for the slap, as DeAndre's large hand smacked her directly across the face. Blood began to escape from her nose.

"Lulu, I'm sorry," DeAndre said, trying to see about her nose.

"Don't touch me," Lulu screamed. "Now get out!"

"Not before I get Andre."

"Andre is not going anywhere with you. Now get your ass out of here before I call the police."

At those words, DeAndre left. When she looked up she saw her son Andre crying at the top of the stairs. Before she had a chance to say anything to him, he ran to his room and slammed the door.

"Andre, I'm sorry," Lulu yelled.

She stuffed some tissue in her bloody nose and then ran up the steps to see about him.

"Mommy, why did Daddy hit you?"

"Honey, I said something that upset your daddy."

"Daddy was angry at you?"

"Yes, he was, but that is never a reason to hit someone. Violence is never the answer," Lulu said, wrapping her arms around him.

"Are you okay, Mommy?"

"Yes, mommy will be fine. Now get your Halloween costume out of your bag and put it on."

"Yeah, we're still going trick or treating?" Andre smiled.

"Yes. Now get on that costume while I go open the door for Keith.

Tears fell down Lulu's cheeks as she made her way down the steps.

"What in the world happened?" Keith asked.

The smile on his face quickly vanished when Lulu told him what was going on.

"Are you all right?"

"No," Lulu cried. "I had special plans for us tonight. That damn DeAndre always messes things up."

"Everything is going to be fine," Keith said.

He left out the room and returned with a wet cloth in his hand. The warm cloth felt good as he wiped away any traces of blood from her nose.

"Keith, I'm sorry."

"Stop apologizing. You have no control over somebody else's actions. When I see that poor excuse of a man, he's going to wish he never laid his hands on you."

"Keith, no. I don't want you getting into a confrontation with DeAndre."

"Lulu, let a man take care of his business. Just know that this will be the only and last time DeAndre ever lays his hands on you."

"Do you know how much I love you?" Lulu told him.

"I love you, too. Now get little Andre down here so we can fill our buckets with candy."

By the time Lulu, Keith, and Andre walked from house to house trick-or-treating, they were all exhausted. Lulu fed Andre, let him eat a few pieces of candy, and then put him to bed. He didn't fuss about going to sleep; he was out like a light before his head could even hit the pillow.

"Keith, make love to me."

"Not now, Lulu. The time isn't right," he said, embracing her in his arms.

They talked and cuddled the rest of the night until they both drifted off to sleep.

Chapter 35

Delana

Delana was a happy woman. Her life was finally starting to look up. She had a great job that paid her plenty of money and a handsome man that worshipped the ground she walked on. How could she ask for anything more?

"Corey, are you ready yet?" Delana asked.

"In a second, honey."

"Well hurry. How long do you expect a woman to wait?"

"All night if you have to. Besides it will definitely be worth the wait," Corey said, coming into the room.

Delana relished the feeling while Corey planted kisses all over her face.

"Forget going out. We can have our party right here," Delana said, running her hand over his chest.

"Greedy woman. In due time," Corey said, opening the door.

He helped Delana into her red Mercedes Benz and then headed off to a night full of surprises.

Their first stop was a romantic dinner. Delana was thrilled to be dining among the upper echelon, where plates started at a hundred dollars and up. The gourmet food was excellent and she even saved room for the chocolate cake smothered in rich chocolate syrup and mousse toping.

"Corey you've outdone yourself with this dinner," Delana told him.

"Well don't get used to it, because it won't happen often."

"I'm not crazy," Delana responded. "It's okay, however, to splurge every once in a while."

"I agree, but we have to stop spending everything that comes in and start saving our money."

"That's funny coming from you after what you've been through," Delana said.

"What do you mean by that?" Corey asked defensively.

"Nothing. I can see that you're irritated by my remark."

"Delana, never mind my mood. If you have something to say, out with it."

"Look, I don't want to ruin this evening by getting into an argument. All I was going to say was it is hard for us to save, especially when we lag so far behind on an economic level. We've all been in that predicament at one point in time."

"Well, I agree with you there."

"Good, now let's change the subject."

"And that would be?"

"Corey, don't tease me. Tell me what we're doing next."

"Nope. Just sit back and relax."

Delana did not like having control. She always took charge of her affairs. She dominated every aspect of her life, including her men. Delana never trusted anyone to have her best interests at heart because the minute she did was the minute she got burned.

"Delana, it's going to be all right," Corey said, seeing her reservations.

"I know it's just hard for me— "

"To trust anyone," Corey replied, completing her sentence.

"Yes."

"Well I told you before that you're going to have to start to trust me."

"All right," Delana sighed. "I'm just afraid of being hurt."

"I understand, but life isn't perfect. We all have our ups and downs throughout life but you have to be able to pick up the pieces and move on."

"I'm really trying," Delana replied. "I've even agreed to mend fences with Lulu and work on our relationship again."

"That's wonderful, because you could really lose out if you had not at least given it a try," Corey smiled.

Delana nodded and went on about the plans she and Lulu had made for the coming week. They were going to spend the whole weekend together, which was a stretch for Delana considering she gave no one that amount of her time besides Corey.

"Okay, we're here," Corey said, pulling into the parking lot.

"Downtown?"

"Yes, we're going to take a cruise on Lake Erie."

"In that case, I'd better grab my jacket," Delana responded.

She enjoyed the boat ride as they nestled in a corner section of the boat and watched the continuous motion of water going back and forth. Corey had his arms wrapped around her waist and the jazz music nestled softly in their ears. All was perfect.

"I love you, Delana Smith."

"I love you, too," Delana smiled, as they indulged in a passionate kiss.

****

Delana didn't think the night could get any better but Corey booked a night at a five star hotel. They went up to their suite and he blind folded her before they went in.

"Corey, I can't believe the magical night we're having."

"It only gets better," he said, leading her in.

"Oh my goodness," Delana gasped.

The Jacuzzi was bubbling with beautiful red rose petals floating on top of the water. On the side there was a tray of fresh fruit, a vase of long stem roses, and a bottle of chilled champagne. Delana was still in shock as Corey undressed her from head to toe. He whisked her off her feet and gently sat her on top of him in the heated water.

"You are really tense," Corey said, continuing to massage Delana's back.

"Yes, between my new job and trying to keep my own business going, I'm doing a lot."

"Have you thought about hiring an extra assistant?"

"I have spoken to my assistant Natasha about bringing someone else on board to help out, but I haven't had a chance to finalize any plans."

"Well, don't take too long because I don't want you under all this stress."

"I hear you," Delana sighed.

She enjoyed letting the warm bubbles and Corey's hands relax her body. Today couldn't have been more perfect. Delana needed this extra boost before the start of a new workweek. She laid her head back in Corey's chest and closed her eyes. After an hour of relaxation and playing in the Jacuzzi, Corey toweled the both of them down.

"Close your eyes," he told Delana.

Delana didn't question him and complied. She held on to his arms while he led the way.

"Okay, you can open up now."

Delana was speechless. Corey really did listen to the things she said. Spread across the entire span of the bed was money. There were one, ten, twenty, fifty, and hundred dollar bills spread across the rich white bedspread.

"Corey!"

"You've always wanted to make love on top of a bed filled with money."

"Yes. I like feeling rich even though I'm not."

"Well you're doing quite well for yourself," Corey said, scooping her into his arms.

"Yes I am. Having you in my life is all the richness I need."

"And money don't hurt."

"It sure doesn't," Delana smiled. "Now make love to me."

"You don't have to ask twice," Corey replied.

He slid the bathrobe off Delana's cinnamon brown skin and pleasured her for the rest of the night.

Chapter 36

<u>*Turner*</u>

November was already here and Turner was a nervous wreck. He and Cynthia would be walking down the aisle before the New Year, meanwhile he still couldn't get Karen off of his mind. In all the years since high school their friendship had been strictly platonic. Sure they had flirted with each other from time to time, but they had never made love. Turner didn't know what to think. Was there the slightest chance that he and Karen could get back together? Maybe Karen was just vulnerable and wanted to get back at her husband Jason for cheating on her. These thoughts had been invading his mind for the past two months. He had to see Karen before they all met up for Thanksgiving dinner.

Turner picked up the phone. "Yes, I would like to make plane reservations for Cleveland, Ohio, roundtrip same day."

After Turner got his flight schedule he grabbed his things and headed out the door to catch a flight that was departing in the next few hours.

"Hello, Karen— "

"Turner, is that you?"

"Yes," he replied. "I need to speak with you."

"Now is not a good time Turner."

"Well make time. I'm on a plane as we speak and will be in Cleveland in the next hour."

"Turner, why didn't you tell me you were coming to town?"

"I didn't know it myself until now. We need to talk face to face, so I'll see you soon," he said, telling her where to meet him.

****

For some reason the flight seemed like it took an eternity, Turner thought as he checked into his hotel suite. He was anxious to meet with Karen. He poured a glass of cognac to

154

sooth his nerves. A half hour later Karen was knocking at the door.

"Turner, I'm surprised to see you," she said, giving him a kiss on the cheek.

"Sorry for the short notice. I didn't get you in any trouble?"

"No, Jason just left for work. Now what is so urgent that you had to fly way up to Cleveland just to speak with me?"

"Karen, I'm still in love with you."

Silence.

"You're about to get married in less than two months. Turner, what's going on?" she asked, with a confused look on her face.

"Karen, we haven't made love in over fifteen years. Ever since September when we were together, I haven't been able to get it off my mind."

Karen sat on the bed. She didn't know what to say. In less than two months Turner was going to be a married man and she was scheduled to have her baby soon after.

"Turner, I had no idea you felt this way."

"You know I've always loved you."

"Yes, but I thought from our past conversation you wanted us to stick with being friends."

"I know I told you that but things have changed."

"Turner, I'm married and six months pregnant with my husband's child."

"I know," Turner said, pacing back and forth. "I'm just trying to sort everything out before I make the biggest commitment of my life."

"You mean marriage? Yes, it is a commitment," Karen said, thinking of her own failed marriage.

"Yes, that's exactly why I'm here. The bottom line is I love you. If there is any chance of us ever being together then let me know now."

"Turner, what are you saying?"

"Karen, I can't be any clearer than this. I'm asking you point blank if you see us being together again in the future."

Silence.

Karen couldn't believe what was coming out of Turner's mouth. Was he serious? Maybe this was some tactic for him to get out of marrying Cynthia. Turner did have a history of leaving women behind that he loved. He felt more comfortable in a relationship that he could control.

"Turner, I don't know what to say."

Turner sat on the bed next to Karen. He took her hands in his and gently kissed the top of them.

"Karen, I need for you to help me put the pieces of my life back together again. Please answer my question honestly."

"Do you love Cynthia?"

"Yes, I love Cynthia, but I also love you. Our history runs too deep and I can't just bypass my feelings for you."

"I don't like being put on the spot like this."

"I'm sorry if you feel uncomfortable, especially since you're pregnant but I have to know."

Karen hoped she wouldn't live to regret what she had to say. Yes, she loved Turner with all her heart but right now her baby came first. She couldn't put her needs before the baby's needs, even if it meant losing the chance of being with Turner forever.

"Turner, you know I love you," Karen said, looking him in the eyes.

How could she explain herself? Karen took a deep breath before continuing.

"If you had come to me over two years ago, before I got married, then yes I would have not even hesitated to be in a relationship with you. Things have changed now," Karen said, rubbing her stomach.

"I would never ask you to leave your marriage if you were truly happy, but you're not. You have been living with an abusive husband who has been cheating on you on more than one occasion."

"Don't forget I cheated on him with you. Two wrongs don't make it right."

"And you made love to me to get back at your husband?" Turner asked.

"NO. How could you even ask me that?"

"Karen, before that day it had been over fifteen years since we were together intimately."

"I understand, but I would never selfishly put you in the middle just to get back at Jason."

Tears began to escape Karen's eyes. "Turner, I would never do anything to hurt you. When we made love it was because I needed you. I needed to feel loved; I needed to feel like a woman again."

"I know that. You shouldn't have to beg your husband to love you. It should come freely. Karen, I just want you to be happy. If that means staying with your husband then just tell me."

"Jason's really trying. I love him and can't throw our marriage away, especially now that I'm pregnant."

"I understand. I just had to be sure."

"Are we still going to be best friends?"

"Always," Turner said, kissing the back of her hand.

"Are you going to tell Cynthia about us?"

"No. Are you going to tell Jason?"

"No. If I did that he would forbid me from ever seeing you again. It's best that we keep this between us. I'll always cherish the times we were together. I have no regrets."

"Me neither," Turner replied, holding Karen in his arms.

They spent the rest of the afternoon talking. Turner savored every minute knowing it would be the last time that they would ever be alone together like this again.

Chapter 37

<u>*Ray Ray*</u>

It was finally over; Jim's case was closed. Ray Ray couldn't count all the times he sat in the police station. He was glad it was over. In the end they stamped Jim's file as a suicide and Ray Ray was free to go. He could put this whole ordeal behind him and move on.

"Demetrius, lets go celebrate."

"A man's death is no reason to celebrate," Demetrius responded.

"What's wrong with you?"

"I can't get over shooting Jim."

"For the hundredth time, you didn't kill Jim. He was alive when you left my shop. In fact the bullet that you fired only pierced him; Jim took his own life right in front of me and the police officers."

"But— "

"Let it go," Ray Ray said. "Jim didn't want you and me to suffer for his sins. If he could live with it then why can't you?"

"Give me time."

"No Demetrius, you don't have time. I'm not about to let you fall into some depressed state and slip up. We could be sitting behind bars or on trial but that's not how it was supposed to be. Besides, you were defending me. No jury in the world would have convicted you. Jim saved us the trouble from going through this. He was dying anyway."

"I know. I just need to refocus. Instead of celebrating let's just spend some quality time together."

"That works for me. What did you have in mind?"

"A quiet dinner here at home. We can order some movies."

"Fine, " Ray Ray said. "Let's order Chinese."

Ray Ray couldn't believe how hungry he was. He loaded his plate with some shrimp fried rice, shrimp egg foo yung, pepper steak, and an egg roll to go along. After eating all that, he quenched his thirst with an ice-cold beer.

"Come over here, I made a nice warm fire for us," Demetrius told him.

"Okay, let me grab another beer. Do you want one?"

"Nope. I just want you."

"Demetrius, we're supposed to be watching movies."

"The movies can watch us, now hurry along."

Ray Ray cracked a smile and then hurried to retrieve his belongings. He joined Demetrius on the fur spread and enjoyed their night of intimacy together.

****

Ray Ray was awakened by the sound of the phone. He didn't want to wake Demetrius so he answered it by the second ring.

"Hello."

"Is this Ray Ray Fields?"

"Yes, it is."

"My name is Sandy Meyers from Meyers and Associates. I'm calling because your name is listed as a beneficiary in Jim Medley's trust."

"Trust," Ray Ray repeated.

"Yes, can you meet with me to go over Jim's final wishes?"

"Is this some kind of joke?" Ray Ray asked, getting up.

He tried to tip toe into the kitchen but Demetrius rolled over on the fur rug and looked at him to see what was going on.

"No, this is not a joke. Can you come in at 1:00 today?"

"Yes, I'll be there," Ray Ray, agreed reluctantly.

When he hung up the phone he filled Demetrius in on what was going on. He called and cancelled all his hair appointments for the day. Ray Ray wondered what this meeting was really about. Did someone else know what happened the night Jim killed himself and now was coming forward? The lawyer said it was regarding Jim's trust but he didn't have any money. Was this some kind of prank? Maybe one of his lovers was trying to get revenge.

"I'm not going to this meeting," Ray Ray said, frustrated.

"Well if it makes you feel any better, Meyers & Associates is listed in the phone book. I even called to make sure Sandy Meyers worked there and she does."

"Really?"

"Yes."

"Do you think I should go?" Ray Ray asked.

"If you don't then you'll always wonder what this meeting would have been about."

"You're right."

Demetrius smiled. "If you feel that uncomfortable about this meeting, I'll ride with you and wait in the car."

"I would like that," Ray Ray said, grabbing his coat.

Ray Ray was relatively quiet on the ride downtown. He slid the window in Demetirus's new car down halfway and let the cold air hit his face. Winter was right around the corner and soon the snow would be falling. Cleveland was notorious for its frigid winters and as many years as Ray Ray lived here, he would never get used to the winter weather.

"This must be the place," Demetrius said, breaking the long silence.

Ray Ray looked at him and wondered if he should get out. He still had time to change his mind.

"It's going to be okay," Demetrius said, seeing Ray Ray's reservations.

"I just want to put this all behind me. Every time I think things are going to be okay, Jim still finds a way to get at me and he isn't even here anymore."

"Well this is the last chapter of Jim's story. Go in and see what this is all about. If you feel uncomfortable at any time, you have the choice of leaving."

"You're right, again."

"I know," Demetrius responded, as he watched Ray Ray get out of the car.

" Don't sign anything— and Ray Ray, I love you."

"Same here," Ray Ray said, going into the office.

"Can I help you?"

"Yes, I have a 1:00 appointment to see Sandy Meyers."

Ray Ray watched as the receptionist clicked the buttons on her computer. She was a young woman in her early twenties with cocoa butter skin and light brown eyes. Her hair hung down her back and when she spoke, she brightened the room with her pretty smile.

"You can have a seat. Ms. Meyers will be with you shortly."

"Thank you," Ray Ray said.

He sat down and picked a magazine up off the table. Anything to get his mind from the very reason he was sitting in this office.

"Mr. Fields, you can go in now."

"Thank you," Ray Ray said.

On his way into the office he slid the receptionist his business card.

"Come let me work on that fabulous hair of yours," he whispered before going in.

After the formal introduction, they began discussing Jim's trust. It seemed that he had a million dollars, half of which he left to Ray Ray.

"I can't believe this," Ray Ray said, stunned.

"Well it's true. Under the law you are entitled to half of Jim Medley's trust."

"Are you positive we're speaking of the same person? I never knew Jim to have money."

"Yes, Jim was a modest man. He only lived for what he needed. In fact, he brought this package over to me a week before his death back in September. Now that his case is officially closed, we can proceed with his trust."

"Why would Jim leave me all this money?"

"I don't know."

Ray Ray took the sealed packet from Sandy and held it in his hand.

"I'll give you a few moments alone."

"Thank you," Ray Ray smiled.

When he opened the package there was a note and a few of Jim's personal items. Ray Ray tore open the note and began to read:

Ray Ray, if you're reading this then I'm gone. I still have a few things to say, I just regret I could not speak with you while I was alive. Please know that I never meant to rape you back in May. I relive that night in my mind over and over and over again. Something in me snapped. All I ever wanted was to be loved. Since this horrid HIV disease, now full-blown AIDS, has been invading my body, no one has even come close to me, including my own family. Ever since I came out of the closet my family has looked down on me. When I told them of this disease, they said, "What do you expect?" They never understood my feelings, the same thing you went through with your father. I guess that's why I felt so close with you. We kind of have been through the same thing though I was stupid not to practice safe sex. Who knew that the first man I made love to would pass this horrible disease to me. For over ten years I have been living a miserable life, even all my money can't make this go away. You're probably surprised that I have money. Ha ha— boy I would love to see the look on your face. Your friendship meant the world to me even though I wanted more. Your commitment to Demetrius only made me jealous. Why couldn't we have hooked up before all this happened to me? Well it's no use going on about what could've been. The fact of the matter is you're a good person and my last intentions were not for you to ever hate me. I want you to have half of my trust. The only thing that I request is that you take it and get an upscale salon.

"No he didn't," Ray Ray fanned. He shook his head and continued to read on.

Don't be upset but that storefront shop of yours has to go. People are probably scared to come in so go get a place where you can fully blossom the talents you have. In case you're wondering, because my attorney will not tell you, the remaining portion of my trust will go towards AIDS research and legal fees. In closing, please take this money as my apology. I can never rest in peace knowing that you hate me. You're a good person so I know all is forgiven.

James Medley, aka Jim

Ray Ray walked out of Meyers & Associates a half a million dollars richer. He still couldn't believe it as he filled Demetrius in on the story.

"You have to be kidding me," Demetrius said.

"No, it's true. Should I accept the money?"

"Hell yes, after what Jim has put you through. Besides, why let all that good money go to waste. Take it and open up you another shop and invest the rest."

"I think I'll do that."

Ray Ray was glad he decided to come to Meyers & Associates after all, he thought smiling as they drove back home.

Chapter 38

Lulu

Lulu wasn't looking forward to spending the whole weekend with Delana. There were a million other things she could be doing but she had to make an effort, especially considering Delana wanted to give their friendship a second try.

"Well look who's here," Lulu said, looking at her watch.

"Don't start," DeAndre replied, with a conspicuous stare.

"Start what?" Lulu smiled.

She was in no mood to argue with DeAndre. She called Andre down the steps, gave her son a kiss and sent them on their way. She shut the door and laughed. Lulu told DeAndre to be here at two o' clock. It was now going on four-thirty but she and Delana hadn't scheduled getting together for at least another couple of hours. Why hadn't Lulu thought of doing this before? DeAndre was just always looking for a fight. As much as Lulu wanted to go upside his head, she refrained. She was a changed woman, besides she liked seeing the look on DeAndre's face when she didn't take his bait. She wasn't going to stoop down to his level anymore. As far as she was concerned he was the father to one of her children, nothing more and nothing less. Lulu went into the kitchen to prepare dinner.

The ring of her doorbell interrupted Lulu. She turned the oven off then went to open the door.

"Delana, come in."

"I'm afraid I can't stay."

"What's going on?" Lulu asked.

"We have an emergency at work. Of all times for things to go wrong."

"Don't beat yourself up. You have to do what you have to in a position like yours. Besides, you're black and you know they're going to work the hell out of you for the money you're making."

"Yes they are," Delana agreed, but it was all worth it when she received her paycheck.

"Do you at least have time to stay for a quick meal? I made lasagna, salad, and breadsticks."

"Sounds great," Delana said.

Instead of wine, Lulu poured Delana a tall glass of mineral water. She fixed their plates and they both sat down to a delicious meal.

"You sure did put your foot in this," Delana said, in between bites of food.

"Thank you."

"So how is your relationship going with Keith?"

"I love him. It's hard to believe that I have a good man."

"Why is that?"

"Good things never happen to me. Sometimes, I'm afraid that I will wake up and this has all been a dream."

"Well it's not a dream. I'm glad you found happiness," Delana said, finishing the last of her meal.

"And what about you?" Lulu asked.

"As you know things are hectic at work because of the holiday season coming up. On the other hand my relationship with Corey is going great."

Delana filled Lulu in on her and Corey's last romantic date.

"Girl, you have to be kidding. You and Corey made out on a bed full of money?"

"Yep, and it was all good. I'm still hanging on cloud nine from that night."

"Well I hope that happens to me soon."

"Hold up, you mean to tell me that you and Keith haven't knocked boots yet?" Delana asked, surprised.

"Nope, he said the time wasn't right."

"Wow, you certainly seem to have a good one there," Delana said, refilling her glass of mineral water.

Lulu agreed and they spent the next hour talking before Delana had to pack up and leave. Even though they couldn't spend the whole weekend together, she was pleased that they had a pleasant dinner. They promised to pick back up on their time after things settled down with Delana's job, which would probably be after the holiday season.

****

"Are your bags all packed?"

"Yes. Where are we going?"

"Over to my place," Keith told her.

Lulu was glad to be able to spend some quality time alone with Keith. Between work, school, and the kids, she hardly had a minute to herself.

Keith lived in a nice town house in the city of Bedford Heights. After his divorce, he and his wife had to sell their house and he was building up his income to put down on another house in a few years.

"I see you decided to go ahead and purchase the flat screen television," Lulu said, admiring his new system.

"Yes. I was really debating on whether to get it but the television went on sale; besides it's a good investment."

"I agree," Lulu replied. She sat on his black leather sofa and reclined back.

"Here, let me turn on the massager."

"Oh, just what I needed. This really feels good."

"Wonderful, then you're in store for some treats tonight because I'm going to work my hands all over your body."

Lulu growled in pleasure. It had been over two and a half months since they had started dating. She followed Keith up the stairs and the game was on. They first started with a series of kisses but that wasn't enough. Keith pulled off her shirt, unsnapped her lace bra, and let her double D breast fall in his hands. He kissed both of her nipples as they hardened to his touch.

"You are so beautiful."

Lulu smiled. He really meant those words. She had never really saw her size 16 body frame as beautiful, but ever since she had been with Keith her attitude towards herself had changed. For the first time ever Lulu had began to like herself.

"Keith, I love you."

"I love you, too," he said, lifting her into his arms.

He laid her on his bed and slid off her panties. She was a work of art, her cream colored body looked perfect against his black silk sheets. Keith was going to take his time showing Lulu how a man really loved a woman. Tonight wasn't just about sex, it was about expressing his love for her and his commitment to the relationship he wanted with her.

Chapter 39

Turner

Turner was excited that he would be able to see everyone again at Thanksgiving dinner. He retrieved their luggage from the airport, rented a truck, and he and Cynthia was on their way. This year Ray Ray insisted that dinner be served at his house.

"I'm so glad Thanksgiving is here. This time next month we'll be husband and wife," Cynthia said, with a smile.

"Yes, we will. I'll be a happy man," Turner replied.

He gave Cynthia a wink and eased his hand up her thigh.

"Turner."

"Sorry, I can't resist," he said, inching his way into her panties.

Turner let his finger mingle in her wetness as they drove down the highway. The moan escaping her mouth sent his hormones into overload. He pulled over to the emergency lane, put the truck in park and pulled Cynthia on top of his hard shaft. They were detained for at least a half hour before they merged back onto traffic again.

"You are so bad," Cynthia crooned, slapping his hand.

"Well you just wait until tonight and I'll show you how bad I can be."

****

"About time," Ray Ray hissed, motioning them to come in.

This was the first time Turner had been in Demetrius and Ray Ray's home. It was a two-story house, the outside all brick, and the inside was covered with beautiful hardwood floors. The living room had enough space to fit ten people on the large sectional Chanel sofa. There were four ottomans and two additional fabric recliners for more seating. All in all, there was enough room to fit sixteen people comfortably.

"This is a nice place you have here," Turner told Ray Ray.

"Yes, it's much better than the home I used to live in. I'm glad Demetrius asked me to move in with him."

Turner just smiled as he joined the others. Delana, Corey, Lulu and Keith were all chit chatting. Karen and Jason were in a private conversation on the other side of the room.

"I'm glad everyone was able to make it," Ray Ray said aloud.

"Now we can begin our festivities."

Everyone looked in curiosity as Ray Ray went around and handed envelopes to his best friends.

"Please wait before opening," Ray Ray announced excitedly.

"I just want to thank you all for being my friend, especially through these hard times I've been through lately. You can now open."

All at once, Turner, Karen, Delana and Lulu opened their envelopes. They were all surprised to have a check for twenty thousand dollars sitting in their hands. Almost instantaneously everyone looked up puzzled for an explanation, so Ray Ray told them the story.

"Ray Ray, can I speak to you for a moment?" Turner asked.

They stepped into the hallway for a little privacy.

"Ray Ray, I just wanted to make sure everything is all right with you."

"Yes— yes, things are perfect. I'm so blessed that Jim didn't pass that horrible HIV disease to me. The money I can deal with and I intend on putting it to good use," he said, filling him in on his plans to open a new shop.

"Well I'm glad things are working out for you. How is Demetrius handling all of this?"

"He's fine. In fact, he helped me through this whole ordeal every step of the way. I really appreciate everyone standing behind me, especially you, Turner."

"What are friends for?"

"No, I'm serious. You saved me when I tried to commit suicide. You were there to help me mend fences with my father and there to help me get my life back on track. This money is just a small token of my appreciation. I'm so glad to have you as my friend, my family."

"I'm glad, too," Turner replied.

They joined the others back in the living room. Turner's attention went directly over to Jason. He would love to slug that sucker in the face. He was disgusted at how phony he was acting, being so attentive to Karen. He was caressing her belly. Turner wondered how long it would be before those hands turned abusive again. He couldn't stand the thought of it but what could he do? Karen wanted to stand by her husband's side and so he had to move on. He had a wonderful woman as he went over and kissed his wife to be.

"Can I have everyone's attention?" Turner asked, wiping his lips.

"Before we began dinner, I want to tell everyone how excited I am about my upcoming nuptials," he said, kissing Cynthia again.

"This woman here has made me a very happy man. There's only been a select few women in my life that I've truly loved. One being my mother, Cynthia, well you all know who," he said, glancing over at Karen.

"Anyway, I just hope all of you will be able to join us next month for our wedding nuptials."

"Of course," Ray Ray said. "Now let's bless the food and eat."

The food looked delicious and Ray Ray had the whole Thanksgiving meal catered. Turner had a mound of food on his plate. He couldn't wait to dive into the succulent turkey, dressing, honey baked ham, green beans, greens, macaroni and cheese, potato salad and cranberry sauce. He even went back to the buffet table and grabbed some sweet potato pie, because once he sat down he did not want to get back up until his plate was empty. He looked over at Cynthia whose plate had just a little of everything. Turner was sure glad he didn't have to worry about fitting into a wedding gown because people usually gained most of those unnecessary pounds during the holiday season.

"So Cynthia, where are you two love birds going for your honeymoon?" Delana asked.

"We're going to the islands of Jamaica for two weeks."

"Girl, I'm jealous," Delana responded. "That's the best place to be during this frigid winter weather here."

"I know. I'm really looking forward to it."

"I can imagine. Now after dinner, you and I have to go over some last minute details," Delana told her excitedly. She was glad they had let her business plan their wedding day. Delana was only charging Turner for the materials and not labor, which would have been a fortune considering the short time frame they had to prepare for this event.

"So Karen, any names for the baby?" Turner asked, changing the subject.

"Of course," Jason said, cutting in. "If it's a boy, he'll definitely be a junior. If the baby is a girl than we're going to name her Katherine, a.k.a. Katie," he said, rubbing his wife on the back.

Karen just looked at her husband with a false smile. How rude of him to cut her off when the question was directed at her. This was just another way of Jason trying to control her. She prayed to God she hadn't made the mistake of letting Turner get away. She rubbed her stomach for assurance that she was making the right decision. Even if she hadn't it was too late, because Turner had truly moved on with his life. She had turned down the one and last opportunity of them ever being together. Deep down it hurt her knowing that Cynthia could make him happy. You could see the love in their eyes, the same love they once shared. It was the same love they still shared but circumstances had broken their lives apart. She had too much baggage on her shoulders and could never consciously put Turner in the middle of having to deal with Jason. It would be explosive and she would not jeopardize Turner or the baby growing inside her belly for her happiness.

"Those are beautiful names," Cynthia smiled. "I can't wait to be in your shoes," she added.

Karen just grinned at her pleasant remarks. Obviously she had no idea the mess her life was in. Karen would love to be standing in Cynthia's shoes but right now was not the time or place to be having these feelings.

"I can't wait either," Turner cut in. He could see the pain in Karen eyes. He was the only one who could read and touch her soul. He knew deep down she had a lot of issues to resolve. Turner had only hoped she could live with the decision of staying in an abusive relationship because Jason was a ticking time bomb. They needed intensive therapy if they had any hopes of saving their marriage. Although Turner could not stand the sight of Jason, at least he had begun treatment, which was the only way he could ever hold on to his wife and child.

"Hey, enough about relationships. Lets watch some football," Lulu said.

Everyone agreed and they enjoyed watching the game on the flat screen theater television mounted on the wall.

Chapter 40

<u>*Karen*</u>

Karen was glad to walk out the last guest from her baby shower. She closed the door, sank into the couch, and looked at all the gifts that were spread out all over the floor. This should have been a happy occasion for her but deep down she was miserable. Karen couldn't understand her depression. Jason had been acting like a changed man, the perfect husband. She just wondered how much of it was really genuine.

"Honey, are you okay?" Jason asked.

Startled, Karen jumped to her feet.

"Are you sure you're okay?"

"Yes, I just didn't hear you come in."

"Were you sleep?"

"No, just deep in thought. I'm exhausted," she told him.

"Well, get some rest."

"Okay, but first come and see all the gifts."

By the time Karen showed Jason each and every gift and cleaned up the house, a few hours had passed by.

"I'm going to go out with the fellows for awhile. Will you be okay?"

"Sure."

Karen was glad to have the house all to herself again. She was just about to climb the steps and head to bed when the doorbell rang.

"What now!" Karen said in a faint tone.

"Can I help you?"

"It's me, Monique."

Karen body froze in place. She stood there and looked at the woman whom her husband cheated with. Her belly protruded out more than Karen's.

"It's cold out here. May I come in?"

"Sure," Karen said, hesitantly.

Monique was the exact opposite of her. She damn near looked white with short curly hair. Even though she was pregnant, Karen could tell she had a slender body frame. Her eyes were a hazel green and she was a few inches taller than Karen. Karen took her coat and then escorted her to the living room.

"Why are you here?" Karen asked.

"We need to talk— woman to woman."

"Why now? You didn't want to be bothered when I contacted you months back."

"That's because I was at risk of loosing the babies."

"Babies?"

"Yes, I'm expecting twin boys. My due date is in two weeks, December 19."

Tears rushed to the corner of Karen's eyes. Jason grandfather was a twin. Were these her husband babies growing inside of her? She had to hear it from Monique's mouth.

"Is Jason the father?"

"Yes, although he thinks otherwise."

"Does he have reason to think otherwise?"

"No. Believe it or not, I don't chase after married men. When I met Jason he never mentioned having a wife."

"That doesn't surprise me."

"Why do you say that?"

"Because Jason will do anything to get what he wants. If that means lying and cheating, it doesn't bother his conscience in the least bit."

"Wow, that's pretty cold coming from his wife."

"It's the truth. You really don't know the man you have chosen to be the father of your children."

"No, but I'm learning."

"Do you know Jason is abusive," Karen told her.

"Yes I know. I wouldn't have believed it until I saw it with my own two eyes."

"What happened?"

"Jason was furious when I wrote you back in the summer. He all but insisted I get an abortion and from the crazed look in his eyes, I believed he would have forced these babies out of me with his bare hands if I had not agreed."

"So he believes you're no longer carrying his babies?"

"Yes, he doesn't even know that there are two lives growing inside me. Besides, he does not want to acknowledge that he's the father. After the last time I spoke to him, I packed my bags and moved out of town with my sister."

"It's been nearly six months. Why are you back? Why would you put yourself and the babies at risk?"

"Because I can't afford to raise these babies on my own."

"So you're looking for money? What?" Karen asked.

"First of all, I'm not looking to rekindle or steal your husband. I was shocked to find out he had a wife. It was all so convenient for Jason to walk away and deny me when he learned of my pregnancy. I no longer suited his needs and he was gone just like that. Six months of being together went down the drain. Secondly, I'm not going to lie, Jason do need to take care of his children financially. He can take a paternity test or whatever but he definitely is the father."

Karen actually felt sorry for Monique. How could she be mad at her? Monique was going through just as much agony and pain as she was, but the only difference Monique was alone. Her children would be brought into the world as bastards. Why should they suffer? All of this was overwhelming. Karen felt a twinge of pain in her stomach.

"Are you okay?" Monique asked.

"Yes."

"When are you due?"

"January 15," Karen replied.

"You know I was really nervous about coming over here. When I finally found out about you, Jason portrayed you as a bitch."

"That doesn't surprise me. He probably was trying to ease what little conscience if any for going outside his marriage."

"What are we going to do?" Monique cried. "I can't possibly take care of two babies alone."

"You won't have to," Karen said, picking up the phone.

"What are you doing?"

"Calling Jason," Karen told her.

"Maybe I should go."

"No, sit here. We are going to work things out right here and right now," Karen assured her. "I promise I won't let anything happen to you."

Monique must have taken comfort in her words because she sat back down. Karen could tell she was nervous as she looked into her hazel green eyes. She looked lost, scared for the future of her and the unborn babies.

"Jason, it's me."

"Is everything all right?"

"Monique is here with me."

Silence.

"I'm on my way home."

It took Karen a few moments to realize Jason had already clicked her off the phone. She took a deep breath and prepared herself of what was to come next. It wasn't going to be pretty but they had to resolve this once and for all. The lies and deceptions had to stop. Karen couldn't possibly move on with her life, her marriage, not knowing the truth. She always wondered in the back of her mind about Monique and whether Jason was the father of her kids.

Karen jumped to her feet as Jason nearly toppled down the door.

"Karen," Jason called out.

"We're in the living room," she responded.

Now was not the time to get nervous. You would think she would be used to his mood swings but Jason always found a way to unravel her nerves.

"What in the world is going on?" Jason asked.

He couldn't believe Monique was in his house. What was she up to? What in the hell did she want? And why couldn't she just leave him alone. When he walked into the living room he was shocked at what he saw. Monique stomach was hanging further out than his wife's. He looked at Karen who was sitting on the couch calmly.

"Join us," Karen told him calmly.

Jason eased on the couch next to his wife. He never imagined he would be facing this problem again. Monique was nothing more than a good fuck. She was good looking, had a nice body, and dropped her panties anytime he wanted to go up inside her. She was definitely not the type he would be with on a long- term basis and certainly not the type he would leave his wife and family for.

"Monique is pregnant," Karen said, as if he didn't know.

"Well it's not mine and what the hell are you doing in my house?" Jason asked, glaring toward Monique with an evil eye.

"First of all, we're going to be civil in here," Karen cut in. "Jason, we're both expecting so please be respectful enough not to upset us more than we already are."

"Baby, whose side are you on? You should have never let her into our house. Monique is just after our money— can't you see that?"

"I see that Monique is pregnant with twins. She is alone, upset, and has every reason in the world to claim you as the father considering the time frame. You did have sex with her, right?"

Jason just sat there and pouted like a child. He had absolutely no control and could not even try to wiggle himself out of this situation.

"If you really believed Monique was not carrying your children, why did you ask her to have an abortion?"

"Because, I'm married, damn it! Why should I lose everything? I could give a damn about Monique." Jason shouted.

He stood and paced back and forth. Twins. What in the hell had he gotten himself into? In less than a month he would be a father to three children.

"I'm going to leave now," Monique said, standing.

"Yeah, get your ass out of here. You should have done what I told you to do but you didn't. Don't be expecting me to be here for you because you can forget it. I love my wife," he yelled, throwing his hands up in the air.

"Monique, please stay," Karen said.

"Are you crazy?" Jason asked his wife.

"No, I just need to deal with reality and so do you," Karen replied.

"I can't believe this shit."

"Jason, please! Either way you're going to have to deal with this. If I can sit here and be civil, then why can't you?"

"Because I don't want to lose you or our way of life," Jason replied. "I just want it to be the three of us— you, me, and our baby."

"And what about these babies?" Monique asked.

"What about them?"

"Jason, how can you be so callous? It's one thing to hate me but how can you act that way towards your children."

"She's right," Karen cut in.

"First, I don't even know if I'm the father. Monique, if you let me slide up so easily in you then how do I know you haven't let some other brother do the same?"

Tears began to spiral down Monique eyes. "I'm having stomach pains. I need to go."

"No, you can't leave out by yourself, especially if you're having stomach pains."

Karen didn't even have a chance to ask how severe the pains were. Monique's water broke right inside their living room. She grabbed her purse and demanded Jason take Monique to the hospital as she followed behind them.

Chapter 41

Delana

"What do you want?" Delana snapped at Corey.

"What's wrong with you?"

"I'm busy. Between work, my business, and trying to coordinate the last minute details for Turner's wedding, I'm burnt out."

"Well don't take it out on me," Corey said.

"I'm sorry," Delana replied.

She couldn't believe Corey hung the phone up on her. Angry, she dialed the number to his cell phone.

"Hello."

"Damn it, don't you ever hang up on me again."

"Who are you talking to in that tone?"

"Who else," Delana's voice was agitated?

Again, Delana's face turned red when a dial tone registered through the phone. She slammed her fist down on the table and threw a stack of papers to the floor.

"Upset?" Corey asked, coming into her office. He shut the door and twisted the lock.

Delana didn't respond, surprised he was standing in her office. Angry, she got up from behind her desk, walked over to Corey and slapped him across the face.

"Did that make you feel better?" Corey asked.

"Yes."

"Yes!" Corey repeated. "Have you lost your mind?"

"YES," Delana cried.

She apologized and threw her arms around Corey. "I've had a bad day," Delana sobbed.

"What can I do to help?"

"You want to help?" Delana asked surprised.

"Anything to please you," Corey replied with a kiss.

Delana relished the warmth of his tongue gliding across hers. She pulled him into her private bathroom, pushed him onto the toilet stool and eased on top of him. Delana's body instantly became heated as Corey continued with his passionate kisses. He unbuttoned the top of her blouse and lifted her bra up and traced his tongue across her hardened nipples. Delana purred in pleasure while Corey eased her skirt up, inched her panties down and sat her on top of his hard shaft. Delana then took control and rode him like a mad woman. She released all her frustration and worries and when it was over she felt like a new woman— all refreshed and energized.

Delana wondered who was knocking at her office door. It was after hours and everyone had pretty much left for the day. She insisted Corey stay in the bathroom until they were alone again.

"Mr. Henderson," Delana said surprised. "How can I help you?"

"Just one moment," he told her, answering his cell phone. "I'll have to take this privately. I should be back in about ten minutes," he said, leaving her office.

Delana watched Mr. Henderson until he disappeared from sight. She pulled Corey out of her bathroom and politely kicked him out of her office. If Mr. Henderson had come anytime sooner he would have caught her in an uncompromising position. Delana wiped the sweat beads from her forehead and sat behind her desk and wondered what her boss wanted. True to his word, Mr. Henderson was back in her office in ten minutes.

"So, how is everything going?"

"Quite well," Delana responded. "If you're looking for the marketing report, I will have it done shortly."

"Whenever you hand it in is fine," Mr. Henderson replied. "I need to speak with you on a personal matter."

"Personal matter?" Delana repeated.

Delana's heart began to pound. Did Mr. Henderson catch her and Corey together? What did he have to talk with her about on a personal matter?

"My wife and I would like to invite you out to dinner and to a musical concert."

"Oh," Delana smiled. "That would be wonderful."

"Good. I hope you have a special someone to bring along," Mr. Henderson said. "We'll have a great time and this will be a great way for me to learn more about you on a personal level."

"Yes, well I look forward to it. Thank you," Delana said, as she watched Mr. Henderson disappear from her office. Thank goodness he had not seen Corey just race out of her office. Delana sat back in her leather chair and breathed a sigh of relief. That was to close to call, Delana thought, smirking to herself.

Chapter 42

<u>*Lulu*</u>

"DeAndre, take your drunk ass on," Lulu said, pushing him away.

"Don't act like you're going all suburban on me," he slurred, grabbing her by the arms.

"Damn it— take your hands off me," Lulu yelled.

If DeAndre thought they were going to rekindle any type of relationship, he was dead wrong. There was no way in hell she was going to mess up the good relationship she had with Keith.

"Have you forgotten how good this is?" DeAndre said, grabbing between his legs. He pushed Lulu on the couch, forced her hands up over her head and took what was his. Lulu was the mother of his child. He had every right to have what was his. DeAndre didn't understand why Lulu had been pulling back from him lately. She never had a problem with opening her legs up for him before and he wasn't going to give her the excuse to do so now. Lulu and him had a special bond, like husband and wife, only they weren't married. Maybe one day he could make that commitment to her but not now. At this moment he just wanted to feel his throbbing manhood inside of her.

Lulu couldn't believe DeAndre had just raped her. She pulled herself off the couch, but he grabbed her around the waist and began his thrusting all over again. Lulu's cries for help went unanswered. The kids were gone and she was all alone and helpless to defend herself.

After DeAndre had his way with her, he went into the kitchen, grabbed a beer and then sat back on the couch beside her.

"What's wrong with you?" he asked.

Lulu didn't move. The tears kept rolling down her face as she starred at DeAndre.

184

"You raped me," Lulu finally said.

"Oh, hell no," he replied, sipping the last of his beer.

"Get out! You'd better leave before I call the police."

"What. Girl, stop tripping, you know you wanted that."

"No I didn't," Lulu yelled. "I hate you," she said, slapping him across the face.

"Why can't you just accept the fact that I have moved on with my life? I'm in love with another man. How could you do this to me?"

Silence.

"You're serious?" DeAndre asked.

"Yes, now please leave," Lulu cried.

DeAndre put his hand to her face as if to apologize but the damage had already been done. Lulu just sank back into the couch and continued to cry. With nothing left to say, DeAndre grabbed his things and left. Lulu ran and locked the door behind him. She picked up the phone and began pressing the buttons with her shaking hands.

"Hello."

"Delana, can you come over?"

"It's been a long day."

"DeAndre raped me," Lulu cried.

"I'm on my way."

"Lulu couldn't move. She just sat there until Delana began ringing her doorbell.

"Are you okay?"

"No."

"What happened?"

Lulu went over the events that had just transpired. The thought of what happened made her sick to her stomach.

"That bastard."

"I know. I can't believe it myself."

"Are you going to call the police?"

"No."

"Are you going to tell Keith?" Delana asked.

"No. How can I tell the man I love that my ex-lover forced himself on me? He's either not going to not believe me or kill DeAndre."

"I understand your point," Delana said, wrapping her arms around Lulu.

"Is there anything I can do?"

"Just being here helps," Lulu cried.

Delana grabbed the phone and scrolled through the pre-programmed numbers. When she came down to DeAndre's name she clicked the button.

"Hello."

"DeAndre, this is Delana," she snapped angrily.

"What."

"If you ever put your hands on my friend again, I will personally kill you myself."

Silence.

Delana listened as a dial tone registered on the line. What was it about men hanging the damn phone up on her today?

"Girl, you're crazy," Lulu told her.

"That bastard has not seen crazy. If he ever touches you again then I'll go straight to Keith myself, and DeAndre will have the both of us to deal with."

"Thank you."

"For what?" Delana asked.

"For being a friend."

"Always," Delana replied, gently squeezing her hand.

****

"Keith, I love you," Lulu said, snuggling in his arms.

She needed all the love and affection he had to offer right now. Lulu felt protected when she was in Keith arms.

"Is everything okay?"

"Why do you ask?"

"Because you seem different," Keith told her.

"I've just had a difficult day," Lulu said, contemplating on whether to change her mind and tell him what had happened.

"Let me guess, DeAndre?"

"How did you know?" Lulu asked.

"Because he's the only one who can get under your skin like this. What happened today?"

"It's nothing. Honestly, I'm just tired of being around him," Lulu said.

"Are you sure that's all it is? If he has so much as laid a hand on you I will kill him with my own bare hands."

"I'm okay. I promise," Lulu told him.

The last thing she wanted was for Keith to get into an altercation with DeAndre. She couldn't live with herself if something happened to Keith because of her. She wished DeAndre would just leave her alone; the way she was feeling right now she wished he was dead.

"Who could this be calling so late?" Lulu said, picking up the phone.

"Hello, Lulu."

"Yes."

"It's me, Andrea. DeAndre's dead."

"What!"

"Oh, Lord. I've lost my husband and now my son all in the same year," Andrea cried.

"What happened?"

"DeAndre was driving while intoxicated," she answered. "He was pronounced dead at the scene of the accident."

"I can't believe this," Lulu gasped. "I'm on my way over," she said, before hanging up the phone.

"What's wrong?" Keith asked, sitting up in the bed.

"DeAndre's dead. That was his mother. I have to go and see about her," Lulu said, slipping her clothes on.

"Okay, I'm going with you."

Lulu didn't protest when Keith wanted to go along. Right now she thought she should have been careful what she wished for. As much as DeAndre got under her skin she never actually wished he were dead.

Chapter 43

Turner

The early weeks in December rolled by quickly and Turner was back in Cleveland for his wedding day. It was Friday, December 24, a day Turner thought he would never live to see. For all of his life he had built up a brick wall around his heart. He never in his wildest dreams thought he would find someone whom he could spend the rest of his life with. Cynthia was the perfect woman; fun, loving, and one who could truly understand his needs. Yes, today was a special day, one his mother would have been proud of. He took a last glance in the mirror and then joined the pastor at the altar. He couldn't wait for his beautiful bride to come marching down the aisle.

Nervous, Turner looked upon his friends in the front pew to comfort his anxiety. He was surprised to see his father sitting there, since Turner had shut him out of his life up until today. Now he was glad he had taken Cynthia's advice and invited his father to take part in this special occasion. Maybe it was just the right way to begin the healing process between the two of them. He knew his relationship with his father wouldn't get back on track overnight, but at least they both had taken the first step in moving forward. This year had been especially difficult for him and all of his friends.

Turner glanced over at Ray Ray who was snuggled close to Demetrius. Ray Ray had been raped, forced to face the possibility of contracting HIV; he had almost committed suicide, and was in a gun show with his deranged stalker friend Jim, who left him a half million dollars upon his death. Turner didn't know how, but fortunately Ray Ray was able to quickly put the pieces of his life back together. He had many positive things to help him along the way, such as counseling, mending fences with his father, moving in with Demetrius, and opening up an upscale shop in a new development plaza in the inner city of Cleveland. Ray Ray seemed so happy today and Turner hoped he would remain that way. He smiled at Ray Ray who gave him a wink. Ray Ray was definitely back to his old self, such a pleasant friend to be around.

Next, Turner eyes met Lulu's. She was sitting next to her boyfriend, Keith, well soon-to-be fiancé. Lulu would be in for the surprise of her life on Christmas morning, when Keith would get down on one knee and propose to her. Keith was a good man and after dealing with DeAndre's foolishness and sudden death, she deserved all the happiness life had to offer. Turner was so proud of Lulu. Once a person with low self-esteem, Lulu had turned her life around. No more would she continue to be the mamma to all these different *baby daddies*. He was glad she finally took an interest in herself by going back to school, mending fences with Delana, and, of course, meeting a good man like Keith. When it all boiled down, he thought, women wanted to be taken care of, not just financially, but emotionally and physically as well. It seemed that for half of Lulu's life men just had been interested in what she had to offer physically, and he was glad Keith stepped up to the plate to convince her that there were still some good men out there who could take care of all her needs. The way Lulu's life was going Turner knew she would be fine. She smiled at him.

Next, Turner eyes met with Delana's. She was smart, sassy, and able to take care of herself. Delana owned her own business plus worked for a fortune 500 company making a six digit salary. Delana knew exactly what she wanted out of life and her only short fall was her relationship with men. After Lulu's deception of sleeping with her ex-boyfriend and bearing a child from the affair, Delana had built a concrete wall around her heart, much like Turner had done himself before finding Cynthia. Delana could trust no one, which in the end was a raw deal for her because everyone needs somebody. Maybe Corey would be that somebody. He had been the only man thus far who could contain Delana's over bearing personality, which wasn't a bad thing. Delana was just strong and remained true to the game, being herself.

Karen, on the other hand, was a different story. Turner really worried about her as their eyes met. She was near the end of her pregnancy and looked pretty much miserable, not from the body change that came along with pregnancy, but from a failed marriage. Anyone else would not have been able to see it by just looking at her but Turner could. He could read her heart, mind, and soul. That knowledge of intimacy only came through love, something he once shared with her. Turner only wanted her happiness, but right now that seemed to be out of the question. Karen had a lot on her plate, dealing with an abusive and cheating husband who brought twin boys into the world by another woman before Karen could have her own. As much as her husband, Jason, would have liked to have swept that secret under the rug, paternity test did not lie. He was ninety-nine percent likely to be the father to those twin boys, and now Karen had to deal with that, and the other woman by the name of Monique, for the rest of her life. It would have been easier if Karen had just walked away from it all, Turner thought, thinking back to when he asked her to be with him again. As much as he loved Cynthia, he and Karen were soul mates. He would have given up everything to be with her again but she was persistent on working through her marital problems with that snake of a husband. It nearly killed Turner that she had made that decision, but what could he do about it? He couldn't come between her marriage; if she wanted to stay in it, he had to walk away. Sometimes, Turner wondered if that had been the right thing to do, but when the wedding song began he focused his attention back to the present. He looked up as the church doors opened. Cynthia took Turner's breath away. She was absolutely beautiful and Turner was glad he had made the decision to make her his wife. They stood before God, surrounded by family, and made their wedding vows.

The Bachelor's Fool

Chapter 1

Ken could not breathe; the cold gun barrel was rammed down his throat. A tear of anger escaped his eye.

"Yeah, bastard, it doesn't feel good, do it?" Sheryl asked.

Ken did not respond.

"Answer me," Sheryl said, removing the gun from his throat and slapping the hard medal against his face.

"And give you the satisfaction? Never," Ken responded, feeling the blood rush from his face.

"Get up," Sheryl screamed. "You're going to pay for leaving me and our daughter."

"Can you blame me? You've been nothing but abusive, intolerant, and crazy. I never should have married your crazy ass in the first place."

"Oh, really! You didn't say that when we had sex last week. And now that you have a new wife, you think you can conveniently get rid of me?"

"Sure do. The sex was merely a quick fix. I just wanted one last farewell to all the misery you put my ass through."

"You son of a bitch," Sheryl spat.

Ken laughed. He felt exhilarated to finally be able say what the hell he wanted. For eight years he had been living a life of misery. Every day of their marriage, they were either fighting or she was laying her hands on him. Now, if he had defended himself, he would have been in jail for murder, so he just took her abuse day after day until he could take no more. When she bluffed one day and said she was moving out, he helped her pack. It felt good getting her out of his home, and if it wasn't for their daughter, he would have had Sheryl permanently out of his life.

"Why, Ken? How could you marry someone else so quickly? We haven't even been divorced two months and you already have someone in the home we picked together.

"The same way I married my new wife is the same way I married you, so I don't understand your question."

Sheryl just stood there while tears began to roll from her eyes. She loved Ken despite whatever problems they had, but she would be damned if he just abandoned her and their five-year-old daughter, Katrina. She gripped the gun, pointed and squeezed the trigger.

Ken jumped up in a pool of sweat. He looked over at his wife Tamia to make sure this horrible nightmare was just a dream. Yes, Tamia was sleeping peacefully next to him. She opened her eyes at his sudden movement.

"Is everything all right?"

"Yes, baby, I just had a nightmare," Ken responded.

"Want to talk about it?"

"Not really. You go back to sleep," he said, kissing her forehead. It was 3:30 a.m. and he did not want to upset her with talk of his ex-wife.

"Are you sure?" Tamia asked, running her hand along his sweaty forehead.

"Positive," he said, wrapping his arms around her. "I love you; I love the way you feel lying up against me," Ken whispered, as his shaft became rock hard.

"Now, how am I supposed to go back to sleep?"

"Good question," Ken responded, lowering his lips to meet hers.

"Umm, I love the way your tongue feel against mine," Tamia said.

She let her husband's tongue intertwine with hers as she massaged the hard shaft bulging between his legs. Tamia let her head fall back to the pillow as his lips made their way down to her hardened nipples. He then ran his tongue down to suckle the flowing juices between her legs. When she could hold it no more, she released and then positioned his swollen muscle to relieve his build up. Tamia always enjoyed making love with her husband. It relaxed her nerves from the everyday stress they dealt with in life.

****

The next morning, Ken was excited about the day's activities. He was going to pick up his daughter Katrina and she would be joining his new family for an outing at one of the large theme water parks.

"What time are you picking Katrina up?" Tamia asked.

"I thought we'd just pick her up on our way to the park," Ken responded, sipping his morning cup of orange juice.

"Are you kidding me? I'm not trying to ruin my day by dealing with the likes of your ex-wife."

"Tamia, you're going to have to deal with her sooner or later. You knew the deal when we got married. I know it is difficult having a ready made family, but I love my daughter and I will not put her in the middle of any family rivalry."

Tamia just shook her head. Her day was already starting to turn downhill. Ken had always talked about how crazy his ex-wife Sheryl was, and for the world Tamia could not understand why he wanted to put her smack dead in the middle of things. She didn't want to be bothered with her or his daughter Katrina. The last time Katrina was over, she gave Tamia hell. She was rude and smart-mouthed, and knew way too much about things to be only five years old. If Tamia had her way, she would straighten that child up real quick because the road she was taking, she would undoubtedly be just as crazy as Sheryl when she grew up. How in the world did Ken ever bring that woman into his family? It is said that opposites attract but damn, their past relationship was way off the charts and that's exactly why it was in the past, because Sheryl was one nutcase of a woman.

"Are you ready to go?" Ken asked.

"Sure, why not."

"Tamia—"

"Look, you're making a huge mistake," Tamia said, cutting his sentence off.

"And everyone told me I was making a big mistake by marrying you two months after getting a divorce from my ex-wife," Ken responded.

"What's that supposed to mean?"

"It means sometimes we have to make sacrifices. I made a big one being with you, so I expect the same loyalty in return."

"Well, who said we should not have gotten married?"

"Let's not go there," Ken said, thinking about how upset all his family and friends were with his marriage to Tamia.

"You brought up the subject."

"Yes, but it was only to point out the sacrifices I have made to be with you. Now come on, I don't want you getting all upset about things. We're a family and that includes my daughter Katrina. Let's head out so we can pick her up."

"Fine," Tamia said angrily.

Tamia had a straight up attitude from the moment she set foot in the truck. Ken looked over at her and brushed her lips with the tip of his hand.

"Oh, you think your loving can resolve everything?"

"It must be good or you would not have bothered to be with me and all my *so called* baggage."

"Funny," Tamia smirked, while they merged onto the highway.

The Florida weather was absolutely perfect this time of year. It was sunny with a nice breeze for a mid-September day.

It was pleasant to have the breeze caress her face rather than the cold air conditioning they needed during most of the hot days they get.

"We're here," Ken said, pulling up to the apartment building.

"I'll just wait in the car while you go up and get Katrina."

"No, we're both going. Now come on," Ken stated, opening the passenger side door.

Reluctantly Tamia got out and followed her husband up to the fifth floor.

"Oh, no you didn't bring that heifer over to my place," Sheryl said, standing at the door.

"Sheryl, what is your problem?" Ken said, in a scolding tone.

"My problem is I don't want your new wife no where near my place. How ass backwards are you going to get?"

"Now, let's not start on a rampage," Ken told her. "I thought it would be good for you to meet my wife. She will be spending a lot of time with our daughter."

"Yes, our daughter— the one we made together when you stuck your dick up me."

"Oh my goodness! Ken, I am going to wait downstairs," Tamia gasped.

"Since you're up here bitch, you might as well stay so we can get a few things straight," Sheryl said, pushing the door closed.

Sheryl didn't give either one of them a chance to respond to her remark.

"Now, first of all, how do you like having my leftovers?" Sheryl asked.

"Sheryl—"

"Shut the hell up, Ken. You wanted me to meet this heifer, so let me talk," Sheryl interrupted.

"Just let her say what she has to," Tamia said.

"No, I'm not about to let her speak to you in this kind of tone."

"Fuck you, Ken. I'll speak in whatever damn tone I want to. If you think you're going to get our daughter and play the happy family, you're dead wrong."

For a brief moment the room fell silent. Sheryl smiled.

"Now, as I was saying— if you want my leftovers, fine. Just know that Ken and I fucked on every inch of that house that you now call home."

"Excuse me."

"You heard me right. Every inch of that house has been claimed with my DNA."

"And what does that have to do with Katrina?" Tamia asked upset.

"This new wife of yours is a stupid one at that," Sheryl spat, rolling her eyes over to Ken. "It means that we fucked on every inch of that house, dummy. How do you think Katrina got here?" Sheryl said, shaking her head. "Just know that every time you look at our daughter that my legs were spread all over the house that you're now living in."

"This is nonsense," Ken interrupted. "Where is Katrina? We're ready to go."

"Don't interrupt me, you selfish bastard. You were bold enough to bring this woman in my house so deal with what I have to say."

"I'm going to ask you again, where is Katrina?"

"Don't worry about where she is at. You weren't worried about her when you were running up and down that highway visiting this piece of trash," Sheryl ranted.

"Look, if you don't get my daughter—"

"What?" Sheryl said, jumping like she was going to hit him.

Ken jumped back from his ex-wife sprawling hands.

"Yeah, still a wimp," Sheryl laughed.

"I don't see anything funny," Tamia cut in. "You played these silly games with Ken but don't think I'll let you put your hands on me. I'll whoop you until there's no tomorrow," Tamia said, rolling up her arm sleeves.

"Ghetto fabulous," Sheryl clapped. "The cherry don't fall far from the tree. You better be careful because just like Ken up and left me, he'll do the same thing to you."

Tamia just rolled her eyes. She would not stand here and be humiliated any longer.

"Let's go," Tamia hollered.

"Where is Katrina?" Ken asked for what seemed like the thousandth time.

"She's not here. Do you think I would let her go to your perfect little family outing?"

"It's my visitation weekend?"

"The hell with your visitation weekend," Sheryl scolded. "You should have thought about all this when you deserted our family. If you think I'm going to sit here and be cooperative, you have another thing coming, you idiot."

It took all Ken's strength not to haul off and punch Sheryl. He didn't resort to violence when they were married and he was not about to do it now. He had too much going for himself to be sitting in jail over her.

Chapter 2

Tamia was not in the mood to be bothered. After this fiasco, she resented even looking at Katrina, who was an exact mini replica of her mother. Tamia wished they had just left, but Ken took out his cell phone and called the police. Ken had partial custody of his daughter and he was not about to let his ex-wife play games with his child. When the police showed up, Sheryl had no problems handing Katrina over. She was a few apartments down the hall at one of Sheryl's friend's apartment.

"So, are you excited about going to the water park?" Ken asked his daughter.

"Yes, Katrina" shouted excitedly.

"And what about you?" Ken said, looking over at his wife.

Tamia was too angry to reply. She just rolled her eyes and looked out the window in disgust.

"Don't do this, baby," Ken said, patting his wife on the leg.

"You should have thought about that about that before you dragged me over here. I told you from the start that this was not a good idea. All you had to do was pick her up and then come back and get me."

"You're right, maybe I should have. I just thought this was the right thing. The sooner everyone accepts our marriage, the better things will be."

"Do you honestly think that heathen is going to accept our marriage?"

"Tamia, now is not the time to discuss this," Ken said, looking back at his daughter.

Katrina was too busy watching her portable DVD player to notice them bickering.

"Fine," Tamia gasped. "We'll definitely talk about this later," she said, pushing her hair away from her forehead.

Ken tried his best to get Tamia on his good side but it was not going to happen today. They spent nearly five hours riding on every imaginable water slide they could go on. Katrina was happy, but his wife had let the spoiled mood from earlier this morning carry on throughout the rest of the day. It was upsetting to Ken that Tamia could not overlook their problems and put on a happy face for his daughter.

"I'm hungry, daddy," Katrina told him.

"We just had something to eat a few hours ago," Tamia said, pointing at her watch. "We'll get something to eat on the way back."

"Let's just grab a little something now," Ken cut in.

"Ken, do you know how expensive this food is. We've already spent over a hundred dollars."

"Tamia, if my daughter is hungry, we're going to eat."

He pulled Tamia to the side, out of hearing distance from his daughter. "What the hell is wrong with you?"

"Nothing is wrong with me. I'm just telling you it is cheaper for us to eat outside the water park."

"We'll be fine."

"Fine— I just had to help you pay the mortgage."

"Are you not living in the house?" Ken asked angrily.

"Yes, but I can do bad all by my damn self," Tamia said. "You're the man of the house. I should not have to be stuck helping pay for a mortgage because a third of your check is going to your ex-wife for child support. This is my money we're spending here and I do not want to waste it on food we can get for much cheaper."

It took everything in Ken not to scream at Tamia. He turned away and walked to his daughter.

"Let's get something to eat," Ken said, looking down at his daughter.

They went to the nearest hot-dog stand and piled their tray up with food. Tamia could not believe her husband. She sat there in disgust while Ken and his daughter stuffed food down their throats. To be honest, Katrina did not need to be having this junk food with her added weight. For her age, she could certainly stand to lose a few pounds. Not being able to take any more, Tamia stood up.

"I'll be waiting in the car."

Ken did not even respond to his wife. He and Katrina finished up their food and then he spent the next few hours taking his daughter on some more rides. It was impossible to get on everything in one day and by the time evening came, he was ready to go. It was six o' clock by the time he made it to the truck. Tamia was sitting there watching a movie on Katrina's portable DVD player.

"Tamia, can I have my DVD player back?" Katrina asked.

"Not now," Tamia scolded. "I'm in the middle of watching a movie," she told her.

"Daddy— I want to watch my cartoons."

"Katrina, not now," Ken told his daughter.

He looked over at his wife to see she was watching a movie that they had just seen last week. Now that was just being petty. She could have given the DVD player back to his daughter to occupy her time. She was a child and that was just the way his wife seemed to be acting.

****

Normally Ken would have taken Katrina back home Sunday evening but her mother was taking her to early morning church service and then to her best friend's birthday party. He was actually glad to be dropping her back off at home because he had to get some things straightened out with Tamia. As soon as he stepped foot back in the truck, the argument began.

"Tamia, don't you ever disrespect me like that again in front of my daughter."

"Disrespect—"

"Yes. You have been nasty since earlier this morning," Ken said angrily.

"Well, you should have thought about that before you dragged me over to your ex-wife's place."

"Fine, maybe it was not the best time, but why were you taking your frustrations out on my daughter?"

"This is not about your daughter. If you had only listened to me, this would have never happened. All I asked is that you pick up your daughter and then we could have gone to the water park. Instead, you put me in the middle of your daughter and ex-wife and believe me this better never happen again."

"Look, I cannot predict what my ex-wife Sheryl is going to do. All I wanted was for Sheryl to meet you since you are Katrina's step-mom."

Tamia just sat there and pouted. Ken's rationale did make sense but she did not want to admit it. It did not matter whether she met Sheryl today or a year from now, the explosive outcome would have been the same.

"I'm sorry," Tamia finally said. "It's just hard dealing with your ex-wife."

"I know, but you cannot let Sheryl get to you like that. Sheryl loves a good fight; don't give in to her pettiness or it will drive us all insane."

Instead of going home, Ken checked in for the night at a luxury hotel. He thought his wife needed pampering as he filled the Jacuzzi.

"You didn't have to do this," Tamia said, stepping in the hot water.

"All I want is for us to be happy. I'll do whatever it takes," Ken replied, stepping into the Jacuzzi after her. He wrapped his arms around Tamia and they let the shooting bubbles ease their tension away.

Chapter 3

"Kenneth Jackson, long time no see," Greg said.

Ken had not heard his real name in years. He turned around to see his best friend coming down the aisle.

"Greg, it's good to see you," Ken smiled.

"Is it? Everyone thinks you have dropped off the face of the earth. What's going on with you, man?"

"Just trying to get adjusted to married life again," Ken told him.

Ken knew Greg wanted to scold him for disappearing from his family and friends. They had been friends since grade school and now Ken had acted like he didn't even want to be bothered. It wasn't that, he just was tired of hearing the negative comments about him getting married again, so he just backed away from everybody.

"Our basketball tournament is starting up next week. Hope you will be part of the team," Greg said.

"Yeah, I miss playing ball," Ken said. "It's been so long, I feel a little sluggish about getting back on the court."

"I can see that," Greg laughed, tapping at Ken's protruding stomach. "You need to get back with the program before you become a couch potato."

"Oh, my feelings are hurt," Ken told him.

"Well, they should be. Just think about how you hurt everyone else's feelings. Man you did not have to disappear just because you remarried. We all know you're crazy but we still care. You're like a brother to me; I would have never imagined you acting like this."

Ken just stood there and pondered Greg's words. He missed his family and friends and felt torn about the whole ordeal. On one hand, he really wanted for everyone to meet his wife, but on the other hand, would they be receptive to Tamia?

Ken did not want to put her in the middle of the "gossip" and negativity of them getting married so quickly after his divorce from his first wife. Tamia had enough dealing with his ex-wife, and he did not want her dealing with any other problems right now.

"Let's get together soon, so we can talk," Ken suggested.

"Whatever is good for you," Greg said. "You know how to reach me," he told him before walking away.

Ken went back to looking for the DVDs that Tamia wanted to watch. He found all of them and headed to the checkout line.

When Ken got home, Tamia had already popped some fresh popcorn and had ice cold beverages waiting for him. He put in the movie and they sat down in front of his fifty-inch plasma television to watch the newest releases.

"Is everything okay?" Tamia asked.

"Yeah, why do you ask?" Ken said.

"It just seems like you're preoccupied with something. You're not into the movie at all."

"I ran into my best friend Greg at the video store," Ken told her.

"I see. So, what did Greg have to say to get your mind all twisted up?"

"Why does my mind have to be all twisted up?" Ken asked. "We just made small talk. Actually we spoke about the basketball league starting next week."

"I know you're not about to start that back up again," Tamia said, putting the movie on pause.

"Is there a problem if I get back on the basketball league?"

"Yes, it is," Tamia pouted, rolling her eyes. "You're already busy with work and your daughter. If you join the basketball league, when will you have time for me?"

"So, you expect for me to give up everything I did before we met?" Ken asked.

"No, but you need to get your priorities straight. I should come first, remember our wedding vows."

"Okay, honey," Ken said, not wanting to get into a heated argument. He grabbed the remote control and started the movie back again.

Five minutes had not even gone by before the doorbell rang. All Ken heard was commotion at the door. He got up quickly and ran to see what was going on.

"Sheryl, what are you doing here?" Ken asked.

"It is your visitation weekend, right?"

"Yes, but you said you wanted Katrina to be with you this Sunday."

"No, that's not what I said," Sheryl snapped. "I told you that I wanted Katrina to go to church and then attend a birthday party. Now, it's only four o'clock and I have plenty enough time left of the day to get what I need done."

"This is bullshit," Tamia cut in. "Ken, you better get this schedule straight with this hoodlum because I do not want her nowhere near my house."

"Your house! Bitch this was my house before it was your house. I lived here for five years before Ken decided to kick me and his daughter out for the likes of you. How do you think our daughter feels living in a scraggly little apartment? Ken you ought to be ashamed of yourself. You play this innocent role but you don't give a shit about our family."

Ken just stood there stunned. As much as he hated the words coming from Sheryl's mouth, she was right about one thing— Katrina. He never thought about how this divorce would impact her. Sure, he knew it was difficult now that her mommy and daddy were no longer together but to uproot her from the only place she knew as home struck a cord within him.

"I want you out of here," Tamia demanded.

"Fine, as soon as I get Katrina and her bags from the car. Ken, you can drop her off later tonight or just let her spend the night and take her to school tomorrow morning."

"I can't believe this," Tamia screamed. "What the hell— what have I gotten myself into."

"Lower your tone," Ken said to his wife.

"Lower my tone," Tamia repeated back. "Have you lost your mind? Do you think I'm going to stand here and let your ex-wife dictate things over here?"

"Tamia, it is my weekend to have Katrina. What do you want me to do? I can't just leave my daughter out on the street. We have argued enough, so when she comes in here I don't want to hear it from you, understand!"

Tamia just flung her hair back and walked away mumbling underneath her breath. Ken was not sure how to smooth things over with his wife. It seemed like they were always arguing, much like his days with Sheryl. Maybe he should not have gotten married so quickly. Maybe he should have just taken the time to get to know Tamia, or better yet get to know himself. Greg had said he was a *Bachelor's Fool*; now he was beginning to think that was true. Ken was so afraid of being alone that life without someone was unimaginable. Was he a fool for not being a bachelor? Yes, maybe he was because he certainly would not have these problems if he had been alone.

****

Ken ended up sleeping on the couch. Tamia was in such a bad mood that he wanted to avoid an argument at all cost. He had a restless night and when morning came, he got Katrina ready for school and then headed off for work. At the office, Ken was no good. His concentration was shot, thinking about all the problems that were going on in his life.

"Excuse me, is it all right to come in."

"Sure," Ken told the new secretary.

Kathy had started at Welds Communications two weeks ago. He was happy the small media firm had finally hired a secretary. As lead designer for web and software development, Ken found it hard to keep a clean office doing work that a secretary should do.

"My first assignment is to centralize all the office files into one location," Kathy smiled. "Since you're closest to me, I thought I'd start with your office first."

"That is fine with me," Ken laughed. "It will be nice to actually free up some space."

"Yes, clutter is not a good thing. If you're not organized, then you'll never be able to find things when you're looking for them."

What a breath of fresh air, Ken thought to himself. Kathy was a very pleasant person to be around. The small office was finally becoming a little diverse, the two of them being the only African Americans. Kathy was medium height, slender, long hair, and had the smoothest chocolate brown skin he had ever seen. Her bulging chest and thick derriere was an added plus. If Ken was a bachelor then maybe he could have talked to this fine woman, he thought, looking down at his wedding band.

"So, Kathy, would you like to go out to lunch with us?" Ken asked.

"I would but I have to work two weeks in the hole before I even get paid," Kathy said.

"Don't worry about it," Ken told her. "It's my treat. Jim and I normally go to lunch twice a month to get out of the office and it is my turn to treat."

"Okay, sure then," Kathy said. She gathered the rest of the files and headed out the office.

Damn, Ken thought to himself. What a fine woman. Kathy had all the curves in the right places. Kathy's look of perfection was far better than his ex-wife Sheryl or his new wife Tamia. Had he not been married, would Kathy even give him the time of day? Ken wasn't ugly but he did not consider himself fine either. He was about six-one in height, ebony jet black skin, a clean shaven head, and the prettiest white teeth; everybody always complimented him about them. Ken used to be in better physical shape but since his marriage, he kind of let his body go. He had a small beer belly that he had to get off. Ken made up his mind right then and there at the office that he would get back on the basketball league. He knew Tamia would not be happy about that but she was not about to run his life like his ex-wife had.

Ken was not upset that his manager, Jim, had to skip out on lunch. An emergency came up with a client that Jim had to deal with. Ken headed to a small coffee shop that served the best sandwiches he had ever tasted. The shop was normally crowded at lunch but Ken managed to find a corner seat in the shop that offered a small sense of privacy.

"Thanks for inviting me to lunch," Kathy said.

"No problem. We make this a ritual practice in the office, so we can talk about things other than the office."

"That is actually a good idea," Kathy smiled. "So, tell me about yourself. I see from your ring that you are married."

"Yeah, I just got married two months ago," Ken said.

"Congratulations."

"Thank you," Ken replied. "So, tell me a little about yourself."

"Where do I begin? Well, for starters I just moved here from Chicago. I graduated from a community college with an Associate's degree and I'm enrolled part-time at Florida State University for my Bachelor's degree in Computer Technology."

"Oh, wonderful— let me know if you need help with anything."

"I'll take you up on that offer. I applied for this position because I have to start somewhere. I figured as secretary, I could learn the business but not be too busy with client projects, since I'm in school."

Ken spent the rest of their lunch hour talking. He learned so much about Kathy at lunch than he knew when she started over two weeks ago. When they got back to the office he was more focused and able to get some work done. It was nice being with someone without all the arguing and bickering. Ken was glad he did not call off of work after all.

Chapter 4

By the time Ken came home, Tamia had dinner on the table. The lights were turned down low and the scented candles burning sent off an aroma that eased any tensions Ken had thought about coming home to his argumentative wife.

"What's the occasion?" Ken asked.

"I just want you to know how much I love you," Tamia said, circling her arms around his neck.

You have beautiful eyes," Ken said, kissing the softness of her lips. He let his tongue slid into her mouth.

"Ken, you're a dirty man," Tamia teased, easing his neck tie off.

"Yes, I am."

It did not take long for things to heat up. Ken eased his wife's clothes off and then took her right there in the kitchen. His hard shaft felt relieved as he slid in and out of Tamia, whose front side was pressed up against the kitchen cabinet. Ken loved being spontaneous as he pleasured his wife. When they were done, they redressed and sat to the kitchen table for dinner.

"My favorite, steak and potatoes," Ken said, stuffing his mouth full.

After the energy he just used making love to his wife, the food going into his stomach replenished his stamina.

"How was your day at work?" Tamia asked.

"It was good," Ken told her. "The firm actually hired a secretary two weeks ago to help around the office"

"Oh, really," Tamia said.

"Yes, it will be good to finally have a clutter-free office," Ken replied, thinking back to the lunch he had with Kathy earlier today.

"Is she white or black?" Tamia asked.

"What difference does that make?" Ken said, puzzled.

"I was just wondering if they were going to get some diversity in that office since you are the only black."

"Well I guess you can call the office diverse," Ken smiled.

"Oh," Tamia said, biting into her baked potato. She made a mental note to get to his office to see what this sister looked like for herself.

"So, enough about my work. How was your day?" Ken asked.

"It was fine. I got off a few hours early so I could come home and prepare dinner for you."

"I appreciate it," Ken smiled.

It really felt good walking through the front door and having dinner already done. The love making with his wife was an added bonus. He really loved his wife for going the extra mile to make him happy.

"How about a back and foot massage," Ken suggested to his wife.

Tamia did not refuse his offer. She quickly loaded the dishwasher, ran upstairs to get her oils, and then they settled on the couch were she let Ken's magical hands go to work.

"You like this, baby?" Ken whispered in her ear.

"Yes," Tamia moaned softly.

"Do you like this?" Ken asked, letting his tongue slid down in between her legs.

Tamia didn't have to answer. Her body's excitement was all he needed as he moved in for more. The aftermath of their sexual engagements tired the both of them out. They flicked on the television and settled down to watch some movies on cable.

****

Tamia made sure she put on some professional clothes the next work day. Today she would be taking her husband some lunch and to meet this new secretary working in her husband's office. Tamia was not jealous or anything but she had to protect her property, because too many times you hear of these sleazy secretaries sleeping their way up to the top; and if that meant sleeping with your husband, they would not think twice about sinning in adultery.

Tamia was on edge all morning at work. When eleven o' clock came, she high-tailed it from her office and picked up some hot corned beef sandwiches and ice cold lemonade for lunch. When she got to Ken's office, she checked herself in the mirror to make sure her makeup and hair were perfect.

"Is Ken here?" Tamia asked, staring the secretary down from head to toe.

"Yes, he is, may I tell him who's here?" Kathy said.

"His wife," Tamia smiled. "I just wanted to drop by and bring him some lunch since he is always busy and all."

"That is so thoughtful of you," Kathy responded.

Tamia just smiled as Kathy picked up the phone to dial her husband. What a bitch, Tamia thought to herself. Kathy probably was some pompous Ms. Know It All with her brown skin that looked smooth as a chocolate candy bar. Tamia would kill for her slender frame and the beautiful long hair that hung down her back. Envy rose in the pit of Tamia's stomach as Kathy got up to retrieve a file. Not only did she have perfect breasts, that she did not have to wear a push up bra for, she also had an ass that would make any man turn twice. How could someone be that beautiful? Had Ken looked at Kathy the way she was doing now? Would he even think about having an affair? What if Kathy came on to her husband? Would he be able to resist her temptations? All these thoughts were going through her mind as Ken came out into the reception area.

"Tamia, this is a surprise," Ken said, kissing her on the cheek. "I see you have met our assistant, Kathy."

"Yes," Tamia smiled.

Tamia made sure Kathy got a good look at how happy they were. "After last night, I just wanted to continue what we started by bringing lunch," Tamia said.

"Well come on into my office," Ken smiled. "What do we have here?" he said, opening the brown paper bag.

"Two hot corned beef sandwiches," Tamia responded.

Tamia must have been reading his mind, Ken thought. He was starved. He pulled his wife a chair next to him so they could eat. She was purposely loud with her conversation and laughter with her husband. She wanted to send a message to Kathy that they were a happily married couple and that she better not even think about trying to take something that was not hers. After lunch was over, Ken walked Tamia out into the reception area.

"Ken, you have a call on line one," Kathy said.

"Who is it?" Ken asked.

"It's Mr. Thomas."

"Oh, I've got to take this," Ken told his wife.

"Yes, go ahead and handle your business," Tamia said, kissing her husband.

She watched Ken as he disappeared into his office and shut the door. When her husband was no longer in sight, she turned her eyes back to Kathy.

"Next time I'll have to remember to bring you a corned beef sandwich," Tamia said.

"No, thank you. I do not eat meat, it puts on too many pounds," Kathy smiled, before getting back to work.

Tamia did not open her mouth. She turned and walked out the office. That smart bitch, she thought angrily to herself. She looked at her thick frame and felt guilty for just having eaten a whole corned beef sandwich.

Chapter 5

"Ken, I cannot believe you are here," Greg said.

"I told you a few days back that I would join this year's basketball league."

Ken was excited about his first game. He had been working out since Greg had mentioned about the team starting back up again. Ken was not in perfect shape but this was a great way for him to lose the few pounds that he had put on.

"These are some nice jerseys we have," Ken said.

"I agree. The league has come a long way. I feel like an NBA player," Greg said, suiting up.

Ken took a few deep breaths before heading out to the court. He had to get his mind mentally prepared for the game. When he followed his team to the court, a crowd of fans were cheering them on. Ken smiled, thankful that he had decided to come back. He had missed being with his friends and just doing the things he loved to do. Ken saw his wife Tamia waving out the corner of his eye. He smiled and gave her a wink as he went to sit down. His smile quickly vanished when he saw his ex-wife Sheryl coming into the bleachers with Katrina. Ken wondered what mess Sheryl was trying to start now. When they were married, she never came to any of his games; in fact, she gave him a hard time about participating since she tried to control every aspect of his life from the activities he was in and the friends he had. Ken knew his wife Tamia sensed his change in mood because her eyes turned to Sheryl.

Tamia could not believe what she was seeing. What the hell was Sheryl doing here? She had some nerve showing up to the game with a posse of her ghetto ass friends.

"Hello, Tamia," Sheryl said in a condescending tone.

Tamia just rolled her eyes. "What are you doing here?"

"Do you own this here auditorium?" Sheryl asked with a snap of her hands.

"No."

"Then don't worry about what I'm doing here. This is a free country last time I checked."

"Hi Tamia," Katrina smiled, cutting in.

"Hello," Tamia replied. "Come here and give your step-mommy a hug."

Tamia smiled as Katrina came over with her. "Do you want to sit with me?" Tamia asked, holding out a bag full of fresh popcorn.

"Yes," Katrina said.

Tamia was relieved that Katrina had come over to sit with her. With Sheryl's posse of friends, she needed someone to be near her. Tamia saw that Ken kept looking back from time to time to check on her. She did not want him to be worried, so she smiled and blew him a kiss before he walked on the court to play ball. Tamia was nervous and excited about him playing. Within the first minute, Ken had already scored six points for the team. He was good at shooting from the three point line and the crowd was loud with cheers every time the basketball swooshed through the net. The adrenaline in the crowd sent the players on a winning streak because they kept on scoring throughout the entire game, as they ran back and forth up the court. The team playing against them could not get their momentum going and lagged behind ten points and ultimately ended up losing the game.

When the game was over Ken headed to the locker room to shower and change. He wanted to get back to Tamia quickly, so he did not spend much time socializing with the guys. When he returned to the court, many of the fans were still there talking with each other. Sheryl and her group of friends were among the people sitting and gossiping. Her loud voice seemed to echo in his ears as Ken's lips turned in disgust. He shook his head wondering why Sheryl was even here. Thoughts of his ex-wife quickly vanished when his eyes locked with his wife Tamia. Ken saw the relief in her eyes as he came over and wrapped his arms around her and then his daughter.

"Ken, I'm so glad you decided to play," Tamia told him.

"Me too, and how is my little girl?" he asked, scooping Katrina up in the air.

"Daddy, you won the game," Katrina said excitely.

"We sure did," Ken smiled.

"Excuse me," Sheryl said, interrupting them. The thought of their happiness made her sick to the stomach.

"What are you doing here?" Ken asked.

"Oh, is it a problem for me to bring your daughter here to watch you play basketball?"

"No, it's not," Ken told her. "You never have been at any of my games before and if Katrina wanted to come, she could have come with Tamia."

"No, no, no! This is my weekend. In fact, I came to tell you that we are heading out of town right now for the next two weeks."

"The next two weeks. You cannot take Katrina, she is in school," Ken voiced angrily.

"Do not tell me what I can do with my daughter," Sheryl hollered. "You should have thought about things like this before you just up and left our family."

Ken was embarrassed as some of the crowd members in the gym began to look on.

"Let's go outside," Ken motioned.

"Outside, oh you embarrassed of me?" Sheryl asked.

"Of your behavior, yes," Ken told her. "Now stop putting up this façade in front of your friends. Anything we need to speak about in regards to our daughter can remain between us," he said grabbing her by the arm.

"Don't touch me," Sheryl hollered. "I'm not talking to you about nothing. I'm taking Katrina out of town and that is final."

Tamia could not believe the commotion going on. Ken ran right behind Sheryl as she headed out the gym with their daughter and posse of friends.

"Sheryl—"

"What!"

"You cannot just pick up and leave out of town with our daughter," Ken said.

"Just watch me," she hollered, putting Katrina in the car.

Tamia just looked on as she watched tears stream down Katrina's eyes. She felt awful that Sheryl used her daughter to get back at Ken for divorcing her. Tamia wanted to go over and slap that silly grin off Sheryl's face but Katrina had seen enough and besides that would only make matters worse.

"Sheryl, where are you going?" Tamia cut in. "Is everything all right?"

"Oh, the concerned little bitch. What do you care?" Sheryl asked in disgust.

"I care about Katrina. Besides, we have a right to know where you are taking her. Ken does have rights," Tamia told her.

"Rights, he did not seem to care about his rights when he was busy chasing you," Sheryl said.

"That's not the point," Tamia said. "And if you had any sense you would know that you're hurting your daughter with all this bickering back and forth."

Tamia watched as Sheryl looked at her daughter and back at them again. She must have felt a twinge of guilt because she raced over to her daughter and picked Katrina up to comfort her.

"Mommy did not mean to upset you," Sheryl said, patting Katrina on the back.

Tamia watched as Ken went over and took his daughter in his arms. Katrina calmed down instantly once she was with her daddy.

"Look, we're going to Alabama to visit my mamma," Sheryl said.

"Is everything all right?" Ken asked.

"No, mamma fell. Her diabetes and old age is starting to make her health decline. I'm going to talk with her doctors and make sure she gets the proper medical treatment she needs. You know I'm the only person mamma has to depend on," Sheryl told him.

"Do you want Katrina to stay with us?" Ken asked.

"No, mamma really wants to see her. I've spoken with the school and got all of Katrina's homework assignments. I will make sure she does not fall behind on her work."

As much as Ken wanted Katrina to stay, how could he argue about letting his daughter be with her grandmother? Unlike Sheryl, Betsy Mallock was a good person and had always treated Ken well. He never could figure out where Sheryl's craziness came from. Despite the good raising, she had been the black sheep of the family. Something went on in Sheryl's life to turn her cold and Ken wished he had figured that out before he had married her so quickly, which was the same way he had married his new wife Tamia.

"Give Daddy a kiss," Ken said, twirling his daughter around. "You make sure to be a good girl for Mommy," he whispered in her ear.

Ken put his daughter back in the car and spoke with Sheryl a few minutes before they left. He then opened the door to the truck and helped his wife Tamia in. As he was walking around the car to the driver's side, Ken quickly wiped away the tears that formed at the corner of his eyes. Ken could not come to terms that his daughter was suffering from their divorce. He hated that Katrina's life had been turned upside down.

Chapter 6

Ken thought with his daughter and ex-wife in Alabama that Tamia and he would have some quality time together. That was furthest from the truth and another night sleeping on the couch began to become the norm for Ken. Tamia and he had been arguing again over money. She was livid that Ken had given his ex-wife Sheryl an extra two-hundred dollars in addition to the child support and alimony money she was already getting. Ken understood her frustrations but how was he going to deny helping Sheryl out when it was for her rent? Since she had been out of town for two weeks helping her mom, she was not able to make the over time she normally made to supplement her income. Now Ken could have been an ass about things, but he was not giving Sheryl the extra money to help her, he was giving it to help his daughter. Katrina had already been uprooted from the only home she lived in and he was not about to let her be moved again because Sheryl could not pay the rent.

Ken hoped Tamia was still asleep as he quietly went to his room to gather up some clothes for work.

"You can get all your clothes out of here as far as I'm concerned," Tamia said.

Ken nearly jumped, surprised she was awake. "This is my room, too. How are you going to kick me out? In fact, this is my house; you better remember that," Ken told her.

"And you think I care about this house," Tamia said rolling her eyes. "You better recognize that I help you pay for this house because evidently you don't have enough income to support me, your daughter, and your ex-wife."

"Look, Tamia, I'm not trying to argue with you this morning. I told you the extra two hundred dollars I gave to Sheryl was an emergency."

"And why did she have to ask you? She could have asked her family, hell anyone besides you. That extra money was supposed to be for the fertility monitor you promised to buy me last month."

"Well I'm trying to do the best I can. I do not understand why you're in such a rush to get pregnant considering the financial situation we're in. Yes, you're right; I don't make enough to support you, my daughter, and ex-wife. The alimony check Sheryl is getting is only for another year, why can't we wait until then to start a family?"

"Because I want us to have a baby now. I want my own family," Tamia cried. "Do you know how stressful it is, knowing I have a hard time getting pregnant?'

"Tamia, just let things happen naturally. The doctors said nothing was wrong with you. I think you've been so stressed in your past relationships about getting pregnant that it consumes and probably is a factor of why you have not become pregnant."

"Ken, you're not a doctor. The fact of the matter is, this money was supposed to go towards the fertility monitor. I do not like being second to no one. I'm your wife and you better start acting like it."

"Why are you putting all this stress on me?" Ken hollered, losing control. "We should be enjoying our marriage, not arguing all the damn time about money, about my daughter or ex-wife, or silly shit that is trivial. I'm tired of your nagging ass," Ken said, grabbing his clothes.

Ken quickly showered and then got out the house and headed for work. At the office he buried himself in his work so he would not have to think about all the problems that were going on at home.

"Ken, you have a phone call on line one," Kathy said.

"Who is it?" Ken asked.

"Greg Blackwell."

"Oh, okay, go ahead and put the call through," Ken told her.

Ken was glad his best friend Greg had called. Today he needed the diversion and was glad Greg had invited him to a night out on the town with just the fellows. At the end of the day Tamia had not called and Ken was not about to call her. He did not feel like hearing her mouth and quite frankly did not want to be bothered with her much at all. In fact, the thought of being married had been a pain lately and Ken kept thinking time and time again if he had made a mistake.

He truly thought he was in love with Tamia but at times like this he really doubted his decisions. Ken kept trying to internalize his best friend Greg's words: are you in love with Tamia or are you in love with the thought of always being with someone? Ken did love the fact of having someone by his side all the time, to talk, to laugh, to make love to, to cook, to clean, all those things that married couples did together. However, getting to know his wife was not measuring up to what he thought it was going to be. Ken should have taken the time to know his wife before marrying her. What was he thinking marrying Tamia two months after divorcing his first wife Sheryl?

Ken's thoughts were interrupted by the fine woman stepping out of a mid-night blue Mercedes Benz. She was tall, slender, had ebony skin and a body that would make any man's head turn twice.

"Hello," Ken smiled.

Ken was all teeth when the woman slid him her phone number but when she saw the wedding band on his finger, she snatched it back. Her words rang through his ears as he made his way up to the night club: *Sorry, I don't mess with married men.* Damn, Ken thought to himself. Now he would have had a good time slapping that fat ass but again his marriage blew that from existence. The thought of being rejected and the problems in his marriage caused Ken to go on a drinking binge. The smooth VSOP felt good gliding softly down his throat. The laughter and good time he had with his friends were refreshing. The fellows talked shit to each other, to any women giving them the time of day, and just had a good old fuckin' time. When the bar got ready to close, Ken was not looking forward to going home. Right now he envied his friends who all seemed to be happy. Greg had a good strong marriage and his other friends were either happily married or happy being single.

Ken sat in his truck for a few minutes trying to gather his composure. Before he took off, the lady he had met when they first arrived with the Mercedes Benz was walking to her car.

"You never did tell me your name," Ken said, rolling down his window.

"Bernice," she grinned, coming over to him.

Ken could smell the liquor on her breath. For her to even be talking to him was a surprise. Liquor sure did have a way a distorting people's minds because Bernice got in his truck and was all up on him. Ken did not turn her away as he slid her panties off and glided his hard shaft in and out of her. When their twenty minute escapade was over, she took the card she had taken back from him earlier and handed it to him again. Ken started up his truck and headed home. A huge smile was glued to face because he still had it going on.

****

"What the fuck!" Ken said, jingling his key in the door.

He never had a problem before, and now all of a sudden the lock did not work. Ken ran out the garage and tried his key in the front door with no luck. He ran back in the garage, let the garage door down and then fumbled for his cell phone.

"Hello."

"Tamia, open the door, the locks don't work."

"That's because I changed the locks," Tamia replied.

"Changed the locks! Are you crazy?" Ken hollered. "Open the fuckin' door, you crazy bitch."

"And you think talking to me in that tone is going to get you through the door."

"It's my house," Ken hollered like a two year old baby.

"Your house! Do you pay all the bills for this house? Let's get this straight; if it was not for me, you could not afford this house."

"Tamia, I warning you, you better open this door."

"It's four o' clock in the morning. If you think you're going to come in this house any time of day, you're dead wrong."

Ken had enough. With all the years of Sheryl's abuse and now this, Ken totally lost control. He threw his cell phone against the garage wall and began slamming his six foot frame into the door. When the door refused to open, he grabbed his axe, screamed "If you're behind the door, move back," and began chipping away the wood door. All Ken could hear was Tamia screaming for him to leave, which increased his desire to break through the door. Ken hit the door about ten times with the axe and then kicked the door down. When he stepped foot in the house, Tamia was holding a kitchen knife. Her body was trembling so much that Ken just grabbed the knife from her hand and threw it across the room from arm's reach. Ken didn't care about the knife blade ripping through his skin, all he wanted was to get a hold of his wife.

"What the hell is wrong with you?" Ken screamed, grabbing Tamia by the shoulders. He pushed her body up against the wall.

"There is nothing wrong with me. I should be asking you that question. Now let me go," Tamia demanded, trying to wiggle free.

"Don't you ever lock me out of my own damn house again," Ken hollered.

"That's the problem, Ken, everything seems to be singular with you, *my house, my truck*. When are you going to realize that we are married? This is our house, our truck. Get your English straight and add the pluralism to this because all the shit you think is yours is mine too."

"Oh, really," Ken said.

"Yes, really," Tamia hollered back. "If you think you are going to leave me without nothing you are wrong. All the bullshit I put up with from your ex-wife, your spoiled smart mouthed daughter, I deserve something and rest assured I will get it. Unlike your ex-wife Sheryl, I will not just walk away and leave you with all this," Tamia said, pointing to the house and everything in it.

Tears started to spill from Ken's eyes. He wanted to hit his wife so bad but instead he punched a hole in the wall and kept banging through the plaster until all the hurt and anger inside of him released. When he was done, he went upstairs, packed his bags and left.

Chapter 7

The hotel became Ken's home for the next few weeks. The one room had a big comfortable bed, a kitchen with a full refrigerator, stove, micro-wave, and a clean bathroom. Ken had the basic necessities to get him through the rough period he was going through right now. His marriage to Tamia had fallen on the rocks before it even began and now he had to figure out what steps to take next. Ken could either go back to her or have the marriage annulled. Unlike what Tamia had said, if he got the marriage annulled at this point she probably would not be entitled to much of anything since they had not even been married for six months.

"What does Tamia want?" Ken said, looking at the caller ID on his cell phone. He hesitated before picking up the phone.

"What do you want?" Ken asked.

"We need to talk. Can you come home?"

"No, I need more time to think. Tamia, when you locked me out of the house I nearly lost my mind. I wanted to hit you. I never want to feel like that, ever."

"I know you would never hurt me," Tamia said.

"No, I've never laid a hand on a woman before and I'm not about to start now," Ken said.

"Ken, please come home."

"I can't"

"I'm pregnant. I guess I did not need that fertility monitor after all," Tamia told him.

"Pregnant," Ken repeated.

"Yes. Ken we are going to be parents; can you believe it?"

Ken was at a loss of words. His marriage was on the rocks and now he had a child on the way. Was this his fate to go back and try to work his marriage out with Tamia? How could he even think about annulling his marriage with a child on the way? Ken did not believe in having children out of wedlock so this news was pretty much the decision maker on what he had to do. Ken packed up his bags, checked out the hotel, and headed back home to the suburbs.

"Ken, you're home," Tamia said, greeting him with a kiss.

"Yes, we need to talk."

"You're not going to walk out on our marriage?" Tamia asked.

"No."

Ken saw the relief in his wife's eyes. She wrapped her arms around him and kissed him some more as if nothing ever happened.

"Not now, Tamia."

"I'm trying to put the problems we are having in the past. Let's start over," Tamia told him.

"How can we put our problems in the past without bringing a resolution to them? If we don't talk about our problems now, they are only going to surface back up later."

"Right now I just want to be happy. Come on in and get settled in," Tamia told him.

Ken was surprised that in two weeks Tamia had the garage entrance door replaced and the hole he had punched through the wall fixed and painted. Other than the two of them, no one would have ever known what happened in the house.

"Here are the new keys," Tamia said. "I'm sorry about changing those locks. I was just mad about things but I understand now that I went about things the wrong way."

"And I'm sorry that I lost control," Ken said, wrapping her in his arms.

For the next few hours, Ken enjoyed being pampered by his wife. While Tamia was making his favorite dinner, Ken went upstairs to enjoy a hot soothing bath. He hadn't soaked in the water fifteen minutes before his cell phone began beeping. He looked at the caller ID and did not recognize the number.

"Hello."

"Ken."

"Yes, who is this?" Ken asked.

"Bernice."

"Bernice," Ken repeated out loud.

"Yes, the woman you fucked in the back of your truck two weeks ago.

Silence.

"How did you get my number?" Ken asked.

"It took me some time but I got your number, your address, and much more," Bernice said.

"And what do you mean by much more?"

"Look, let's not beat around the bush. You took advantage of me, because I'm not the kind of woman that sleeps around in the back of people's trucks."

"What!" Ken said, in disbelief. "You were a willing participant."

"Was I?" Bernice asked him.

"You damn straight. In fact, you were the one who got in my truck and was all up on me."

"That is not how I remember things."

"You've got to be kidding me," Ken said, standing up out the water.

Ken's head began spinning as Bernice went on with what she thought happened two weeks ago. Twenty minutes of sex was going to cost him a life time of pain if he did not get this straightened out quick.

"Bernice, look, I don't know where you are getting this but we need to talk," Ken told her.

"I agree. Meet me in an hour at the Breakfast Barn.

"I cannot just up and leave. I'm a married man," Ken reminded her.

"You should have thought about that before you went up in me. Either meet me on my terms or suffer the consequences."

"Okay, I'll be there," Ken said, hanging up the phone.

Ken half dried off and slipped into some clothes. He ran down stairs, told his wife that Greg had an emergency, and then sped out the house like a bat out of hell. When he was a good mile from the house, he dialed Greg and filled him in on what had just happened. He thought his best friend was going to flip out but he was cool and told him to calm down and see what Bernice wanted before he came to any conclusions. Ken was at the Breakfast Barn a half hour early. When he pulled up in the parking lot, Bernice's midnight blue Mercedes was already parked in the driveway.

Ken took a deep breath, stepped out of his truck and headed into the small restaurant where Bernice insisted he meet her at. At this time of night the restaurant was half empty and Ken had no problem spotting Bernice sitting at the far left of the room in a small booth. She was sipping on a small cup of coffee when he walked up to her.

"Bernice, let's talk," Ken said, sliding into the chair.

"That's him," Bernice nodded, cutting her eyes to the right.

Before Ken knew it, there were two men with police badges hanging from their neck coming towards him. They cuffed Ken's hands behind his back and then charged him with the rape of Bernice Wellington. Ken was in total shock.

"You're making a mistake," Ken told the officers. "Bernice, tell them the truth," he pleaded with her.

Ken saw the cold look in Bernice eyes. She did not open her mouth as the officers read him his rights. Never in his life had Ken been handcuffed, stuffed in the back of an unmarked police car, and taken to jail. What started off as a good day had turned into a nightmare? How was he going to tell his wife of his one night stand? He really had not planned on telling her especially now that she was pregnant but he had no choice. What happened to Ken's rights? He never forced Bernice to have sex with him and yet he was headed down town to be booked and put in jail for a crime he did not commit. They never once asked him his side of the story. Ken closed his eyes hoping this nightmare would go away.

At the police station, Ken was forced in front of a camera for a picture and then fingerprinted as a criminal. His personal information would now be logged into a nationwide criminal database that held millions of data records on crimes people committed. Ken's whole life flashed before his eyes. If he was in jail, who would take care of his daughter Katrina? What about the baby he had on the way? What about his job? If he had a felony on his record he would definitely be discriminated against in the workplace. Would he lose his job? Without a job, he would not be able to pay the mortgage and could possibly lose the house he worked so hard to get. What the hell was going on? What about his rights? A tear of frustration escaped Ken's eyes as he was led into a holding cell.

"Do I get to make a phone call?" Ken asked the officer.

"Not now. You have to wait your turn," the officer replied.

Ken waited for over two hours before he was able to make his one phone called. He slowly took a deep breath and dialed home.

"Tamia—"

"Ken, where are you? I've been worried out of my mind. You have not returned any of my phone calls."

"Tamia, I'm in jail."

Chapter 8

For the next month Ken went through hell at home. Tamia was hollering and screaming at him every chance she got. He never could do anything right and going to work every day was his only refuge.

"Ken, is everything all right?" Kathy asked, coming into his office.

"No, I going through some marital problems," Ken replied.

Ken watched Kathy push the door closed for some privacy and for the next hour he dumped all his problems out on the table. Ken left nothing out, and when he was done there was a moment of silence. He knew Kathy probably thought he was a crazy SOB but he did not care. It felt good to talk to someone.

"Ken, I think it would be good for you and your wife to go to counseling."

"Oh no—Tamia would never agree to that."

"Why, counseling is not a bad thing. If Tamia does not agree then I suggest you go. Just like you're talking to me, you can see a clinical practitioner who will be able to give you some sound advice."

"That may not be a bad idea. It does feel good to talk and get my problems out. I hope you don't think the worst of me."

"No, Ken, it is not my place to judge. However, I believe after your divorce from your first wife, you should have taken some time for yourself instead of jumping right back into marriage. You never gave yourself time to heal."

"That is something my best friend Greg would say. Heck, my whole family has basically felt the same way."

"I think your best friend and your family are right," Kathy told him. "I hope you can get things straightened out between you and your wife."

"Thanks, Kathy."

"No problem, and what we just talked about will stay in here," Kathy assured him before walking out.

****

Over the next couple of weeks Ken took refuge in his therapist's office. Tamia had refused to get counseling and thought everything should be her way or no way. If it was not for the pregnancy, Ken would have had no problems walking out and annulling this marriage.

"Tamia, how long do you expect me to put up with your intolerable behavior?"

"Intolerable behavior! You are the one who cheated on me with somebody you did not even know."

"Are you going to hold this against me the rest of my life?" Ken said.

Ken was appalled that Tamia did not answer his question. She just shrugged her shoulders and walked out of the room. Ken paced the floor wondering what to do. He could have burned a hole in the carpet, seeing how angry he was. Upset, Ken grabbed his keys and headed out the door.

"I hope you don't mind me coming over," Ken said, in a defeated tone.

"Not at all," Kathy replied. "I told you I'm here if you ever need to talk."

"Well, I do, but not about my problems. I just wanted to go somewhere to get a little peace of mind and I ended up at your doorstep."

"Well, come on in. I was just about to eat dinner. Do you want to join me?"

Ken never had vegetable lasagna but it was good. The salad and red wine to wash everything down with was soothing to his nerves. He had not had a good, home cooked meal since he was released from jail. His wife Tamia had stopped everything from sex, cleaning, and cooking. His house was like a battlefield with dishes piled up, clothes unwashed, and the refrigerator empty. Tamia was making a point of what a wife normally does by not keeping the house together.

"So, Ken, other than work and married life, tell me something about you? Kathy asked.

"I like to ride bikes," Ken told her.

"Really—what kind of bikes do you ride?"

"Well in my younger days, I had a sports bike. I really wanted to get a Harley Davidson but my ex-wife Sheryl forbid me from getting what I wanted."

"Can I ask you a question without you getting offended?" Kathy asked.

"Yes."

"Why do you let women run over you? It seems like from your first wife to your current wife, that they have been doing everything and making all the decisions."

Ken just sat there dumbfounded. It took someone from the outside looking in to make him realize the truth. Sure, his best friend and family had told him this a thousand times, but he thought they were being intrusive. Now, he could not say Kathy was being intrusive because she barely knew him, and what reason would she have to make him think otherwise?

"Your absolutely right," Ken said. "I control my own destiny and I'd better start acting like it."

"That's the first positive thing I've heard you say about yourself," Kathy replied. "Now, getting back to Harley Davidson bikes, I have one."

"No, get out!" Ken gasped.

"Sure do. My ex-boyfriend got me hooked on riding. At first I was scared to ride on the back of his bike but when I finally got up the nerve, it was the best thing ever. When I'm on that bike, it's just me and the open road. You see everything in a different perspective. It is just beautiful."

"Wow, I know what you mean," Ken said.

"Do you want to go for a ride? I have an extra helmet."

"Now how can I turn down that offer," Ken said.

For the next couple of hours, Ken enjoyed holding his arms around Kathy. He wished it was the other way around but it didn't matter because he was having fun. They took some scenic routes and enjoyed the Florida weather. They stopped at a park, grabbed some cold raspberry flavored water, and headed to sit down by the lake.

"Now, this is the life," Ken said, gulping down his water.

"I'm glad you've enjoyed this," Kathy smiled.

"Can I ask you a question without you getting offended?" Ken asked.

"Sure."

"You have never mentioned anyone in your life besides your ex-boyfriend. What happened between the two of you?"

"A bunch of nonsense," Kathy said. "I know what you're going through. I certainly can relate. My problems were different but all the same, they were problems that eventually caused the break-up between me and my ex. His family had money and they did not like me at all. They thought I was some homeless fool looking to live their lifestyle."

"How could your ex let his family come between the two of you?" Ken asked.

"He didn't, but after a while you get tired of all the games. Life is too short to put up with a bunch of mess *all* the time. I just got tired and decided to part ways. It was hard but I did it. I moved from Chicago to Florida and I am enjoying every minute."

"That took a lot of courage." Ken said.

"Yeah, it was more like a peace of mind. I have not told you the whole story. His family actually had one of their rich friend's daughter try to hook up with my ex, John. When we got into an argument, he made the mistake of running into her arms and getting her pregnant. That pretty much ended things because as much as I loved him, I could not put myself through dealing with a child that was not mine."

"I wish we could have met six months ago. Would you have even given me the time of day?" Ken asked.

"I am now," Kathy responded. "Maybe we could have been more than friends but not now. Ken you are a married man with a child on the way."

"I know," Ken responded, shaking his head.

The reality of his marriage came crashing back to his forethoughts but he pushed them aside and enjoyed the rest of the evening with Kathy. When they returned to her place, he kissed her on the hand and then left. Ken was going to take back his life. He was in control of his destiny, so when he returned back home, he loaded the dishwasher, washed his clothes, cleaned the house, and then collapsed on the couch, which had become his bed. It was three o'clock in the morning but since it was the weekend, he didn't care.

It seemed like Ken had just closed his eyes for some sleep when the doorbell rang.

"Sheryl, what are you doing here?" Ken asked.

"I have an emergency, can you watch Katrina?"

"What's going on?" Ken said looking at his watch. It was 7:30 Saturday morning.

"I don't have time to explain. Either you watch her or I'll ask my boyfriend," Sheryl snapped.

"Boyfriend!"

"And what do you mean by that," Sheryl hissed. "Do you think nobody else would want me?"

"Look, let's not argue," Ken said.

"Good, because I really need to go," Sheryl said, kissing her daughter on the forehead.

Ken watched as Sheryl sped out of his driveway. She almost ran over their freshly cut lawn as her tattered red car disappear from sight. Normally Ken would have been upset at Sheryl's tactics but for her to even be here this early on a Saturday morning really must have constituted an emergency on her end. Besides, he did not want his daughter sitting up with another man. Ken prayed his crazy ex-wife would speak with him about things like this, because he could not even imagine the kind of company Sheryl would bring home in her house. Every since their divorce, she had been acting crazier, making decisions that he certainly would think questionable.

"You want some breakfast?" Ken asked his daughter.

"Yes, Daddy. Can you make me those good Belgian waffles you always make?"

Ken turned and saw Tamia standing on the stairwell. She did not even bother responding to his daughter. She just stared, tuned up her lips, and then turned and walked away.

"Of course I can make you those Belgian waffles," Ken smiled.

After breakfast, Ken cleaned up their mess, put on a video for Katrina to watch and then marched upstairs.

"Don't you ever disrespect my daughter again," Ken said, yanking Tamia out of the bed.

"What is wrong with you?" Tamia hollered. "Don't you ever put your hands on me like that again unless you want to be back behind bars again?"

"No, I'm not going to be behind bars again. I am not going to let you or any other woman dictate my life. Marrying you was the worst mistake I could have made," Ken yelled.

"I agree. What was I thinking marrying some low life loser?" Tamia spat back. "You can't even contain you ex-wife or anything in your life for the matter."

"Yes, you're right. I married you because I could not stand the thought of being alone. Are you happy? I just needed a woman to talk to, someone to clean, cook, and fuck. Hell, I could have hired a prostitute rather than be bothered with all this shit that you have been taking me through."

"You son-of-a-bitch," Tamia raged, slapping him across the face. "If you wanted a prostitute then you should have hired one because I am nobody's maid or a woman who spreads her legs because a man tells her to."

"Tamia, I'm not going to continue to argue with you. I want you out of my house," Ken said, grabbing a suitcases out the closet. "Pack your shit and get out!"

"You have got to be kidding me," Tamia hollered. "I am not going anywhere."

"Oh, really. Either you get out peacefully or I will throw you out of here. You're name is not signed on a damn thing— not the mortgage, not the utilities, or anything. The only thing with your name is the truck sitting out in the garage and that has wheels, so you can spin on and get the hell out of here."

Ken was not playing. Tamia just stood there as he started throwing her things in a suitcase. She was yelling, screaming, and taunting him, any excuse to call the police. When the police arrived, Ken came down with all of Tamia's bags.

"What seems to be the problem here?"

"There is no problem, officer," Ken said calmly.

"He hit me," Tamia yelled.

"Is that true?" the officer asked.

"Absolutely not. Do you see any marks on her? I just want her out of here," Ken said. "This is my house— I just want her gone."

"Look, we're not here to make court decisions. Obviously, there are some problems. I'm going to ask that one of you leave."

Tamia just grabbed her bags and stormed out the door. As upsetting as this whole ordeal was, Ken was relieved. For the first time in a long time, there was peace in his house.

Chapter 9

Ken enjoyed having his independence back. It had been two whole quiet weeks since Tamia had left the house. Actually, he kicked her out. He could no longer be held captive to a life of misery and pain. Sure he had made some serious mistakes but he was willing to work on them. Ken was willing to go half the mile but if Tamia did not want to make things work then there was nothing else he could possibly do. It took two people to make a marriage work and his wife was absent from the picture.

Ken's thoughts were interrupted by the sound of the telephone. "Hello."

"Hey, Ken, I'm on my way."

"Okay, man. See you when you get here," Ken said, hanging up the phone.

Ken rushed upstairs to get his bag together. Greg was going to pick him up for their basketball game. This afternoon they would be playing against one of the better teams in the league. The sound of the doorbell surprised Ken.

"I know that couldn't be Greg already," Ken said, grabbing his bag and heading downstairs.

Ken could hardly maintain his balance as the screen door was nearly ripped off its hinges.

"You think you're going to kick my pregnant sister out of this house?"

"Look Tony, I don't want any trouble," Ken said.

"Trouble! You have not seen trouble," Tony raged, pushing his way in the house.

"Leave now or I am going to have the police arrest your ass," Ken threatened. The last thing he expected was for Tamia's crazed brother to be standing in his house. Tamia had

241

never invited him or any of her family for the matter over here before, so why the problem now.

"Just like a girl,' Tony hissed. "Why don't you handle things like a man?"

"A man," Ken repeated. "Do not come over my house and insult me."

"Insult you, I didn't come over here to insult you. I came over here to whip your ass," Tony said.

Ken fought as Tony's fist came smashing against his head. Tony's large body frame overpowered Ken as blood starting pouring out from a gash in his forehead.

"Tony, stop," Tamia yelled, running in.

Ken saw Tamia coming towards them from the corner of his eye. "Get back, Tamia."

Within seconds, the damage was done. Tamia had tried to step in between her brother's raging fist and Ken. Unaware, Tony's fist became the batting cage on Tamia. It took a few seconds for Tony to realize what he was doing before he stopped. Tamia sank to the floor holding her stomach.

"What have you done?" Ken yelled out, circling his arms around his wife.

"Ken, the baby—oh my God, the baby."

By now Greg had run through the door and bomb rushed Tony. Ken wanted to join his friend in kicking Tony's ass but his wife was his first priority as he dialed 911. By the time the police and ambulance arrived, Ken's house looked like it had been through a tornado. Tony was arrested and Tamia had been rushed to the hospital.

Ken was devastated when the doctors told them the baby was gone. Tears started to trickle from the corner of his eyes.

"Tamia, I'm sorry," Ken said, caressing her hands.

"No you're not. This is just what you wanted. You did not want me or this baby," Tamia yelled in a fit of rage.

"That's not true."

"Just get out, Ken. You've got what you wanted. I hate you."

"No, I am not going to leave you like this," Ken said.

He was surprised when Tamia did not push him away. He circled his arms around her and cried that he could not have done more to protect her and his unborn baby.

****

After everything that had happened, Ken only thought it appropriate to have his wife come back home. Tamia's attitude had changed dramatically and she was now acting the way a wife normally acts. She just wanted a fresh start and Ken gave her that. He wanted a clean slate as well, and the first thing he did was put his house up for sale. Memories of this house belonged to him and his ex-wife. It was hard for Tamia to be comfortable here knowing this was a part of Ken's past with another woman. It all boiled down to Tamia's having security and if that meant getting another place, he would do it.

Everyone from family and friends thought he was crazy for taking Tamia back but she was his wife. He took vows that he would be with her through better or worse and through sickness and health. A part of him also felt guilty for the loss of their unborn child. If he had not kicked Tamia out in the first place, then none of this would have happened.

Ken found himself giving up a lot to try and mend fences with his wife. He had to drop from the basketball team so he could pick up a part-time job to help pay for their new house. He had not planned on spending more than his old house but Tamia fell in love with the thirty-five hundred square foot home that they were now moving into. With their incomes combined, they would just have enough to pay their expenses, including child support for his daughter Katrina.

The new home, furniture, and car had Ken sweating bullets. He was not rich and hated penny pinching. Even with his part-time job things were close. To make matters worse, everyone from the outside looking in was envious. They had no problems voicing how he was letting Tamia make a fool of him. Sheryl was one of them. When she found out where they were living, she assumed they had hit the lottery. He never imagined her going to court to increase child support. The courts awarded her more money based off his and Tamia's income rather than his alone. Ken was so upset that he went for full custody of Katrina. Tamia was not happy about this but when she saw all the money they could save in child support, she realized how much less they would have to struggle.

Ken dressed in his best suit as he and Tamia made his way to court.

"Well—well, from rags to riches," Sheryl interrupted.

"Sheryl, how could you do this? You never can leave things well enough alone."

"Well enough alone. You dumb bastard, do you think I'm going to live in the poor house while your ass is in a mansion?"

"We do not live in a mansion," Ken responded.

"Oh, the hell if it ain't, and I'm just doing what is best for our daughter," Sheryl said. "If you are going to be living well off then so will our daughter and me."

"We'll see about that," Ken said. "I hope the courts grant Tamia and me full custody of Katrina."

"You have got to be kidding," Sheryl gasped. "It will be a cold day in hell before I let my daughter live permanently with that snooty bitch. Besides, she does not like our daughter anyway. Katrina tells me what goes on over there and believe me it takes all my strength not to come over and beat her ass."

"Are you going to let her continue talking to us this way," Tamia cut in.

"What the hell you think he's going to do?" Sheryl asked. "I'll beat both of your asses."

"Are you threatening us?" Tamia asked.

Sheryl did not even respond. She just turned and walked away when she saw her lawyer approaching them.

Ken was in the court room for over two hours and was livid when the judge denied his request for full custody of his daughter. How could the judge make a decision about his daughter's well being so quickly? What about a father's rights? As long as Sheryl was working and was not doing anything illegal or on drugs, the judge did not feel a need to remove Katrina from Sheryl's care. Ken wanted to slap that silly smile off Sheryl's face but he was not willing to go back to jail over something he had no control over.

"I cannot believe the judge's decision," Tamia said.

"Neither can I," Ken responded, pulling out the parking lot.

Ken was pissed that he had just wasted fifteen-hundred dollars in attorney's fees. He should have just presented the information in court himself because either way, the judge was going to side in Sheryl's favor. *Life, nothing but drama* was all Ken could equate to this whole situation.

"Why did you have to marry that low life?" Tamia screamed. "Sheryl is making our life a living hell."

"Everything is going to be okay."

"No, it's not. Just look at us, you are working two jobs just to make ends meet. You were already paying Sheryl a thousand dollars a month and now that scum is taking fifteen-hundred dollars from our pocket. That is a house note."

"Don't worry. You won't have to suffer any," Ken said. "I've been working to get my side business up."

"Side business," Tamia repeated.

"Yes. I'm going to be doing computer work on the side."

"Oh, Ken, that may conflict with your regular job."

"No. I'm targeting an entirely different market then Welds Communication. I will be working with smaller businesses who can't afford to get work done like larger companies."

"Hmm. That actually is not a bad idea," Tamia responded.

"And the best part is, Sheryl do not have to know about any of this. The money generated from this business will go straight in our pocket."

It was good to see a smile on Tamia face, Ken thought to himself. He had been working on his side company for the past six months. He had his company name, logo, and website already completed. His first few clients had already contacted him, which sparked this whole idea to do something for himself. When they reached home, they stripped naked and enjoyed a relaxing evening at the pool.

Ken could not believe it. He just saw his wife flush her birth control pills down the toilet. They had both agreed to wait a year before trying to have another baby. With all the expenses of the new house and money going to his ex-wife, they could not afford a baby of their own right now. Ken eased back into bed in disbelief.

"Do you like this new night gown?" Tamia asked, slipping into bed.

"How could I not," Ken replied, running her hand over his hard shaft.

Ken took pleasure in rubbing and kissing the softness of her body. When he was ready to make love to her, he slipped on a condom.

"Oh, you don't have to wear those anymore," Tamia said, with a kiss.

"I'd better," Ken replied.

"But I'm on the pill."

Ken smiled knowing her little deceptive secret. "It's better to have two forms of protection."

Ken took pleasure in their love-making and knowing that he had just avoided the possibility of becoming a father. He could not get over his wife flushing those pills down the toilet. Why did women think he was such a fool? Was he that easy to take advantage of? Whatever the case, he would be more careful from here on out. Even though he had mended fences with his wife, he had an invisible wall built around himself to shield from the hurt that both his ex-wife Sheryl and Tamia had put him through recently. When their love-making was over, Ken curled his wife in his arms and went into a deep sleep.

"What are you doing?" Ken asked rubbing his eyes.

"Ssshh—just relax," Tamia responded.

Ken thought he was dreaming but Tamia had gone down on him and then got on top and was riding his hard shaft. By the time he realized what was going on, he had released from the pleasure he thought he was dreaming about.

"I love you," Tamia said.

Ken grabbed his clothes and headed out the bedroom door.

"Where are you going?" Tamia asked.

"To get some air," Ken responded in disbelief.

Outside, Ken paced back and forth. It was 3:00 a.m. Saturday morning and in a few hours his daughter Katrina would be coming over.

"Ken, what's wrong?" Tamia asked, coming outside to join him.

"What's wrong? What's wrong is you trying to get pregnant behind my back. I thought we had both agreed to wait a year."

"We did."

"Don't lie to me," Ken said, cutting her sentence off. "I saw you flush your birth control pills down the toilet earlier. When that did not work, you took advantage of me in my sleep. Nothing is ever good enough for you," Ken said, pointing to this big house that he had sacrificed for her.

"I can explain," Tamia said.

"Explain what. The bottom line is you trying to deceive me. I'm working two jobs right now to try and pay for this house we are living in. Why are you trying to play me for a fool?"

"Fine, I want a baby. You made me lose our first child so no sacrifice is too much."

"Are you kidding me!" Ken said. "You're blaming me for losing our child?"

"If you had not kicked me out then none of this would have happened."

"And what about your crazy ass brother? No one told him to come over to my place and attack me. Maybe you should blame yourself because if you took one moment to think about someone other than yourself then maybe our baby would still be alive."

"You bastard," Tamia said, slapping him across the face.

"If I'm a bastard then you are a bitch. I admit I have made some mistakes but instead of working through them, you treated me like some third wheel. You refused counseling, and just outright rejected being a wife until you decided you could get what you wanted out of me."

Ken watched as his wife ran into the house. He was frightened when she came back to the door with a knife to her throat.

"Is this what you want?" Tamia asked.

"Baby, put that knife down," Ken said, coming inside.

Ken shut the door to keep their problems inside closed doors. Somehow he managed to get Tamia to drop the knife. She sank to the floor in tears.

"Tamia, I think you need to get some help," Ken told her.

"I'm not crazy," Tamia shouted back.

"Neither am I, but counseling has helped me a lot. I tried to convince you to come when we were going through our problems earlier. Tamia, you just lost a child. Please take my advice and see someone. I promise you it will help."

Ken just watched as Tamia shook her head in acceptance. He reached his hand to her and then helped her off the floor. Right now was not the time to continue arguing. Tamia needed help and he would be there to help her.

"Ken, I'm sorry," Tamia cried.

"It's okay. We are going to be fine," he reassured her.

Things had to be okay because there was no way he could afford to live on his own now with all the expenses they had.

****

Ken had very little time for relaxation but the few moments he could find, he enjoyed the most.

"Kathy, thanks for everything," Ken said.

"It's no problem at all. We both enjoy riding motorcycles, so this is nice for me as well."

Ken smiled as they made their way to a secluded space on the beach. He unfolded a blanket and the lunch they brought along.

"I thought you had your daughter this week."

"I do. Sheryl had to change their hair appointment to this morning so she is going to bring her over this evening."

"Oh, so how are things at home?"

"You do not even want to know," Ken responded.

"Now you have me intrigued, but I won't push if you don't want to talk about it," Kathy said.

"Actually, I do, but I do not want you to become the dumping ground for all my problems. I really value our friendship."

"Hey, it's okay to talk. In fact I know that really helps."

Ken told Kathy some things about Tamia flushing her birth control pills down the toilet and the argument they had gotten into. He did not feel it necessary to tell her about how Tamia lost control with the knife. Some things you just had to keep to yourself, Ken thought as he threw a pebble in the ocean. He watched the pebble as it skidded across the water before sinking below the surface.

"Ken, I lost a child before," Kathy told him.

Ken was surprised as he looked into her eyes. "I'm sorry."

"Thanks," Kathy replied, as tears rolled down her eyes. "This happened over ten years ago but it still seems as if it happened yesterday. You never forget and sometimes you go into a state of shock and do things you normally would not do."

"So, then I should not be mad at Tamia?" Ken asked.

"No, I'm not telling you how you should feel. I just want you to know that miscarriages can take a toll on a woman. The separation of a baby that was developing in your body is such a miracle and for it to be taken away."

"I never looked at it from that point of view," Ken said.

"Most men don't. It's hard to explain but I do understand your wife's pain. I'm really sorry this all happened. I think she is so traumatized that she will do anything to get pregnant again. Just be patient and talk with her. Things will be all right."

"I wish I had met you earlier," Ken said.

"Now you know we could not have an office affair," Kathy laughed. "We both would be out of a job."

"You got that right," Ken smiled.

Ken and Kathy enjoyed a picnic lunch and then spent the rest of the afternoon riding on the motorcycle. It was a hot day and the open wind felt exhilarating against his body and the fact that Kathy had her arms wrapped around him as they rode. Today, she let Ken ride them and it felt good to be back on the front seat. As soon as Ken could, he was going to invest in a Harley Davidson. There was nothing like being out on the road on one of the best made motorcycles.

****

At home Ken had to come back down to reality. It was four o' clock and his daughter would be coming over soon. Ken was just about to catch a quick nap when the doorbell rang.

"Daddy—"

"Hey, sweetie," Ken said, swooping his daughter into his arms.

Ken's smile immediately disappeared.

"Here is Katrina's overnight bag."

"Who are you?" Ken asked.

"Ron."

"Ron. What the hell are you doing with my daughter and where is Sheryl?"

"Excuse me. I don't like your tone of voice."

Ken told his daughter to run and put her things upstairs.

"Why is Sheryl having you drop my daughter off?"

Ken listened as this rugged old man talked. He was old enough to be Ken's father and it took everything in him to contain his anger, after all, it was Sheryl who sent him over here and it would be Sheryl who he had it out with. As soon as Ken shut the door, he grabbed the phone.

"Hello."

"Sheryl, why the hell do you have another man dropping my daughter off over here?"

"Hold up. First of all I don't like your tone of voice. When you're ready to talk in a decent manner then we can talk."

Dial tone. Ken could not believe Sheryl had just hung up on him. He pressed the redial button.

"Sheryl—"

"Ken, I don't have time for your foolishness right now. I'm still getting my hair done, that's why Ron dropped Katrina off. He's going to come back for me and we're going out of town."

"I really don't care where you go," Ken lied.

"What ever. Would you like to know anything else?"

"Yes. I'd like to know who you have my daughter around," Ken said.

"It's not your daughter, it's our daughter, and I'm not going to put Katrina in harm's way, if that is what you are worried about."

"Yes, I do worry," Ken responded. "Sometimes I question your judgment."

"My judgment! What about your judgment, Ken. What about you sleeping around on Tamia with some woman you didn't even know? What about the rape charges that were brought against you? You should be glad the police found those allegations to be untrue. Your stupid judgment could have cost you everything, including raising your daughter if you had been sitting behind bars because you were thinking with the wrong head."

Ken did not respond.

"I thought so," Sheryl said. "Don't think I'm going to sit here and put my life on hold because you think I can't make judgments to be with anybody else."

"Tamia— I mean Sheryl, you could have at least called and told me about Ron. Hell, if you needed someone to pick up Katrina, all you had to do was call me."

"Why, so you and your nagging wife can complain," Sheryl snapped.

"Sheryl, why would you say that?" Ken asked.

"You are so blind sided. I know your wife doesn't like our daughter. Katrina tells me things that go on there."

"And what's that?"

"Do you really want to know the truth?"

"Sheryl, I don't have time for your lies."

"Lies, than go ask your daughter," Sheryl said. "Ask her how Tamia says how fat she is for her age, or that she is lazy, or that she wished she did not have to be bothered with her little bad ass."

Once again, Ken was listening to the sound of a dial tone. Sheryl had hung up on him and he just stood there for a moment pondering on what she had just said. Ken went and spoke with his daughter to find out if Sheryl was speaking the truth. It killed him inside to know that his daughter was not happy to come over to his house because Tamia was always mean to her. Was Ken really blind? How could he not see what was going on? All these questions were racing through his mind as he tried to think of a way to resolve the issue.

Chapter 11

Ken thought counseling would help Tamia but after two sessions with a clinical therapist, she refused to go. In her mind she did not see their marriage as a problem and did not feel comfortable in receiving advice. Besides that, after a few visits they were responsible for paying the therapist out of pocket. Tamia could not see wasting money talking with a stranger, but Ken thought otherwise. When it all boiled down to things, it was either Tamia's way or no way. Ken thought giving his wife a new house of her own would change things in their relationship. As usual he was wrong and they continued arguing constantly about his daughter, his ex-wife, and now the added living expenses.

****

Ken was surprised his ex-wife Sheryl was so prompt in picking Katrina up on Sunday. In fact, he hardly recognized Sheryl with the new hair style and suburbanite look. Sheryl actually looked good for a change.

"May we come in?" Sheryl asked.

Ken frowned when he saw Ron stepping out of his car. "Sure."

Tamia had now joined Ken and was about to say something had Ron not followed through the door behind her. Ken offered them a drink but they refused as they sat down to talk.

"Where is Katrina?" Sheryl asked.

"She's taking a nap," Ken responded.

"Good, because Ron and I would like to talk with the both of you."

Ken knew what was coming next. This free loader wanted to move in with Sheryl and his daughter, he thought angrily to himself.

"Ron and I are married," Sheryl said. "We flew to Las Vegas yesterday and tied the knot."

Ken's mouth fell to the floor. "Married! What the hell is wrong with you?" Ken said.

"Look," Ron cut in. "I'm not going to have you continue to insult me or my wife."

"What the hell—"

"Ken!" Tamia snapped.

"Wait a minute," Ken hollered. "Don't tell me how to act in my own damn house," he said to all three of them.

Ken jumped up from his seat as the room fell silent. Did he just hear Sheryl say she got married? What in the hell was wrong with her?

"Sheryl, just because I re-married did not mean that you had to take the first cat off the block to marry."

"Excuse me," Sheryl said, standing up. "First of all, you are the damn one who married the first ho that would drop her panties. Second of all, did you think I would sit here and be by myself for the rest of my life because I'm not with you?"

Ken did not respond. Why was this happening to him? Why would Sheryl do anything to make his life a living hell? Ken had tuned out both Tamia and Sheryl, who were arguing back and forth.

"Get Katrina so we can go," Sheryl spat.

"Katrina is not going anywhere," Ken said. "I will not have my daughter staying under the same roof with some man I don't even know."

"Your dumb ass should have thought about that before you dumped our family on the street for this heifer."

"Get out," Tamia hollered.

"Not until I get my daughter," Sheryl said.

Ken was just about to say something when Ron stood up. He took a wad of money and threw it on the table.

"I'm not just some poor man off the block," Ron cut in. "I work well, get paid well, and I will provide for my wife and daughter."

"Katrina is my daughter," Ken cut back.

"Now she's the daughter of both of us. I suggest you get her or I will have the police over here to force you to give her to us."

Ken watched as Ron picked up the money and put it back in his wallet. He rushed up the steps to get his daughter and then watched them carry her out of the protection of his house. Ken wanted to punch a hole through the wall but instead he sank to the floor and cried.

Monday was especially difficult after the ordeal from the previous night. Kathy's face was the only gleam of sunshine as she came into his office and handed him a new client file.

"Shut the door," Ken told her.

"Is everything all right?" Kathy asked.

"No."

When Kathy shut the door he filled her in on what happened.

"Ken, I am so sorry this is happening to you but right now you have to pull yourself together before your new client gets here."

"I know," Ken said, shaking his head.

"Well, there is more to this on the line," Kathy told him.

As secretary, Kathy many times was privy to information that everyone else was not. She knew if Ken was able to get this new client on board that he would be in for a big promotion. Kathy could not tell Ken the details, but she did give him the heads up, so he could get himself together and focus on the task ahead instead of all the family problems that were going on in his life right now.

With the information Kathy had just told him, Ken pushed all of his problems to the side. He went through his client file and focused on going over the specs for his afternoon meeting. Sealing the deal for Shop-in-Drop food chain would bring in huge earnings for Welds Communications, and maybe in return they would increase his salary. Shop-in-Drop food chain was a five billion dollar industry who was looking to have their company website redesigned. They were a food management company that provided services to large companies, such as restaurants and hotel chains. Ken had taken the last few months learning their business from top to bottom. They had already met and today they would be showing the client the website design they felt would increase their revenues. It was an efficient design to fit the company's needs for the future rather than the design they currently had. Ken had to admit that his work was exciting and he was glad Kathy had given him that extra push to re-focus and get himself together.

The meeting with Shop-in-Drop lasted all afternoon. The four hours seemed like an eternity as Ken presented his ideas. The entire staff from Welds Communication was sitting in on the meeting to offer support. There were twelve people sitting around their conference room table, six from Welds Communication and six from Shop-in-Drop. Ken breezed through his presentation and answered a ton of questions that the client had. He was able to answer every question and show where the solutions would be incorporated into the design of their new website. At the end of the meeting, Ken felt good about the information he had just presented. Everything was out of his hands now as to who Shop-in-Drop would select, but Ken knew he had done an awesome job.

"Kathy thanks for celebrating with me," Ken said, holding up a class of champagne.

"My pleasure," Kathy responded, toasting her glass against Ken's.

Ken was not sure if they would be awarded the account but the staff felt pretty confident in the presentation they had just delivered, and that in itself was cause for celebration. Ken should have been celebrating with his wife but he did not want to bring down his mood, so he invited Kathy instead to a nice quiet dinner. Afterwards, he took her home and was surprised at the unexpected, they kissed.

On the drive home, Ken was so wrapped up in the kiss he and Kathy just shared. To Kathy it probably was nothing more than a victory kiss but Ken took it totally different. He relished the warmth of her breath and her sweet sensual tongue brushing up against his. Had she not told him to leave when she did, Ken knew things might have gotten out of control. Kathy was a smart woman, stay out of trouble and right now that was exactly where Ken's life was. His marriage was in trouble, Sheryl's sudden marriage was troubling, and the fact that his daughter would now be living in the household with another man was definitely troublesome. Ken wished he could erase the past ten years of his life and start over, but that was impossible.

"Where have you been?" Tamia asked.

"At the office," Ken replied. "You know we had the big presentation with Shop-in-Drop," he reminded her.

"Yes, but business do not last until ten o' clock at night," Tamia said, looking at her watch.

"The office went out for cocktails."

"And you could not answer your cell phone?" Tamia asked.

"Look, I guess I forgot to turn my phone back on after the meeting. Please don't bring my mood down," Ken said in disgust.

"Whatever!" Tamia said, angrily. "By the way, my brother is going to be staying with us for the next few weeks."

"The hell he ain't," Ken replied.

"Well, if you would have answered your phone then I could have known your thoughts, but since you were not available, I had to make the decision myself."

"Well you better call him back and tell him my wishes because I do not want that man in my house. For goodness sakes, he came and attacked me and made us lose our baby."

"We all are the blame for that and besides it was an accident. Now the decision for my brother to stay here is final. This is my house, too," Tamia reminded him.

Ken could not believe his wife. How could she make a stupid decision like that knowing how he felt about her brother? Now that they were living in an upscale house, her family was coming around more and more. Ken packed a few things and left. As long as her brother was in this house, he would not be.

Ken was glad his best friend Greg let him crash at his house all week. Greg's wife Tracy and his kids had flown home to Cleveland, Ohio, for a week to visit her parents.

"Now, that we have some time, can we sit down and talk?" Ken asked Greg.

"I told you, I'm here anytime."

"I know but I've just been avoiding everybody because I've been making some stupid mistakes."

"Oh, so you finally admit that you made a mistake?" Greg asked.

"Yes," Ken replied honestly.

For the first time since he married Tamia, he actually could admit to his mistake. It sort of reminded him of an alcoholic going to AA. In order to fully recover, it had to be the person's decision that drinking was wrong and not just because someone forced them to be there. A person had to want to get better and Ken wanted to get his life together and stop living in such chaos all time.

"How do you know you love your wife Tracy?" Ken asked.

"It should be no question when you love a person. When you can't stop thinking about that person or how they make you feel inside is love. Tracy makes me feel whole inside, the way she kisses, makes love, smiles, laughs, talks— just everything about her makes me buckle to my knees. Tracy gave me two beautiful kids. I love her with all my heart. Can you say that about Tamia?"

"No."

"Then you're not in love with her. I think you like the idea of being in love."

"Yes, I'm finally realizing that."

"Have you ever been in love before?" Greg asked.

"Now, you know I have," Ken responded.

Ken could not help but think back to when he was in college. He would never forget how Chi-Anne made him feel. He thought he would marry her but his heart was broken in two when she dumped him for a senior football player.

"I forgot all about Chi-Anne," Greg said.

"I haven't and I have not felt that way about anyone until recently."

"You're kidding," Greg said. "Tell me about it."

Ken talked for the next hour about Kathy. He loved everything about that woman. Kathy never judged him for any of the personal problems he loaded on her day in and day out. He loved the way she looked, smelled, talked. Ken loved the time they spent together riding motorcycles and just taking time out getting to know one another. Quite honestly, he knew more about Kathy than his own wife. Ken knew Kathy's favorite color, favorite foods, perfume, clothing styles, inner-thoughts and views on life. He knew about her past, where she wanted to be in the future, everything that couples knew about one another. The only problem, Ken was not with Kathy.

"So what are you going to do about your feelings for Kathy?"

"What can I do? I'm a married man," Ken reminded Greg.

"Oh, you always can do something. Ken you only have one life. Do you choose to be happy or miserable?" Greg asked.

"I want to be happy."

"Then problem solved. Do whatever it takes to make yourself happy. I would hate to see you spend the rest of your life miserable and from the direction you and Tamia are heading, it is only going to get worse."

"I know you're right about ending things with Tamia, but what if Kathy does not want to be with me?" Ken asked.

"Then you move on. Kathy is only a part of the equation. Regardless of whether you and Kathy ever get together, your relationship with Tamia will never change. You have to get rid of the negative people in your life. I am your best friend and I'm only telling you the truth about things. Now, whether you decide to finally listen is up to you, it's your life."

"My life— yes it is my life," Ken said.

****

Ken took the next few days off of work to see an attorney to file for a divorce. He and Tamia had been married less than a year and he wanted to end the marriage before the stakes became higher than they already were.

"You son of a bitch," Tamia said, slapping him across the face.

"Tamia, I just want to end things peacefully. You know we never really had a marriage to begin with."

"Who is it, Ken?"

"What are you talking about?" Ken asked, puzzled.

"Who is the bitch you're messing around with? Is it that good that you would just give up on our marriage?"

"I'm not with anyone else like you're alluding to. The fact of the matter is we never had a marriage and I just want to move on."

Ken listened to Tamia holler for the next hour. Thank goodness her brother was not there because he had something for him this time. Ken would never be caught off guard again where his life would become endangered.

"Ken, how could you give this all up?"

"Tamia, I never wanted all this. You pushed to get this big house and me like a fool was just trying to please you. I realize now that whatever I do will never be enough for you."

263

"I can't believe you," Tamia screamed for the hundredth time.

"Look, I did not have to come over here and tell you this. I thought it was the right thing to do rather than just have you served with divorce papers."

"You son of a bitch! All the shit I went through with you, your fat ass daughter and crazy ex-wife."

Ken could not believe Tamia started swinging on him. He grabbed her and forced her to the floor.

"Tamia stop."

"You dog, I hate you Kenneth Jackson."

Ken wanted to beat the hell out of her, but instead he got up and left. He did not care about any of the things in that house. All the furniture and fancy things in that home were not worth the headache. Ken just wanted a clean start and it felt refreshing knowing that he did not have to go back into the house of hell. What a deceptive life looking from the outside in. One would imagine they had it all but deep inside no amount of money could buy his happiness. When it boiled down to it, like Greg said: *He did not love Tamia, it was the idea of being in love.* For the past ten years, Ken had been settling for less but no more. From here on out he would do what was best for him and Katrina.

****

Ken headed over to Kathy's place. Right now he needed a smile on his face and he knew Kathy could do that for him.

"Ken I've been worried about you."

"I have a lot going on," Ken told her.

"I figured," Kathy said. "It's not like you to just call off from work."

"I know."

"Well, you know the deal. If you want to talk about it you can and if not then we won't."

"Right now I don't."

"Okay, fine. Let me talk then," Kathy said. "I have some good and bad news."

"Bad news? Give me the good news first," Ken said.

"We won the Shop-in-Drop account?"

"No way," Ken smiled.

"Yes," Kathy said, throwing her arms around him. "It was all you. Ken, you single handedly brought this account to the company."

"I'm in shock. I never imagined they would get back with us so quickly."

"Well, they know a good thing when they have one," Kathy said.

"Wow!"

"Now promise me you'll act surprised when you come in to work tomorrow. Jim will have my behind if he knew I spilled the beans."

"Okay, I promise, but I still can't believe this."

"Believe it," Kathy told him. "Now do you want the bad news?"

"Not really," Ken said.

"Well I'm going to tell you anyway, because I don't want you to hear it from anyone else."

"What's wrong," Ken said, with a concerned look on his face.

"I'm leaving Welds Communication."

"What!"

"Ken, I'm moving back to Chicago," Kathy said, breaking down in tears.

"No, you can't—"

"I have no choice. My father had a stroke and I need to go back and help my mother take care of him."

"I'm sorry to hear that," Ken said, wrapping his arms around her.

"You know who I'll miss most?" Kathy smiled between tears.

"Who?" Ken said.

"You. I have become very fond of you, Kenneth Jackson."

"The feelings are mutual. In fact, I'm in love with you," Ken told her.

Ken had no idea those three little words would make Kathy cry even more. He told her everything that had been going on in the past few days. Ken just wanted to get his life back. He thought Kathy would be a part of his life but now even that may not be possible.

"Come back home to Chicago with me."

"I can't. I have my job, my daughter—"

"But what about you; can you for once put yourself first?"

Ken pondered upon her words for a few moments. Would it be possible to pack up and leave Florida? His parents lived in Indiana, which would make him a whole lot closer to them but what about his daughter?

"I would love to say yes to moving back to Chicago with you," Ken said, wiping the tears from her eyes.

"Then do it."

"Kathy, you said you were fond of me. I just think there would have to be more there between us to even consider the possibility of moving."

"I said I was fond of you, but do you not see it's more to that? Ken, I do love you."

"Why haven't you never told me?"

"Hello, knuckle head—for one you are married; you have baby-mamma-drama, and I didn't want to load my feelings on you."

"Loading your feelings on me would have done me a world of good because I need love in my life. I feel so empty right now."

"You shouldn't feel empty. A wife is supposed to be your best friend, your lover and companion."

Ken broke down in tears, too. For almost a year his wife Tamia had made his life a living hell. Why didn't he end the relationship after they lost the baby? He was so tied up in trying to please her that he pushed his true feelings aside. Deep down he had fallen in love with Kathy. The first time she walked into his office he remembered wishing he had remained a bachelor after his first divorce from Sheryl. Greg had told him he was a *bachelor's fool* but at least now he'd taken his first step to recovery. After he and Kathy talked, they decided to remain friends, and if later they wanted to pursue a deeper relationship then they would. Kathy was genuine in telling him that even though they loved each other, Ken should take this time to find himself. He had to find out what was best for him. After his divorce from Tamia he would remain a bachelor. Ken definitely would not be a fool this time, he thought, as he kissed Kathy goodbye. He headed to a hotel where he would be staying for the next few weeks until he settled matters at home.

Chapter 13

"I told you that heifer was no good," Sheryl said, smacking on some gum.

"Please, let's not go there," Ken said.

All Ken wanted was to have a little peace. He thought it was not in his daughter's best interests to be living out of a hotel with him, so he went to talk to Sheryl about keeping her the next few weeks until he made some living arrangements.

"Well, I would have let you stay here but I'm married now," Sheryl said, holding up her diamond ring.

"Sheryl—"

"Okay, Ken, as much as I would love to gloat, I won't."

"Thank you," Ken said.

Ken tried his best not to let any tears escape his eyes. As hard as he was trying to put his life back together, everything was a mess. There was no way he could afford to pay child support, the house expenses, plus live out of a hotel until he tried to figure things out. His credit cards were just about maxed out and after a couple nights he would be out on the streets. There was no way he was going back home to Tamia and he could not even think about going home to his parents home in Indiana.

"Ken, you've gone silent there on me," Sheryl said.

"Sorry, I'm just thinking."

"Well I'm sure money is at the top of the list," Sheryl responded, pulling out her wallet.

"What's this," Ken said.

"A thousand dollars."

"A thousand dollars! Where did you get this kind of money?" Ken asked.

"Contrary to what you think, my husband Ron has money. You really didn't think I would just marry any man off the street, did you?"

Ken didn't respond.

"Ump," Sheryl smiled. "Whatever, but the fact is I married you for love and I married Ron to take care of me."

"You don't love Ron?"

"I love Ron, but I'm not in love with Ron. As selfish as that may be, I'm not about to struggle for the rest of my life. In fact, we are having a beautiful house built now."

"Sheryl, you sound like me. Do you really want to go that route," Ken said, taking the money.

"The difference is I knew what I was getting into. You on the other hand just went off and married the first thing that came around. Ron and I actually talked. His wife passed away and he needed a companion and I have no problem with that as long as he can take care of me and my daughter."

"Well, who I am I to judge," Ken shrugged.

Ken could not believe what Sheryl had just told him, but if she was happy with things, that was all that mattered. Ken on the other hand wanted to get his life back together. As awkward as it was to accept money from Sheryl, he was grateful to have enough to get him through the next few weeks to pay for hotel expenses.

****

The divorce proceedings were fairly simple. Since Ken and Tamia had not been together long, everything was cut and dry. Tamia could keep the house as long as she paid Ken for his half, but since she could not afford it, the house went up for sale. Ken did not want any of the furniture or anything in the house. Tamia thought she was in for a fight, but in the end Ken just wanted peace. It was a load off of him that he did not have to pay spousal support or for the house. The only expense that

Ken had was the car they had just purchased. Since the car was in his name he would be stuck for the payments even though he had gotten the car for Tamia. All in all, Ken was happy with the outcome. He moved into a two bedroom apartment and was glad he came to his senses to start again, this time on his own.

****

Although Ken had just gone through some personal problems in his life, things at work were great. He was promoted for getting the Shop-in-Drop account and he was paid a big commission bonus.

"Kathy, I still can't believe you're leaving Welds Communication," Ken said.

"Me neither," Kathy responded. "I was just getting my life together with work and school and now I have to leave."

"I know you're going back home to help you father, but don't stop going to school."

"I've already enrolled at a University in Chicago. Luckily, all my credits will transfer."

"Good. I just want the best for you," Ken told her.

"I know. I want you to come over for dinner tonight."

Ken did not have any problems accepting Kathy's dinner invitation. After living off fast food and micro-waved meals, he was glad that someone would cook him some real food. Ken was surprised at how quickly the work day went by. He went to his apartment, showered, and then headed over to Kathy's place.

"I'm glad you could make it," Kathy smiled.

"Turn down a home cooked meal, are you kidding?" Ken laughed.

"Ha—ha," Kathy smiled. "You'll enjoy the steak and potatoes I've prepared for you."

"And what about you," Ken asked.

"I made me some fried egg plants smothered with marina sauce and mozzarella cheese."

"That sounds good," Ken said, sitting to a candle lit table.

"It is. I want you to try some," Kathy said.

"That's not all I want to try," Ken smiled.

"Oh really, well what else would you like to try?"

"I'd better be good," Ken said, stuffing his mouth full with food.

"I give you permission *not* to be good, especially now that you're not wearing a ring on your finger," Kathy said in a seductive tone.

Ken was all smiles. He told Kathy exactly what he wanted and before they had a chance to finish dinner, they were already sharing a passionate kiss. Ken relished the warmth of her breath as he teased her lips apart and traced his tongue over hers.

"You like the way I kiss your lips?" Ken asked in a raspy voice.

"Yes," Kathy replied.

"Good," Ken said, tracing his mouth down to her neck and branding his mark on her.

"Make love to me," Kathy moaned.

Ken had no problems with her request. He blew out the candles, picked Kathy up in his arms and carried her to the bedroom. There Ken stripped her clothes off until she stood nude. Ken just stood there for a few moments to take in her beauty. Kathy was in perfect form from head to toe.

"You are so beautiful," Ken whispered in her ear.

"Thank you," Kathy replied between kisses.

Ken eased her on the silk sheets and began making love to her. He kissed her lips, traced his tongue over her ear lobe and suckled on her ear-ring before moving down to her hardened nipples. Ken couldn't get enough of her as he continued tracing his tongue down to her belly button and then kissing the inside of her thighs. When she arched her legs wider, Ken suckled the juices from her running river. Kathy tasted so good and the cry of her moans increased his tongue movement until she spun out of control. When Kathy settled down, he eased a condom over his hard shaft and then gave her more of his love. Their bodies fit so perfectly together, Ken never wanted this night to end as he eased in and out of her. Kathy's bedroom was heated with passion that they had waited so long to relinquish. When their bodies were in a complete state of satisfaction, Ken wrapped his arms around her and they stayed up talking until they fell asleep.

Ken was happy about their night together but was sad to see Kathy begin to pack her things for her move back to Chicago. After last night, he never wanted to let her go. Ken could not fathom the thought of her being so far away. He knew long-distance relationships usually did not last and wondered if last night would be the only time he had a chance to make love to the woman he had fallen in love with.

"Kathy, I don't want you to leave," Ken whined.

"Me neither, but I have to," Kathy said, kissing him on the lips.

"Will you think about me while you're in Chicago?" Ken asked.

"Sure will," Kathy smiled.

There was a moment of silence that fell over the room. Ken felt like he was losing his best friend. Sure he would be able to talk to Kathy over the phone or send emails, but it was not the same as seeing her beautiful face every day.

"Ken, can I say something without you taking it the wrong way?" Kathy sighed.

"What is it?" Ken asked.

"It's about our feelings. We both know how we feel about one another but I'm not expecting you to be exclusive to me. Be a bachelor, go out, have fun, and at the end of the day if you find that you only want to be with me, then we will go from there."

"I hear you," Ken said, embracing her in his arms.

Ken let his emotions get to him. A tear escaped from his eye.

"What's the matter?" Kathy asked.

"You're the first woman in a long time that has put my needs first," Ken told her.

Quite honestly, Ken knew this would probably be their last time together. He knew the probability of a long distance relationship was highly unlikely. Ken also knew that there was no way he would move to Chicago with his daughter here in Florida. To make matters worse, he knew it would be only a matter of time before another man came along. Although Ken was upset about this, he just wanted to enjoy the moment he had with Kathy right now.

Chapter 14

At the last moment Ken's was surprised that Tamia was able to come up with money to stay in the home they had purchased together. Ken was happy to get a lump sum of one-hundred thousand dollars, which he took and stashed in the bank. He also signed a lease on a comfortable condo where he could begin a new life.

Ken had to purchase new furniture and everything that went with moving into a new home. Tamia had kept everything down to the dishware, so he had to start from scratch. Maybe that was a good thing so he would not have any reminders of the misery he had dealt with living with that woman.

****

It wasn't a month before Ken was out on a date. It actually felt good to be enjoying his bachelorhood and he would hold high standards for anyone he met. His first date was with a woman named Maggie; the first white woman he had ever dated. They met at the park on one of his daily jogging routines. Ken was determined to get his physique back in shape and had started a stringent exercise routine, including eating healthy. He started cooking his own meals and tried to avoid fast food restaurants all together. Ken had actually dropped over ten pounds and was feeling the soreness from the body conditioning classes he was taking. His goal was to get the six pack stomach he once had before married life and all the drama. Boy, life was surely *nothing but drama* but in the end they were life lessons well learned. Ken could honestly say he was happy at this point in his life. Instead of going backwards, he was looking forward to a prosperous future.

Ken could not get Kathy out of his mind. He emailed her daily and they talked almost every day on the cell phone after peak hours. It was good hearing her voice, although she seemed a little stressed from her situation at home. For once it felt good to be able to comfort somebody else in need, because Kathy had definitely helped him through his trying times. In fact, if it were not for Kathy, Ken probably would have been stuck in his marriage to Tamia. It took their relationship for him to realize how a normal relationship should function. His marriage to Tamia had been wrong from the start and his marriage to Sheryl had been even more unsettling. Sheryl had physically abused him but what could a man do? If he fought back he would have been in jail, and at the time he definitely could not tell anyone that a man was a victim of abuse. The only person he had ever confided in was his best friend Greg who had helped him put his life in perspective. He actually looked forwarded to getting together with the fellows tonight.

****

"Ken, is that you," Greg said, waving him over to their table.

Ken nodded as he bopped his head back and forth to the slamming sounds of hip hop music. It was eleven o'clock and Florida's night clubs were in full swing. There were plenty of fine ladies to look at and Ken did not have to feel guilty this time.

Ken enjoyed sitting with the fellows and talking shit. They talked about sports, women, and everything else that friends talked about. Ken got his groove on with the women on the dance floor and collected a few numbers. One hot girl, Natasha, had it going on and Ken was all up on her as the slamming music played. He smothered his nose in the sweet smell of her hair and had his arms wrapped around her curvy hips. Right now, Ken was enjoying the hell out of his freedom.

"Ken, you certainly seem to be happy these days," Greg said.

"I am unbelievably happy," Ken shouted, sitting back down at the table.

Ken got another drink refill and sipped down the smooth VSOP cognac.

"Well, it's good to hear that," Greg smiled.

Ken nodded in agreement as he enjoyed the next several hours at the club. When he got ready to go, Natasha came up and asked him for a ride home.

"Do you really want a ride home or some sex?" Ken asked.

Ken was surprised she wanted both. Ken could have taken Natasha home and screwed the hell out of her, but instead he offered her cab money home and got her phone number. Ken was not about to get caught up in any more rape allegations like he did with Bernice early this year. Ken almost lost everything, he thought, thinking back to when he and Bernice had sex in the back of his truck after leaving a night club. No way, Ken thought to himself. He would have to get to know Natasha first and then he would see where things lead. Actually, he really didn't see much value in her, since she wanted to drop her panties the first night. Sure, the sex would have been a quick fix, but it surely would not have been someone you would bring home to meet your mamma. Natasha looked like she had been with plenty other brothers and a whole lot of drama to go along. Nope, Ken was not going to fall into that disaster mode again.

Ken saw Natasha slip the money he had given her in her bra and then hit up on the next fellow in line. He took her number and tore it up. It was a good thing he stuck with his gut reaction. Some women were just no good.

****

Ken pretty much started to get bored with his job. When he landed the Shop-in-Drop account, his company went out and hired more people to help support the growing company. Even though Ken had been compensated, the hundred of thousands of dollars this account would bring went to the company and not to him. Besides that, he was missing Kathy too much. The secretary they had hired was not friendly and had very few computer skills. She always wore her blonde hair pulled back in a pony tail and wore skirts below the knee like an old grandma. Jennifer was far from Kathy, who he would normally bounce ideas off of since she had the same job background and interest.

Ken picked up his cell phone.

"Kathy, are you free this weekend?"

"Yes, what's going on?"

"I want to fly up to Chicago and see you," Ken told her.

"Are you serious? Kathy asked.

"Serious as ever," Ken said.

Ken spent the next hour talking to Kathy and getting flight and hotel information. Since he was so close to his childhood home, he would visit his family in Indiana as well. Ken was excited about his trip and went home and packed. Come Friday, all he would have to do was grab his bags and head to the airport.

Chapter 15

Ken could not believe he was on his way to Chicago to see Kathy. He had been dreaming about this moment ever since she left over a month ago. It was actually nice to see her right before the holiday season began. When he landed in the windy city, he could not believe all the snow that covered the ground. Living in Florida, Ken did not even own a pair of boots and now he wondered how he would tread through the high pile of snow.

Ken managed to get his luggage with no problems and Kathy was waiting outside for him as he exited the airport terminal.

"It's good to see you," Ken said, kissing her lips.

"Same here—I can't believe you're actually here," Kathy smiled.

"Well I'd rather be no place else," Ken said.

Ken was glad he did not have to be bothered with this treacherous snow every year. He could not believe how cars were sliding from lane to lane trying to avoid hitting the next car.

"Is driving up here this crazy all the time?"

"Just when the roads have not been salted down, otherwise it is okay," Kathy responded.

"So, how is your father doing?" Ken asked.

"Much better," Kathy replied. "He came home a few weeks ago from the long-term care hospital."

"And what about you?" Ken said.

"It's been difficult. My father has to learn how to talk and walk all over again. He goes to therapy every week, and just doing simple, things such as getting dressed or going to the bathroom, we have to help him."

"Well, I hope things get better for your father as quickly as possible. In the meantime, I'm glad you were able to take a break and spend time with me this weekend."

"A much needed break," Kathy smiled. "I can't wait to be in your arms again."

At the hotel Ken sat Kathy on his lap and handed her a gift.

"What is this?"

"An early Christmas gift," Ken replied.

"You didn't have to do this," Kathy smiled.

"I wanted to and besides this will probably be our only time together before the holidays."

Ken watched Kathy peel the wrapping paper off the box. He almost fell over at her expression.

"A Mac computer—my goodness, I've wanted this notebook forever," Kathy cried.

"I know. See, I've been paying attention," Ken told her.

"Yes you have but you did not have to do this. It must have cost a fortune."

"Don't you worry about what this cost," Ken said wrapping his arms around her. "I just want you to get through school."

"I will," Kathy said, kissing his lips.

Ken enjoyed the rest of the night talking. He wanted to know everything about Kathy. For Ken, this was the first time that he actually took time getting to know a woman. He also appreciated the fact that Kathy had no agenda. His ex-wife Sheryl and Tamia were looking for a man who would financially take care of them. They also wanted to control every aspect of his life, the clothing he wore, who his friends could be, and everything in between. Kathy, on the other hand, was different. She was the first woman who put his needs first. Ken appreciated that especially at this point in his life. And how many women would tell you to take your time and date other women to make sure the relationship was what he really wanted. The more time Ken spent with Kathy, the more he knew that this was the woman he wanted to be with. His only problem was her moving back to Chicago. Ken knew a long-distance relationship would only last for so long and he had to convince her to move back to Florida after her father was well enough.

"Do you ever think about coming back to Florida when your father is better?"

"All the time," Kathy replied. "I miss you, the Florida weather, and my freedom."

"Do you see a future for us?" Ken asked.

"Yes and no."

"Tell me why you said no," Ken said, concerned.

"I told myself I would never get involved with a man who already had a family. It always seems to be issues with a ready made family and I don't want to set myself up for failure."

"I can respect that answer but you have to know that I will never put a woman before my daughter. Either you choose the both of us or end things all together."

"I know," Kathy cried. "You did not let me explain my yes. I love you and I would say, yes, we can have a future, if we are open an honest about things."

"I know," Ken said, circling his arms around her.

Maybe there was a future for him and Kathy after all. For now, they would take their relationship one day at a time. Kathy had to continue taking care of her father in Chicago and he would enjoy this time to himself. Ken had finally been able to get his life back under control. Ken was no longer a bachelor's fool. This time he would remain a bachelor and not rush into a marriage anytime soon. If Kathy loved him as she just said, she would be there in the years to come because true love could withstand the test of time.